PENGUIN ⦿ CLASSICS

ARTHUR HUGH CLOUGH: SELECTED POEMS

PENGUIN SELECTED ENGLISH POETS
GENERAL EDITOR: CHRISTOPHER RICKS

Arthur Hugh Clough (1819–61) witnessed at first hand several of the crucial scenes of his age. Son of a cotton merchant who emigrated from Liverpool to Charleston in South Carolina, he was sent back to school in England and rose to be head boy at Dr Arnold's Rugby, where he exuded moral and intellectual earnestness and in 1836 won a scholarship to Balliol. At Oxford he was thrown into the Tractarian debate which was still raging as theological individualism led to authoritarian reaction. He held a fellowship at Oriel from 1842 to 1848, but the implications of subscribing to the Thirty-nine Articles led to his resignation. In 1848 he was in Paris with Emerson during the revolution, and the following year, before taking up his post as Principal of University Hall, London, he spent the summer in Rome, which led to the writing of his epistolary poem *Amours de Voyage*. In 1850 he visited Venice, which is the setting for his uncompleted but remarkable poem *Dipsychus and the Spirit*, a dialogue concerning temptation and conscience. Resigning his post in 1852, he spent a year in the literary salons of Boston, Massachusetts, before returning to England to marry and, like his friends Matthew and Tom Arnold, to work in the service of education.

Jim McCue was educated at Eastbourne College and St Catharine's College, Cambridge. He works for *The Times*.

G000275722

ARTHUR HUGH CLOUGH
SELECTED POEMS

EDITED BY
JIM McCUE

PENGUIN BOOKS

PENGUIN BOOKS

Published by the Penguin Group
Penguin Books Ltd, 27 Wrights Lane, London w8 5tz, England
Viking Penguin, a division of Penguin Books USA Inc.
375 Hudson Street, New York, New York 10014, USA
Penguin Books Australia Ltd, Ringwood, Victoria, Australia
Penguin Books Canada Ltd, 2801 John Street, Markham, Ontario, Canada l3r 1b4
Penguin Books (NZ) Ltd, 182–190 Wairau Road, Auckland 10, New Zealand

Penguin Books Ltd, Registered Offices: Harmondsworth, Middlesex, England

This selection first published 1991
1 3 5 7 9 10 8 6 4 2

Introduction and Notes copyright © Jim McCue, 1991

Printed in England by Clays Ltd, St Ives plc
Filmset in Bembo (Monophoto Lasercomp)

CONTENTS

ACKNOWLEDGEMENTS

For guidance and assistance in the preparation of this volume, it gives me pleasure to thank Dr Archie Burnett, Richard Finn OP, Dr Paul Hartle, Dr Anthony Kenny, Dr Richard Luckett, Mrs Jenny Macrory, Josine Meijer, Dr David Ricks, Dr Patrick Scott, Professor Roger Shattuck and Dr Michael Tanner.

For permission to quote manuscript material, I am grateful to Miss Katharine Duff, and to the Keeper of Western Manuscripts at the Bodleian Library, Mrs Mary Clapinson, and the Master and Fellows of Balliol College, Oxford. I am also grateful to the librarians of the British Library, the Houghton Library at Harvard, the Yale University Library and the English Poetry Collection, Wellesley College, for permission to quote from manuscripts in their care.

INTRODUCTION

Clough wrote as much poetry as Arnold, though less than Tennyson or Browning. Yet, apart from a few early poems, he published only the twenty-nine of *Ambarvalia* (1849) and his two long poems *The Bothie of Tober-na-fuosich* (1848) and *Amours de Voyage* (1858). At his death in 1861 he was working on a collected edition to appear in America, but he would not have sanctioned publication of many poems that are printed here. Most of those that precede *Ambarvalia* but were not included in that volume he would have regarded as private and incomplete jottings.

The work of preparing the collected edition was completed by Clough's widow, Blanche, with transatlantic help from his friend Charles Eliot Norton. A London edition appeared in July 1862 and an American one at Boston, Massachusetts, in August. Although these editions were independently set and in different formats, proofs had been exchanged, and the contents were similar.[1] As well as reprinting *The Bothie* and, for the first time in book form, *Amours de Voyage*, these editions contained *Mari Magno*, on which Clough was working at his death, and a large selection of the shorter poems. Additional poems were printed in editions of 1863, 1865 and 1869.

Naturally enough Mrs Clough aimed to present her husband in a favourable light. She and the friends who reviewed the various early editions suppressed or at least played down his sexual meditations and religious doubts. But many of his poems are, after all, investigations precisely into the consequences of belief or disbelief, and Clough is now perhaps most honoured as an agnostic who couldn't have cared more, to whom religion was a matter of life or death. Equally he is now seen as the Victorian poet who most honestly faced temptation and who best understood how muted is the voice of conscience. So in aiming, like its forerunners, to present him in a favourable light, this selection emphasises other aspects of his achievement.

Particularly vexing to his widow's attempt to make Clough conform to the ethos of his day was the ambivalence towards sexuality in *Dipsychus and the Spirit*, the manuscripts of which are extremely fraught. Mrs Clough published only extracts in 1862, and in a letter of 2 September 1864 to the Revd Percival Graves she wrote:

I cannot help thinking the summing up 'that practical weakness is inseparable from religion' is a little too strong for the meaning – at least of the Epilogue. I thought it was strong and direct *training* into religious feeling and expressions which is there spoken of. No doubt, it is true that there was the tendency to refrain from speaking of religion and to shrink from giving direct doctrinal statements even of the simplest kind which has laid him perhaps open to criticism. I am afraid on the whole that I shall not have the courage to publish it ... I cannot think he meant the feeling of religion in one sort or other to succumb, but that he did think there must be a time of dearth, so to speak, in practical life, especially to a mind somewhat overfed in youth. I grieve so much that he did not live to do more, because I think he would have done differently later. He did change enough to make me think he would have gone further, and this also makes me shrink from giving in to anything which might *look* as if it were the final result at which he had attained. I think the Continuation 30 years after [not printed in this volume], tho' most unsatisfactory, was a sort of returning to commonplace views as having a degree of truth in them ...

A partial text was published in 1865 and 1869, but the true nature of the poem was disguised, so that in 1920 James Insley Osborne could still write of it that 'Clough's idea of sin lacks boldness and definition when compared with Goethe's [*Faust*] because Clough's sins had never been bold and definite. He had quelled his own instincts too early and too successfully to know much about passion' (*Arthur Hugh Clough*, pp. 142–3).

The scenes printed here from *Dipsychus and the Spirit* show, on the contrary, that he knew a great deal about passion. The text followed is that of the first continuous draft, chosen because in later reworkings he began to quell his instincts.

Clough was prone to the 'self-deceiving afterthought' and tended to weaken his verse as he revised it. Of his revisions of *The Bothie*, the anonymous reviewer of *1862* in *Church and State Review* wrote: 'It is a great mistake for a man at forty to think he can improve a poem written before he was thirty. He may make it more elegant and accurate, but every touch will decrease its freshness and vigour.'[2] A century later Richard M. Gollin wrote:

the manuscripts, and even the texts published in Clough's lifetime, often reflect two distinct stages of writing. In the first stage, Clough wrote his poem as it required itself to be written, a poem reflecting the thoughts and feelings he had at the time; in the second, Clough wrote and revised to make the poem respectably presentable to the Victorian tastes and judgements he increasingly accepted after his marriage.

Certainly some of his revisions are weakenings intended merely to make the poems presentable by repressing their sexual content and playing up a wavering faith; but other revisions strengthen by simplification, clarification or compression, or by rhythmic or verbal improvement.

Fortunately many of Clough's manuscripts survive: indeed, given the care with which the family preserved and catalogued his notebooks and papers, few full-length drafts can have been lost. So the discrepancies between the manuscripts and the posthumous texts are more likely to be the results of interference by the editors than readings from manuscripts that have since disappeared. The material available to the modern editor, then, is much the same as that available to Mrs Clough.

All the material was carefully examined by H. F. Lowry, A. L. P. Norrington and F. L. Mulhauser, when they jointly edited *The Poems of Arthur Hugh Clough*, published in the Oxford English Texts series in 1951. An important and detailed critical reassessment of this edition by Richard M. Gollin appeared in *Modern Philology* in November 1962, and in 1974 many of his objections were met – though not acknowledged – when Professor Mulhauser, who had also edited Clough's *Correspondence*, brought out a second, completely revised, Oxford edition. This is now the standard text and lists most of the substantive variants.[3]

In the case of poems from *Ambarvalia*, Clough's joint production with Thomas Burbidge, the present selection departs from *1974* in not incorporating post-publication revisions (though some are noted). Clough annotated three copies of his part of this book, apparently over a considerable period, but the revisions are inconsistent between one copy and another, and since few of them are manifestly improvements, this selection makes available once more the text seen by the first readers.

The text here of *Amours de Voyage* is essentially that of Patrick Scott's edition in the Victorian Texts series published by the University of Queensland, Australia (1974). This reinstates four lines from manuscript, follows the emendations to the *Atlantic Monthly* text given in Clough's letters to Norton of 1859 (including the addition of twenty-seven lines to Canto V) and lightens the punctuation in line with surviving manuscripts. Apart from two additional verbal corrections mentioned in the notes, the only departures from Scott's text are in such minor details as correcting 'Freiberg' to 'Freiburg' and observing modern conventions such as italicising the title of *Childe Harold* and changing 'to-day' to 'today'.

The manuscript poems present a different problem. An editor might print them as though they were prepared for publication in Clough's lifetime, with their punctuation and use of capitals made to conform, but since the use of capitals in *Ambarvalia* is erratic, this would entail guesswork and imposture. At the other extreme he might print a diplomatic transcript of the poems, supplying no punctuation and preserving slips of the pen and deletions. This edition takes a middle course, presenting a reading text which corrects obvious errors and supplies essential punctuation, but is otherwise close to the manuscripts. This has entailed choosing among drafts and variants.

Most of the poems unpublished in Clough's lifetime survive in more than one manuscript, and the text here derives from a fresh examination of those preferred by *1974* (usually the poet's latest draft), except when revisions have weakened the original impetus of a poem. (Departures from the copy-text used by *1974* are listed in the Notes.)

Once the copy-text had been chosen, verbal variants within the manuscript were selected on a slightly different principle. Except where incoherent or evidently incomplete, the latest reading is usually preferred, but where the poet has left earlier readings undeleted for consideration, the choice is inevitably a matter of editorial judgement. (In some cases his apparently final thought was to score the whole poem through.)

The author's spelling is retained except for some light modernising, such as 'recalls' for 'recals' and 'stayed' for 'staid'. For punctuation Clough seems largely to have relied upon his printers, but as the surviving proofs of *The Bothie* show, he was not always happy with what they provided. Here, therefore, the light and incomplete punctuation of manuscript poems is often strengthened for sense, while the heavier – sometimes heavy-handed – punctuation of poems printed in his lifetime is occasionally lightened to conform with the manuscripts and to preserve the riddling, ambiguous quality of the verse. The resulting punctuation is closer to the originals than that of *1974*.

In the text, [   ] indicates a lacuna in manuscript; [word] indicates material supplied by the editors of *1862* or *1869*.

TITLES

Few English poets have been so indecisive about titles as Clough. Most of his poems have no title, others have more than one, and poems published without sometimes had titles added later. Clough used the title *Mari Magno* for two sets of verses at different dates (causing transatlantic confusion after his death) and gave different manuscripts of 'Say not the struggle nought availeth' different titles and none. He wrote two poems with the first line 'Were you with me, or I with you', as well as one beginning 'Were I with you or you with me' and another beginning 'Am I with you, or you with me?' The title *The Bothie of Toper-na-fuosich* turned out to be a Scottish obscenity ('the hut of the bearded well') and had to be changed. Furthermore, titles were invented by Mrs Clough for some poems in *1862* and *1869*. *Adam and Eve*, for instance, she entitled *The Mystery of the Fall*.

This edition uses the title given on the preferred manuscript or the copy-text, except in two cases. The first is 'Easter Day. Naples, 1849' (p. 89), the title of which is probably authorial, although it does not appear on either of Clough's manuscripts (see note on

p. 238). The second is the poem here entitled '*Sectantem levia nervi deficiunt*' (p. 200), where the title has not been copied onto the incomplete revision (in *1869* Mrs Clough gave this poem a title of her own: 'Parting'; *1974*, as is its practice, uses the first line as a title).

ORDER OF THE POEMS

This selection begins with twenty poems that were written before *Ambarvalia* was published but did not gain admission, followed by twenty of those that did, in the order in which they appeared there. The remaining poems, including *Amours de Voyage*, are then printed in the order in which Clough began to compose them, insofar as this can be ascertained. A three-page list of contents for *1862*, apparently in Mrs Clough's hand and now at Harvard, gives dates for a few poems undated in *1974*. The four lyrics comprising '*In stratis viarum*' are gathered together as Clough requested in 1859. Some poems that remain undated are placed next to others with which they invite comparison.

NOTES

1. For the complex textual relationship, see Patrick Scott's *The Early Editions of Arthur Hugh Clough* (New York and London, 1977), pp. 61–73.
2. See *Clough: The Critical Heritage*, ed. Michael Thorpe (1972), pp. 159–60.
3. A few unimportant poetic fragments among the Bodleian and Balliol papers but not mentioned in *1974* are recorded by Paul McGrane in *Victorian Poetry*, vol. 14, no. 4, 1976, pp. 359–64.

LIST OF ABBREVIATIONS

1862   *The Poems of Arthur Hugh Clough* (Ticknor & Fields, Boston, Massachusetts, 1862)

1863   *Poems by Arthur Hugh Clough,* second edition (Macmillan, Cambridge and London, 1863)

1865   *Letters and Remains of Arthur Hugh Clough* (for private circulation; Spottiswoode, London, 1865)

1869   Vol. II (poems) of *The Poems and Prose Remains of Arthur Hugh Clough* (Macmillan, London, 1869)

1974   *The Poems of Arthur Hugh Clough,* second edition, ed. F. L. Mulhauser (Oxford, 1974)

AM   *Atlantic Monthly*

CAKL   Appendix III: Catalogue of All Known Letters in Vol. II of *Corr*

Corr   *The Correspondence of Arthur Hugh Clough,* ed. F. L. Mulhauser, 2 vols. (Oxford, 1957)

Diaries   *The Oxford Diaries of Arthur Hugh Clough,* ed. Anthony Kenny (Oxford, 1990)

Letters to Clough   *The Letters of Matthew Arnold to Arthur Hugh Clough,* ed. Howard Foster Lowry (Oxford, 1932, repr. 1968)

Prose Remains   Vol. I of *The Poems and Prose Remains of Arthur Hugh Clough* (Macmillan, London, 1869)

Revaluation   *The Poetry of Arthur Hugh Clough: An Essay in
Revaluation* by Walter E. Houghton (New Haven and London,
1963)

TLS   *The Times Literary Supplement*

TABLE OF DATES

1819   (1 January) Born in Liverpool, second son of James Butler Clough, cotton merchant, and Ann, *née* Perfect, daughter of a Yorkshire banker.

1822   (December) Family emigrates to Charleston, South Carolina.

1826   Father declared bankrupt.

1828   (July) Returns to England to go to school in Chester.

1829   (July) Enters Rugby with his elder brother, Charles, under Dr Thomas Arnold.

1836   (July) Family returns to England and settles in Liverpool. (October) Elected scholar of Balliol College, Oxford.

1837   Leaves Rugby. (October) Enters Balliol. Member of the newly founded progressive Oxford debating society, The Decade (until 1848).

1838   Attends Newman's services and lectures. Spends summer vacations with friends in the Lake District, Scotland and North Wales (until 1842).

1839   Spends part of summer vacation with W. G. Ward in the Lake District and Scotland; then goes walking in Wales.

1841   Father again declared bankrupt. (June) Gains second-class degree; walks from Oxford to Rugby and announces to Dr Arnold, 'I have failed.'

1842   (Spring) Becomes Fellow of Oriel. Undertakes to write entries for William Smith's *Dictionary of Greek and Roman Biography and Mythology* (1844–9). (11 June) Death of Dr Arnold. (July–September) In Ireland as tutor to Octavius Carey. Performs charitable work for the Oxford Society for the Suppression of Mendicity and Relief of Distressed Travellers.

1843   Travels in Italy. (November) Death of brother George.

1844   (October) Death of father, James.

1845   Ward and then Newman received into the Catholic Church.

1846   Publishes six radical letters in the *Balance*. Visits the Italian Lakes with sister Anne before taking a reading party to Scotland.

1847   Appointed Sub-Dean of Oriel; publishes *A Consideration of Objections against the Retrenchment Association*, advocating sacrifice by the rich on behalf of victims of the Irish Famine. (November) Invites Ralph Waldo Emerson to Oxford.

1848   (March–April) Meets Emerson in Oxford. (May–June) With Emerson in revolutionary Paris. (September–October) Writes *The Bothie* immediately after reading Longfellow's *Evangeline*. (October) Resigns fellowship. (November) *The Bothie* published.

1849   (January) Publishes *Ambarvalia*, with Thomas Burbidge. (April–July) In Rome during the French siege; writes *Amours de Voyage*. (September) Takes up appointment as Principal of University Hall, London.

1850   (Autumn) Visits Venice; writes most of *Dipsychus and the Spirit*. Appointed Professor of English Language and Literature at University College, London.

1850/51   Meets Blanche Smith.

1851   Applies unsuccessfully for professorship in Classics at University College, Sydney. (December) Resigns from University Hall as from January.

1852   (June) Becomes engaged to Blanche Smith. (October) Encouraged by Emerson, sails for New England, with Thackeray and J. R. Lowell as fellow passengers.

1853   (July) Returns from America and becomes Examiner in the Education Office, London.

1854   (13 June) Marries Blanche Smith at Embley. (21 October) Escorts Florence Nightingale to Calais on her way to the Crimea.

1855   (April) First child, a boy, is born and dies soon afterwards.

1856   Tours Europe, inspecting military academies.

1857?   Begins work with Florence Nightingale on her *Notes on . . . Hospital Administration of the British Army*.

1858   (10 February) Daughter, Florence, born. (February–May) *Amours de Voyage* published serially in the *Atlantic Monthly*. Begins to prepare his poems for an American edition.

1859   Publication in the United States of *Plutarch's Lives: The Translation Called Dryden's*, corrected from the Greek and revised by A. H. Clough. (16 December) Son, Arthur, born.

1860   (June) Death of mother, Ann.

1861   Falls ill; travels in Europe; meets the Tennysons; writes *Mari Magno*. (5 August) Daughter, Blanche Athena, born. (13 November) Clough dies in Florence and is buried in the Protestant cemetery opposite Elizabeth Barrett Browning.

1862   *Poems by Arthur Hugh Clough* with a Memoir by F. T. Palgrave published in Britain; *The Poems of Arthur Hugh Clough* with a Memoir by Charles Eliot Norton published in America.

1865   *Letters and Remains of Arthur Hugh Clough* printed for private circulation.

1866   (April) Matthew Arnold's 'Thyrsis: A Monody to Commemorate the author's friend, Arthur Hugh Clough' published in *Macmillan's Magazine*.

1869   *Poems and Prose Remains* published.

O Heaven, and thou most loving family
Of sister stars, whose intermingled light
From the blue home of this most quiet night
Shineth for aye in conscious unity!
Why bend ye thus your kind looks still on me,   5
That am a wretch, whose passions' ceaseless fight,
And gnawing thoughts of self — an inborn blight —
But vex the warmth of your pure sympathy?
Mine is no cup for you, blest stars, to pour
The rich draught of your sympathies therein;   10
It mantled once with all the joys of sin,
And I have quaffed them; now is nothing more,
Save only dregs of bitterness; and woe,
That ever comes when self's brief pleasures go.

I watched them from the window, thy children at their play,
And I thought of all my own dear friends, who were far, oh! far
      away,
And childish loves, and childish cares, and a child's own buoyant
      gladness
Came gushing back again to me with a soft and solemn sadness,
And feelings frozen up full long, and thoughts of long ago,   5
Seemed to be thawing at my heart with a warm and sudden flow.

I looked upon thy children, and I thought of all and each,
Of my brother and my sister, and our rambles on the beach,
Of my mother's gentle voice, and my mother's beckoning hand,
And all the tales she used to tell of the far, far English land,   10
And the happy, happy evening hours when I sat on my father's
      knee, —
Oh! many a wave is rolling now betwixt that seat and me!

And many a day has passed away since I left them o'er the sea,
And I have lived a life since then of boyhood's thoughtless glee,

15 Yet of the blessed times gone by not seldom would I dream,
    And childhood's joy, like faint far stars, in memory's heaven
          would gleam,
    And o'er the sea to those I loved my thoughts would often roam,
    But never knew I until now the blessings of a home!

    I used to think when I was there that my own true home was
          here,
20 But home is not in land or sky, but in those whom each holds dear;
    The evening's cooling breeze is fanning my temples now,
    But then my frame was languid and heated was my brow,
    And I longed for England's cool, and for England's breezes then,
    But now I would give full many a breeze to be back in the heat
          again.

25 But when cold strange looks without, and proud high thoughts
          within,
    Are weaving round my heart the woof of selfishness and sin,
    When self begins to roll a far, a worse and wider sea
    Of careless and unloving thoughts between those friends and me,
    I will think upon these moments, and call to mind the day
30 When I watched them from the window, thy children at their play.

An Incident

              'Twas on a sunny summer day
                 I trod a mighty city's street,
              And when I started on my way,
                 My heart was full of fancies sweet;
5   But soon, as nothing could be seen,
              But countenances sharp and keen,
              Nought heard or seen around, but told
              Of something bought or something sold,
              And none that seemed to think or care
10   That any save himself was there, –

              Full soon my heart began to sink
                 With a strange shame and inward pain,

For I was sad within to think
　　Of this absorbing love of gain,
And various thoughts my bosom tost;
When suddenly my path there crossed,
Locked hand in hand with one another,
A little maiden and her brother –
A little maiden, and she wore
Around her form a pinafore.

And hand in hand along the street
　　This pretty pair did softly go,
And as they went, their little feet
　　Moved in short even steps, and slow:
It was a sight to see and bless,
That little sister's tenderness;
One hand a tidy basket bore
Of flowers and fruit, a chosen store,
Such as kind friends oft send to others;
And one was fastened in her brother's.

It was a voice of meaning sweet,
　　And spake amid that scene of strife
Of home and homely duties meet,
　　And charities of daily life;
And often, should my spirit fail,
And under cold strange glances quail,
'Mid busy shops and busier throng,
That speed upon their ways along
The thick and crowded thoroughfare,
I'll call to mind that little pair.

The Effusions of a School-Patriarch

　　In the days when twenty fellows
　　　　Drank out of one large mug,
　　And pewter were the dishes,
　　　　And a tin can was the jug; –

5 In the days when shoes and boots were
    Three times a week japanned,
And we sate on stools, not sofas, –
    There were giants in the land!

When new boys on the pump were
10   Set to pelt at and to sing,
Or sent from the close to Pendred's
    For a penny-worth of string;
In the days when fags a long hour
    In the passage had to stand,
15 In the days of happy night-fags, –
    There were giants in the land!

When Sixth and Fifth-Form fellows
    Had all been duly 'chaired',
And he who told a falsehood
20   Was 'cobbed' and never spared;
And we walked around the School-field
    With our breakfast in our hand,
Ere the days of tea and coffee, –
    There were giants in the land!

25 In the days when meat was sold in
    The good old dirty shambles,
And the Dunchurch line of houses
    Was a hedge of briars and brambles;
Ere Eldon Row was thought of,
30   Ere Union Street was planned,
Ere the Bilton Road was built on, –
    There were giants in the land!

When the Eagle was a posting place
    Of eminent renown,
And not a single boarding-house
35   Had yet walked out of town;
Ere fellows took to cut-aways
    And rings upon the hand,
Ere frock coats were in fashion, –
40   There were giants in the land!

When Composition Tutors
  Were happily unknown,
And a penchant pour la poesie
  Was a thing you did not own;
When the fags were told to bag the flowers,   45
  And bagged them at command;
When the Island *was* an island, –
  There were giants in the land!

Ere the days of white brick houses,
  Ere the streets were made so clean,   50
Ere the chapel was erected
  Where bloomed 'the tree of Treen',
Ere they built the National School-room
  Where the horse-pond used to stand,
In those days – oh! in those days   55
  There were giants in the land!

He sate, no stiller stands a rock,
And gazed upon an ancient clock;
He heard its steady even tone,
He watched its finger moving on,
From one to five, from five to ten,   5
So through its hourly course again.
Thus sate he through the livelong day,
And as the minutes sped away,
So seemed it to the wretch, he felt
The life that in his members dwelt   10
(Like waxen image set of old
By magic fire with rites untold)
Minute by minute, hour by hour,
Waste and still waste its vital power,
And melt perceptibly away.   15
Thus sate he through the livelong day,
Powerless alike for good or ill,
Bound hand and foot, a captive still;

Wretched and conscious of his lot,
20   And longed to rise and yet did not.
        Oh, what a lesson was there told
In that wise saw that said of old,
'One half they will thou sure wilt win
So soon as e'er thou darest begin!'

Truth is a golden thread seen here and there
In small bright specks upon the visible side
Of our strange Being's party-coloured web.
How rich the converse. 'Tis a vein of ore
5   Emerging now and then on Earth's rude breast,
But flowing full below. Like islands set
At distant intervals on Ocean's face,
We see it on our course; but in the depths
The mystic colonnade unbroken keeps
10   Its faithful way invisible but sure.
O if it be so, wherefore do we men
Pass by so many marks, so little heeding?

Thou bidd'st me mark how swells with rage
      The childish cheek, the childish limb,
How strongly lust and passion wage
      Their strife in every petty whim;
5   Primeval stains from earliest age,
      Thou sayst, our glorious souls bedim;
Yet not, though true thy Wisdom says,
Will I love less the childish days.

Thou askest, ask it as thou wilt,
10   How thus I dare to praise the State
Of Adam's child, an heir of guilt,
      And sin original, innate;
And why the holy blood was spilt
      If sin at last were not so great:

'Tis true, I own; I cannot tell;
Yet still I cherish childhood well.

Perchance, though born twixt good and ill
   To join in warfare through his life,
His heart is in the garden still,
   With Eden thoughts his Spirit rife,
And therefore conquering Passions fill
   His struggling breast with fiercer strife:
It may be – doubtful Wisdom says,
And lets me love the childish days.

With sin innate, that still descends
   On Adam's children one and all,
Perchance innate remembrance blends
   Of Adam's joys before the Fall;
His sinful heart to us he sends
   And we with him his bliss recall:
And so, a truer Wisdom says
Go cherish still the childish days.

We go our worldly ways, and there
   Our Eden thoughts we lose them quite,
Only the quiet Evening air,
   Or dewy Morn, or starry night
Remind us of the Vision fair,
   Or bring it back in living might,
And offer to our tearful gaze
The Paradise of childish days.

Such be the Cause, or be it not,
   Believe, and let the causes go;
New love may every day be got
   So long as here we dwell below;
Of more the heart is ware, I wot,
   Than philosophic systems know;
So heed not what thy Wisdom says,
But cherish thou the childish days.

Oh, I have done those things that my Soul fears
And my whole heart is sick. My Youth hath flown,
The talents thou hast given me are gone,
And I have nought to pay thee but my tears.

Enough, small Room, – though all too true
Much ill in thee I daily do, –
Enough to make thy memory blest,
And thoughts of thee a place of rest,
If, 'midst the ills that crowd me here,
Unvarying clouds that still appear
To dull Life's social atmosphere,
(Oh shame that things so base have power
To bind me down a single hour)
Vainglorious words of fond conceit,
Self-pleasures of successful wit,
And heartless jests and coward lies
And hollow sleek complacencies, –
Enough, – if ever and anon
In thee secluded and alone,
On the dry dust of this weak breast
With conscious faultiness opprest,
And social levities distrest,
Hath fallen from sunny skies above
An April shower of genuine love:
If homeward thoughts and thoughts of one
Sincerely sought nor all unwon,
Of words once said and things once done
'Mid simpler hearts and fresher faces
In happier times and holier places,
With penitential thoughts combine,
And hopes that ere life's day decline
Such lot may yet once more be mine,
And though with toil recalled and pain
My purer Soul return again,
And I be wiser to retain.

Here have I been these one and twenty years
Since first to Being's breeze my Sail unfurled,
A mariner upon the wavy world
Half idling, half in toil: — 'mid empty fears
And emptier hopes, light mirth and fleeting tears   5
Tacking and tossed forever yet in vain
Timidly now retiring, now again
Carelessly, idly mingling with my peers.
Here having done meanwhile as little good
And as much Evil to myself and other   10
As misused strength and guideless frailty could,
Here am I friendless and without a brother,
With faculties developed to no end,
Heart emptied, and faint purpose to amend.

To the Great Metropolis

Traffic, to speak from knowledge but begun,
I saw, and travelling much, and fashion — Yea,
And if that Competition and Display
Make a great Capital, then thou art one,
One, it may be, unrivalled neath the Sun.   5
But sovereign symbol of the Great and Good,
True Royalty, and genuine Statesmanhood,
Nobleness, Learning, Piety was none.
If such realities indeed there are
Working within unsignified, 'tis well;   10
The stranger's fancy of the thing thou art
Is rather truly of a huge Bazaar,
A railway terminus, a gay Hotel,
Anything but a mighty Nation's heart.

About what sort of thing
Do you want me to sing?
And at what sort of times
Indite you rhymes?
5 Until four in the day
We are reading away;
And then after four
It would be but a bore,
For at meal-times I'm talking,
10 As also when walking,
To myself or to Todo;
So that time will no do,
For as now the world goes
My talk's always prose: –
15 Then for subjects – 'Why, twenty, –
Lakes, mountains in plenty!'
Ullswater or Derwent lake
Would a long journey take;
And even Thirl-mere
20 Is not over near;
Grasmere and Rydal
We can walk to, though idle
But for them I must trouble you
To refer to W. W.
25 Who you know very well
Of your own pretty sell'
Has wroot all can be wroot, and said all can be said
Of Grasmere lake-foot, or of Grasmere lake-head.
So in wrath and great sorrow
30 And hopes that tomorrow
Will bring me a letter
From my obstinate debtor,
Which you are as plain's can be,
I remain A. H. C. –
35 (You ungrateful wretch, –
When I sent you such a pretty sketch!)

Do duty feeling nought and truth believe;
Love without feeling give not nor receive.

Like one that in a dream would fain arise,
    Toiling and striving – vainly striving still,
A strange and baffling torpor still replies
    To every restless movement of the will.

If help there is not, but the Muse
Must needs the one or other chuse,
I do prefer, I must confess,
The somewhat slovenly undress
Of slippered slip-slop sentimentals   5
To Philosophic regimentals.

    To be, be thine;
To work, to worship, and to wish be mine.

Irritability unnatural
by slow sure poisons wrought God's death's work, God's doom.

See! the faint green tinge from the western sky has
Faded; not one star but is gaining brightness;
Over dusk hills slowly, to western seas the
                    Moon is retiring.

5   Now, in this deep stillness from tower and steeple
Hark! the loud knell! to the hills it past, and
List! the same sad sound from across the wide bay
                    Faintly re-echoed!

Epi-Strauss-ium

Matthew and Mark and Luke and holy John
Evanished all and gone!
Yea, He that erst, his dusky Curtains quitting,
Through Eastern pictured panes his level beams transmitting,
5   With gorgeous portraits blent,
On them his glories intercepted spent,
Southwestering now, through windows plainly glassed
On the inside face his radiance keen hath cast;
And in the lustre lost, invisible and gone,
10   Are, say you? Matthew, Mark and Luke and holy John.
Lost, is it? lost, to be recovered never?
However,
The Place of Worship the meantime with light
Is, if less richly, more sincerely bright,
15   And in blue skies the Orb is manifest to Sight.

Homo sum, nihil humani –

She had a coarse and common grace
        As ever beggar showed,
It was a coarse but living face,
        I kissed upon the road.

And why have aught to do with her,
　　And what could be the good?
I kissed her, O my questioner,
　　Because I knew I could!

And do you do, or good or bad,
　　Whatever thing you can?
What's healthy freedom of a lad
　　Is licence of a man:

And do you, if you can and will,
　　Kiss any on your way?
I know not; be it well or ill,
　　I did kiss one today.

I kissed her, for her carnalness
　　It could not come to me;
For I in my containedness
　　Was mightier Force than she;

For royal-rich I was of force
　　Exuberant of will;
And carnal if she were and coarse,
　　She was a woman still.

I kissed, and said, – and piercing-in,
　　I looked her through the face, –
I muttered, as I held her chin,
　　God give you of his grace!

But whether virtue from him flowed,
　　And if it did her good,
He did not question, on the road,
　　Who kissed because he could.

And whether heard or not the word,
　　And whether understood,
He doth not wis who gave the kiss
　　Because he knew he could.

AMBARVALIA

The human spirits saw I on a day,
Sitting and looking each a different way;
And hardly tasking, subtly questioning,
Another spirit went around the ring
To each and each: and as he ceased his say,   5
Each after each, I heard them singly sing,
Some querulously high, some softly, sadly low,
We know not, — what avails to know?
We know not, — wherefore need we know?
This answer gave they still unto his suing,   10
We know not, let us do as we are doing.

Dost thou not know that these things only seem? —
I know not, let me dream my dream.
Are dust and ashes fit to make a treasure? —
I know not, let me take my pleasure.   15
What shall avail the knowledge thou hast sought? —
I know not, let me think my thought.
What is the end of strife? —
I know not, let me live my life.
How many days or e'er though mean'st to move? —   20
I know not, let me love my love.
Were not things old once new? —
I know not, let me do as others do.
And when the rest were over past,
I know not, I will do my duty, said the last.   25

Thy duty do? rejoined the voice,
Ah do it, do it, and rejoice;
But shalt thou then, when all is done,
Enjoy a love, embrace a beauty
Like these, that may be seen and won   30
In life, whose course will then be run;
Or wilt thou be where there is none?
I know not, I will do my duty.

And taking up the word around, above, below,
35 Some querulously high, some softly, sadly low,
We know not, sang they all, nor ever need we know!
We know not, sang they, what avails to know?
Whereat the questioning spirit, some short space,
Though unabashed, stood quiet in his place.
40 But as the echoing chorus died away
And to their dreams the rest returned apace,
By the one spirit I saw him kneeling low,
And in a silvery whisper heard him say:
Truly, thou knowst not, and thou needst not know;
45 Hope only, hope thou, and believe alway;
I also know not, and I need not know,
Only with questionings pass I to and fro,
Perplexing these that sleep, and in their folly
Imbreeding doubt and sceptic melancholy;
50 Till that their dreams deserting, they with me,
Come all to this true ignorance and thee.

I

Ah, what is love, our love, she said,
    Ah, what is human love?
A fire, of earthly fuel fed,
    Full fain to soar above.
5 With lambent flame the void it lips,
    And of the impassive air
Would frame for its ambitious steps
    A heaven-attaining stair.
It wrestles and it climbs – Ah me,
10   Go look in little space,
White ash on blackened earth will be
    Sole record of its place.

II

Ah love, high love, she said and sighed,
 She said, the Poet's love!
A star upon a turbid tide, 15
 Reflected from above.
A marvel here, a glory there,
 But clouds will intervene,
And garish earthly noon outglare
 The purity serene. 20

When panting sighs the bosom fill,
And hands by chance united thrill
At once with one delicious pain
The pulses and the nerves of twain;
When eyes that erst could meet with ease, 5
Do seek, yet, seeking, shyly shun
Extatic conscious unison, —
The sure beginnings, say, be these,
Prelusive to the strain of love
Which angels sing in heaven above? 10

Or is it but the vulgar tune,
Which all that breathe beneath the moon
So accurately learn — so soon?
With variations duly blent;
Yet that same song to all intent, 15
Set for the finer instrument;
It is; and it would sound the same
In beasts, were not the bestial frame,
Less subtly organised, to blame;
And but that soul and spirit add 20
To pleasures, even base and bad,
A zest the soulless never had.

It may be — well indeed I deem;
But what if sympathy, it seem,
And admiration and esteem, 25

Commingling therewithal, do make
The passion prized for Reason's sake?
Yet, when my heart would fain rejoice,
A small expostulating voice
Falls in: Of this thou wilt not take
Thy one irrevocable choice?
In accent tremulous and thin
I hear high Prudence deep within,
Pleading the bitter, bitter sting,
Should slow-maturing seasons bring,
Too late, the veritable thing.
For if (the Poet's tale of bliss)
A love, wherewith commeasured this
Is weak, and beggarly, and none,
Exist a treasure to be won,
And if the vision, though it stay,
Be yet for an appointed day, –
This choice, if made, this deed, if done,
The memory of this present past,
With vague foreboding might o'ercast
The heart, or madden it at last.

Let Reason first her office ply;
Esteem, and admiration high,
And mental, moral sympathy,
Exist they first, nor be they brought
By self-deceiving afterthought, –
What if an halo interfuse
With these again its opal hues,
That all o'erspreading and o'erlying,
Transmuting, mingling, glorifying,
About the beauteous various whole,
With beaming smile do dance and quiver;
Yet, is that halo of the soul? –
Or is it, as may sure be said,
Phosphoric exhalation bred
Of vapour, steaming from the bed
Of Fancy's brook, or Passion's river?

So when, as will be by-and-by,
The stream is waterless and dry,
This halo and its hues will die;　　　　　　65
And though the soul contented rest
With those substantial blessings blest,
Will not a longing, half-confest,
Betray that this is not the love,
The gift for which all gifts above　　　　70
Him praise we, Who is Love, the giver?

I cannot say — the things are good:
Bread is it, if not angels' food;
But Love? Alas! I cannot say;
A glory on the vision lay;　　　　　　75
A light of more than mortal day
About it played, upon it rested;
It did not, faltering and weak,
Beg Reason on its side to speak:
Itself was Reason, or, if not,　　　　80
Such substitute as is, I wot,
Of seraph-kind the loftier lot; —
Itself was of itself attested; —
To processes that, hard and dry,
Elaborate truth from fallacy,　　　　85
With modes intuitive succeeding,
Including those and superseding;
Reason sublimed and Love most high
It was, a life that cannot die,
A dream of glory most exceeding.　　　　90

As, at a railway junction, men
Who came together, taking then
One the train up, one down, again

Meet never! Ah, much more as they
Who take one street's two sides, and say
Hard parting words, but walk one way:

Though moving other mates between,
While carts and coaches intervene,
Each to the other goes unseen,

Yet seldom, surely, shall there lack
Knowledge they walk not back to back,
But with an unity of track,

Where common dangers each attend,
And common hopes their guidance lend
To light them to the self-same end.

Whether he then shall cross to thee,
Or thou go thither, or it be
Some midway point, ye yet shall see

Each other, yet again shall meet.
Ah, joy! when with the closing street,
Forgivingly at last ye greet!

When soft September brings again
    To yonder gorse its golden glow,
And Snowdon sends its autumn rain
    To bid thy current livelier flow;
Amid that ashen foliage light
When scarlet beads are glistering bright,
While alder boughs unchanged are seen
In summer livery of green;
When clouds before the cooler breeze
Are flying, white and large; with these
Returning, so may I return,
And find thee changeless, Pont-y-wern.

Oh, ask not what is love, she said,
    Or ask it not of me;
Or of the heart, or of the head,
    Or if at all it be.

Oh, ask it not, she said, she said,
    Thou winn'st not word from me!   5
— Oh, silent as the long long dead,
    I, Lady, learn of thee.

I ask, — thou speakest not, — and still
    I ask, and look to thee;   10
And lo, without or with a will,
    The answer is in me.

Without thy will it came to me?
    Ah, with it let it stay;
Ah, with it, yes, abide in me,   15
    Nor only for today!

Thou claim'st it? nay, the deed is done;
    Ah, leave it with thy leave;
And thou a thousand loves for one
    Shalt day on day receive!   20

Light words they were, and lightly, falsely said;
She heard them, and she started, — and she rose,
As in the act to speak; the sudden thought
And unconsidered impulse led her on.
In act to speak she rose, but with the sense   5
Of all the eyes of that mixed company
Now suddenly turned upon her, some with age
Hardened and dulled, some cold and critical;
Some in whom vapours of their own conceit,
As moist malarious mists the heavenly stars,   10
Still blotted out their good, the best at best
By frivolous laugh and prate conventional
All too untuned for all she thought to say —

With such a thought the mantling blood to her cheek
15 Flushed-up, and o'er-flushed itself, blank night her soul
Made dark, and in her all her purpose swooned.
She stood as if for sinking. Yet anon
With recollections clear, august, sublime,
Of God's great truth, and right immutable,
20 Which, as obedient vassals, to her mind
Came summoned of her will, in self-negation
Quelling her troublous earthy consciousness,
She queened it o'er her weakness. At the spell
Back rolled the ruddy tide, and leaves her cheek
25 Paler than erst, and yet not ebbs so far
But that one pulse of one indignant thought
Might hurry it hither in flood. So as she stood
She spoke. God in her spoke, and made her heard.

Qui laborat, orat

O only Source of all our light and life,
    Whom as our truth, our strength, we see and feel,
But whom the hours of mortal moral strife
    Alone aright reveal!

5   Mine inmost soul, before Thee inly brought,
    Thy presence owns ineffable, divine;
Chastised each rebel self-encentered thought,
    My will adoreth Thine.

With eye down-dropt, if then this earthly mind
10   Speechless abide, or speechless e'en depart;
Nor seek to see – for what of earthly kind,
    Can see Thee as Thou art? –

If sure-assured 'tis but profanely bold
    In thought's abstractest forms to seem to see,
15 It dare not dare the dread communion hold
    In ways unworthy Thee,

O not unowned, Thou shalt unnamed forgive,
   In worldly walks the prayerless heart prepare;
And if in work its life it seem to live,
   Shalt make that work be prayer.   20

Nor times shall lack, when while the work it plies,
   Unsummoned powers the blinding film shall part,
And scarce by happy tears made dim, the eyes
   In recognition start.

As wills Thy will, or give or e'en forbear   25
   The beatific supersensual sight,
So, with Thy blessing blest, that humbler prayer
   Approach Thee morn and night.

When Israel came out of Egypt

Lo, here is God, and there is God!
   Believe it not, O man;
In such vain sort to this and that
   The ancient heathen ran:
Though old Religion shake her head,   5
   And say in bitter grief,
The day behold, at first foretold,
   Of atheist unbelief:
Take better part, with manly heart,
   Thine adult spirit can;   10
Receive it not, believe it not,
   Believe it not, O Man!

As men at dead of night awaked
   With cries, 'The king is here,'
Rush forth and greet whome'er they meet,   15
   Whoe'er shall first appear;
And still repeat, to all the street,
   ' 'Tis he, – the king is here;'
The long procession moveth on,
   Each nobler form they see   20

With changeful suit they still salute,
  And cry, ''Tis he, 'tis he!'

So, even so, when men were young,
  And earth and heaven was new,
And His immediate presence He
  From human hearts withdrew,
The soul perplexed and daily vexed
  With sensuous False and True,
Amazed, bereaved, no less believed,
  And fain would see Him too:
He is! the prophet-tongues proclaimed;
  In joy and hasty fear,
He is! aloud replied the crowd,
  Is, here, and here, and here.

He is! They are! in distance seen
  On yon Olympus high,
In those Avernian woods abide,
  And walk this azure sky:
They are, They are! to every show
  Its eyes the baby turned,
And blazes sacrificial tall
  On thousand altars burned:
They are, They are! — On Sinai's top
  Far seen the lightnings shone,
The thunder broke, a trumpet spoke,
  And God said, I am One.

God spake it out, I, God, am One;
  The unheeding ages ran,
And baby-thoughts again, again,
  Have dogged the growing man:
And as of old from Sinai's top
  God said that God is One,
By science strict so speaks He now
  To tell us, There is None!
Earth goes by chemic forces; Heaven's
  A Mécanique Celeste!

And heart and mind of human kind
  A watch-work as the rest!

Is this a Voice, as was the Voice
  Whose speaking spoke abroad,   60
When thunder pealed, and mountain reeled,
  The ancient Truth of God?
Ah, not the Voice; 'tis but the cloud,
  The cloud of darkness dense,
Where image none, nor e'er was seen   65
  Similitude of sense.
'Tis but the cloudy darkness dense
  That wrapt the Mount around;
With dull amaze the people stays,
  And doubts the Coming Sound.   70

Some chosen prophet-soul the while
  Shall dare, sublimely meek,
Within the shroud of blackest cloud
  The Deity to seek:
'Midst atheistic systems dark,   75
  And darker hearts' despair,
That soul has heard his very word,
  And on the dusky air
His skirts, as passed He by, to see
  Has strained on their behalf,   80
Who on the plain, with dance amain,
  Adore the Golden Calf.

'Tis but the cloudy darkness dense;
  Though blank the tale it tells,
No God, no Truth! yet He, in sooth,   85
  Is there — within it dwells;
Within the sceptic darkness deep
  He dwells that none may see,
Till idol forms and idol thoughts
  Have passed and ceased to be: 90
No God, no Truth! ah though, in sooth,
  So stand the doctrine's half;

On Egypt's track return not back,
　　Nor own the Golden Calf.

95   Take better part, with manlier heart,
　　　Thine adult spirit can;
　　No God, no Truth, receive it ne'er –
　　　Believe it ne'er – O Man!
　　But turn not then to seek again
100　　What first the ill began;
　　No God, it saith; ah, wait in faith
　　　God's self-completing plan;
　　Receive it not, but leave it not,
　　　And wait it out, O Man!

105   The Man that went the cloud within
　　　Is gone and vanished quite;
　　He cometh not, the people cries,
　　　Nor bringeth God to sight:
　　Lo these thy gods, that safety give,
110　　Adore and keep the feast!
　　Deluding and deluded cries
　　　The Prophet's brother-Priest:
　　And Israel all bows down to fall
　　　Before the gilded beast.

115   Devout, indeed! that priestly creed,
　　　O Man, reject as sin;
　　The clouded hill attend thou still,
　　　And him that went within.
　　He yet shall bring some worthy thing
120　　For waiting souls to see;
　　Some sacred word that he hath heard
　　　Their light and life shall be;
　　Some lofty part, than which the heart
　　　Adopt no nobler can,
125   Thou shalt receive, thou shalt believe,
　　　And thou shalt do, O Man!

Sweet streamlet bason! at thy side
Weary and faint within me cried
My longing heart, — In such pure deep
How sweet it were to sit and sleep;
To feel each passage from without   5
Close up, — above me and about,
Those circling waters crystal clear,
That calm impervious atmosphere!
There on thy pearly pavement pure
To lean, and feel myself secure,   10
Or through the dim-lit inter-space,
Afar at whiles upgazing trace
The dimpling bubbles dance around
Upon thy smooth exterior face;
Or idly list the dreamy sound   15
Of ripples lightly flung, above
That home, of peace, if not of love.

Away, haunt not thou me,
Thou vain Philosophy!
Little hast thou bestead,
Save to perplex the head,
And leave the spirit dead.   5
Unto thy broken cisterns wherefore go,
While from the secret treasure-depths below,
Fed by the skiey shower,
And clouds that sink and rest on hill-tops high,
Wisdom at once, and Power,   10
Are welling, bubbling forth, unseen, incessantly?
Why labour at the dull mechanic oar,
When the fresh breeze is blowing,
And the strong current flowing,
Right onward to the Eternal Shore?   15

My wind is turned to bitter north,
   That was so soft a south before;
My sky, that shone so sunny bright,
   With foggy gloom is clouded o'er:
My gay green leaves are yellow-black,
   Upon the dank autumnal floor;
For love, departed once, comes back
   No more again, no more.

A roofless ruin lies my home,
   For winds to blow and rains to pour;
One frosty night befell, and lo,
   I find my summer days are o'er:
The heart bereaved, of why and how
   Unknowing, knows that yet before
It had what e'en to Memory now
   Returns no more, no more.

Look you, my simple friend, 'tis one of those,
(Alack, a common weed of our ill time),
Who, do whate'er they may, go where they will,
Must needs still carry about the looking-glass
Of vain philosophy. And if so be
That some small natural gesture shall escape them,
(Nature will out) straightway about they turn,
And con it duly there, and note it down,
With inward glee and much complacent chuckling,
Part in conceit of their superior science,
Part in forevision of the attentive look
And laughing glance that may one time reward them,
When the fresh ore, this day dug up, at last
Shall, thrice refined and purified, from the mint
Of conversation intellectual
Into the golden currency of wit
Issue — satirical or pointed sentence,
Impromptu, epigram, or it may be sonnet,

Heir undisputed to the pinkiest page
In the album of a literary lady.   20

   And can it be, you ask me, that a man,
With the strong arm, the cunning faculties,
And keenest forethought gifted, and, within,
Longings unspeakable, the lingering echoes
Responsive to the still-still-calling voice   25
Of God Most High, — should disregard all these,
And half-employ all those for such an aim
As the light sympathy of successful wit,
Vain titillation of a moment's praise?
Why, so is good no longer good, but crime   30
Our truest, best advantage, since it lifts us
Out of the stifling gas of men's opinion
Into the vital atmosphere of Truth,
Where He again is visible, though in anger.

Thought may well be ever ranging,
And opinion ever changing,
Task-work be, though ill begun,
Dealt with by experience better;
By the law and by the letter   5
Duty done is duty done:
Do it, Time is on the wing!

Hearts, 'tis quite another thing,
Must or once for all be given,
Or must not at all be given;   10
Hearts, 'tis quite another thing!

To bestow the soul away
In an idle duty-play! —
Why, to trust a life-long bliss
To caprices of a day,   15
Scarce were more depraved than this!

Men and maidens, see you mind it;
Show of love, where'er you find it,
Look if duty lurk behind it!
20   Duty-fancies, urging on
Whither love had never gone!

Loving – if the answering breast
Seem not to be thus possessed,
Still in hoping have a care;
25   If it do, beware, beware!
But if in yourself you find it,
Above all things – mind it, mind it!

Duty – that's to say complying
    With whate'er's expected here;
On your unknown cousin's dying,
    Straight be ready with the tear;
5   Upon etiquette relying,
Unto usage nought denying,
Lend your waist to be embraced,
    Blush not even, never fear;
Claims of kith and kin connection,
10   Claims of manners honour still,
Ready money of affection
    Pay, whoever drew the bill.
With the form conforming duly,
Senseless what it meaneth truly,
15   Go to church – the world require you,
    To balls – the world require you too,
And marry – papa and mamma desire you,
    And your sisters and schoolfellows do.
Duty – 'tis to take on trust
20   What things are good, and right, and just;
    And whether indeed they be or be not,
    Try not, test not, feel not, see not:
    'Tis walk and dance, sit down and rise
    By leading, opening ne'er your eyes;

Stunt sturdy limbs that Nature gave, 25
And be drawn in a Bath chair along to the grave.

'Tis the stern and prompt suppressing,
    As an obvious deadly sin,
All the questing and the guessing
    Of the soul's own soul within: 30
'Tis the coward acquiescence
    In a destiny's behest,
To a shade by terror made,
Sacrificing, aye, the essence
    Of all that's truest, noblest, best: 35
'Tis the blind non-recognition
    Either of goodness, truth, or beauty,
Except by precept and submission;
    Moral blank, and moral void,
    Life at very birth destroyed, 40
Atrophy, exinanition!
Duty! —
Yea, by duty's prime condition
    Pure nonentity of duty!

'Blank Misgivings of a Creature moving about in Worlds not realised'

I

Here am I yet, another twelvemonth spent,
One-third departed of the mortal span,
Carrying on the child into the man,
Nothing into reality. Sails rent,
And rudder broken, — reason impotent, — 5
Affections all unfixed; so forth I fare
On the mid seas unheedingly, so dare
To do and to be done by, well content.
So was it from the first, so is it yet;
Yea, the first kiss that by these lips was set 10

On any human lips, methinks was sin —
Sin, cowardice, and falsehood; for the will
Into a deed e'en then advanced, wherein
God, unidentified, was thought-of still.

II

Though to the vilest things beneath the moon
For poor Ease' sake I give away my heart,
And for the moment's sympathy let part
My sight and sense of truth, Thy precious boon,
5   My painful earnings, lost, all lost, as soon,
Almost, as gained: and though aside I start,
Belie Thee daily, hourly, — still Thou art,
Art surely as in heaven the sun at noon:
How much soe'er I sin, whate'er I do
10   Of evil, still the sky above is blue,
The stars look down in beauty as before:
Is it enough to walk as best we may,
To walk, and sighing, dream of that blest day
When ill we cannot quell shall be no more?

III

Well, well, — Heaven bless you all from day to day!
Forgiveness too, or e'er we part, from each,
As I do give it, so much I beseech:
I owe all much, much more than I can pay;
5   Therefore it is I go; how could I stay
Where every look commits me to fresh debt,
And to pay little I must borrow yet?
Enough of this already, now away!
With silent woods and hills untenanted
10   Let me go commune; under thy sweet gloom,
O kind maternal Darkness, hide my head:
The day may come I yet may reassume
My place, and, these tired limbs recruited, seek
The task for which I now am all too weak.

IV

    Yes, I have lied, and so must walk my way,
Bearing the liar's curse upon my head;
Letting my weak and sickly heart be fed
On food which does the present craving stay,
But may be clean-denied me e'en today,   5
And though 'twere certain, yet were aught but bread;
Letting — for so they say, it seems, I said,
And I am all too weak to disobey!
Therefore for me sweet Nature's scenes reveal not
Their charm; sweet Music greets me and I feel not;   10
    Sweet eyes pass off me uninspired; yea, more,
The golden tide of opportunity
Flows wafting-in friendships and better, — I
Unseeing, listless, pace along the shore.

V

    How often sit I, poring o'er
    My strange distorted youth,
Seeking in vain, in all my store,
    One feeling based on truth;
Amid the maze of petty life   5
    A clue whereby to move,
A spot whereon in toil and strife
    To dare to rest and love.

    So constant as my heart would be,
    So fickle as it must,   10
    'Twere well for others as for me
    'Twere dry as summer dust.
Excitements come, and act and speech
    Flow freely forth; — but no,
Nor they, nor aught beside can reach   15
    The buried world below.

VI

– Like a child
In some strange garden left awhile alone,
I pace about the pathways of the world,
Plucking light hopes and joys from every stem,
With qualms of vague misgiving in my heart
That payment at the last will be required,
Payment I cannot make, or guilt incurred,
And shame to be endured.

VII

– Roused by importunate knocks
I rose, I turned the key, and let them in,
First one, anon another, and at length
In troops they came; for how could I, who once
Had let in one, nor looked him in the face,
Show scruples e'er again? So in they came,
A noisy band of revellers, – vain hopes,
Wild fancies, fitful joys; and there they sit
In my heart's holy place, and through the night
Carouse, to leave it when the cold grey dawn
Gleams from the East, to tell me that the time
For watching and for thought bestowed is gone.

VIII

O kind protecting Darkness! as a child
Flies back to bury in his mother's lap
His shame and his confusion, so to thee,
O Mother Night, come I! within the folds
Of thy dark robe hide thou me close; for I
So long, so heedless, with external things
Have played the liar, that whate'er I see,
E'en these white glimmering curtains, yon bright stars,
Which to the rest rain comfort down, for me
Smiling those smiles, which I may not return,
Or frowning frowns of fierce triumphant malice,

As angry claimants or expectants sure
Of that I promised and may not perform
Look me in the face! O hide me, Mother Night!

IX

Once more the wonted road I tread,
Once more dark heavens above me spread,
Upon the windy down I stand,
My station, whence the circling land
Lies mapped and pictured wide below; —   5
Such as it was, such e'en again,
Long dreary bank, and breadth of plain
By hedge or tree unbroken; — lo,
A few grey woods can only show
How vain their aid, and in the sense   10
Of one unaltering impotence,
Relieving not, meseems enhance
The sovereign dullness of the expanse.
Yet marks where human hand hath been,
Bare house, unsheltered village, space   15
Of ploughed and fenceless tilth between
(Such aspect as methinks may be
In some half-settled colony),
From Nature vindicate the scene;
A wide, and yet disheartening view,   20
A melancholy world.
                    'Tis true,
Most true; and yet, like those strange smiles
By fervent hope or tender thought
From distant happy regions brought,
Which upon some sick bed are seen   25
To glorify a pale worn face
With sudden beauty, — so at whiles
Lights have descended, hues have been,
To clothe with half-celestial grace
The bareness of the desert place.   30

Since so it is, so be it still!
Could only thou, my heart, be taught
To treasure, and in act fulfil
The lesson which the sight has brought;
In thine own dull and dreary state
To work and patiently to wait:
Little thou think'st in thy despair
How soon the o'ershaded sun may shine,
And e'en the dulling clouds combine
To bless with lights and hues divine
That region desolate and bare,
Those sad and sinful thoughts of thine!

Still doth the coward heart complain;
The hour may come, and come in vain;
The branch that withered lies and dead
No suns can force to lift its head.
True! — yet how little thou canst tell
How much in thee is ill or well;
Nor for thy neighbour, nor for thee,
Be sure, was life designed to be
A draught of dull complacency.
One Power too is it, who doth give
The food without us, and within
The strength that makes it nutritive:
He bids the dry bones rise and live,
And e'en in hearts depraved to sin
Some sudden, gracious influence,
May give the long-lost good again,
And wake within the dormant sense
And love of good; — for mortal men,
So but thou strive, thou soon shalt see
Defeat itself is victory.

So be it: yet, O Good and Great,
In whom in this bedarkened state
I fain am struggling to believe,
Let me not ever cease to grieve,
Nor lose the consciousness of ill

Within me; — and refusing still
To recognise in things around
What cannot truly there be found,   70
Let me not feel, nor be it true,
That while their daily task I do
I still am giving day by day
My precious things within away,
(Those thou didst give to keep as thine)   75
And casting, do whate'er I may,
My heavenly pearls to earthly swine.

X

I have seen higher holier things than these,
    And therefore must to these refuse my heart,
Yet am I panting for a little ease;
    I'll take, and so depart.

Ah hold! the heart is prone to fall away,   5
    Her high and cherished visions to forget,
And if thou takest, how wilt thou repay
    So vast, so dread a debt?

How will the heart, which now thou trustest, then
    Corrupt, yet in corruption mindful yet,   10
Turn with sharp stings upon itself! Again,
    Bethink thee of the debt!

— Hast thou seen higher holier things than these,
    And therefore must to these thy heart refuse?
With the true best, alack, how ill agrees   15
    That best that thou wouldst choose!

The Summum Pulchrum rests in heaven above;
    Do thou, as best thou may'st, thy duty do:
Amid the things allowed thee live and love;
    Some day thou shalt it view.   20

Qua cursum ventus

As ships becalmed at eve that lay
    With canvas drooping, side by side,
Two towers of sail at dawn of day
    Are scarce long leagues apart descried;

5   When fell the night, upsprung the breeze,
        And all the darkling hours they plied,
    Nor dreamt but each the self-same seas
        By each was cleaving, side by side:

    E'en so — but why the tale reveal
10   Of those, whom year by year unchanged,
    Brief absence joined anew to feel,
        Astounded, soul from soul estranged.

    At dead of night their sails were filled,
        And onward each rejoicing steered —
15 Ah, neither blame, for neither willed,
        Or wist, what first with dawn appeared!

    To veer, how vain! On, onward strain,
        Brave barks! In light, in darkness too,
    Through winds and tides one compass guides —
20   To that, and your own selves, be true.

    But O blithe breeze! and O great seas,
        Though ne'er, that earliest parting past,
    On your wide plain they join again,
        Together lead them home at last.

25 One port, methought, alike they sought,
        One purpose hold where'er they fare, —
    O bounding breeze, O rushing seas!
        At last, at last, unite them there!

Alcaics

So spake the Voice; and, as with a single life
Instinct, the whole mass, fierce, irretainable,
   Down on that unsuspecting host swept
   Down, with the fury of winds that all night
Up-brimming, sapping slowly the dyke, at dawn   5
Full through the breach, o'er homestead, and harvest, and
   Herd roll a deluge; while the milkmaid
   Trips i'the dew, and remissly guiding
Morn's first uneven furrow, the farmer's boy
Dreams out his dream: — so over the multitude   10
   Safe-tented, uncontrolled and uncon-
   trollably sped the Avenger's fury.

Natura naturans

   Beside me, — in the car, — she sat,
      She spake not, no, nor looked to me:
   From her to me, from me to her,
      What passed so subtly stealthily?
   As rose to rose that by it blows   5
      Its interchanged aroma flings;
   Or wake to sound of one sweet note
      The virtues of disparted strings.

   Beside me, nought but this! — but this,
      That influent as within me dwelt
   Her life, mine too within her breast,   10
      Her brain, her every limb she felt:
   We sat; while o'er and in us, more
      And more, a power unknown prevailed,
   Inhaling, and inhaled, — and still   15
      'Twas one, inhaling or inhaled.

   Beside me, nought but this; — and passed;
      I passed; and know not to this day
   If gold or jet her girlish hair,
      If black, or brown, or lucid-grey   20

Her eye's young glance: the fickle chance
    That joined us, yet may join again;
But I no face again could greet
    As hers, whose life was in me then.

25 As unsuspecting mere a maid
    As, fresh in maidhood's bloomiest bloom,
In casual second-class did e'er
    By casual youth her seat assume;
Or vestal, say, of saintliest clay,
30   For once by balmiest airs betrayed
Unto emotions too too sweet
    To be unlingeringly gainsaid:

Unowning then, confusing soon
    With dreamier dreams that o'er the glass
35 Of shyly ripening woman-sense
    Reflected, scarce reflected, pass,
A wife may-be, a mother she
    In Hymen's shrine recalls not now,
She first in hour, ah, not profane,
40   With me to Hymen learnt to bow.

Ah no! – Yet owned we, fused in one,
    The Power which e'en in stones and earths
By blind elections felt, in forms
    Organic breeds to myriad births;
45 By lichen small on granite wall
    Approved, its faintest feeblest stir
Slow-spreading, strengthening long, at last
    Vibrated full in me and her.

In me and her – sensation strange!
50   The lily grew to pendent head,
To vernal airs the mossy bank
    Its sheeny primrose spangles spread,
In roof o'er roof of shade sun-proof
    Did cedar strong itself outclimb,

And altitude of aloe proud 55
   Aspire in floreal crown sublime;

Flashed flickering forth fantastic flies,
   Big bees their burly bodies swung,
Rooks roused with civic din the elms,
   And lark its wild reveillez rung; 60
In Libyan dell the light gazelle,
   The leopard lithe in Indian glade,
And dolphin, brightening tropic seas,
   In us were living, leapt and played:

Their shells did slow crustacea build, 65
   Their gilded skins did snakes renew,
While mightier spines for loftier kind
   Their types in amplest limbs outgrew;
Yea, close comprest in human breast,
   What moss, and tree, and livelier thing, 70
What Earth, Sun, Star of force possest,
   Lay budding, burgeoning forth for Spring.

Such sweet preluding sense of old
   Led on in Eden's sinless place
The hour when bodies human first
   Combined the primal prime embrace, 75
Such genial heat the blissful seat
   In man and woman owned unblamed,
When, naked both, its garden paths
   They walked unconscious, unashamed: 80

Ere, clouded yet in mistiest dawn,
   Above the horizon dusk and dun,
One mountain crest with light had tipped
   That Orb that is the Spirit's Sun;
Ere dreamed young flowers in vernal showers 85
   Of fruit to rise the flower above,
Or ever yet to young Desire
   Was told the mystic name of Love.

ὁ θεὸς μετὰ σοῦ *

★

Farewell, my Highland lassie! when the year returns around,
Be it Greece, or be it Norway, where my vagrant feet are found,
I shall call to mind the place, I shall call to mind the day,
The day that's gone for ever, and the glen that's far away;
5 I shall mind me, be it Rhine or Rhone, Italian land or France,
Of the laughings, and the whispers, of the pipings and the dance;
I shall see thy soft brown eyes dilate to wakening woman
     thought,
And whiter still the white cheek grow to which the blush was
     brought;
And oh, with mine commixing I thy breath of life shall feel,
10 And clasp the shyly passive hands in joyous Highland reel;
I shall hear, and see, and feel, and in sequence sadly true,
Shall repeat the bitter-sweet of the lingering last adieu;
I shall seem as now to leave thee, with the kiss upon the brow,
And the fervent benediction of − ὁ θεὸς μετὰ σοῦ!

15 Ah me, my Highland lassie! though in winter drear and long
Deep arose the heavy snows, and the stormy winds were strong,
Though the rain, in summer's brightest, it were raining every
     day,
With worldly comforts few and far, how glad were I to stay!
I fall to sleep with dreams of life in some black bothie spent,
Coarse poortith's ware thou changing there to gold of pure
20   content,
With barefoot lads and lassies round, and thee the cheery wife,
In the braes of old Lochaber a laborious homely life;
But I wake − to leave thee, smiling, with the kiss upon the brow,
And the peaceful benediction of − ὁ θεὸς μετὰ σοῦ!

★

* God be with you.

ADAM AND EVE

SCENE I
(*Adam and Eve*)

ADAM

Since that last evening we have fallen indeed.
Yes, we have fallen, my Eve, O yes –
One, two, and three, and four; – the Appetite,
The enjoyment, the aftervoid, the thinking of it,
Specially the latter two, most specially the last.   5
There in synopsis see you have it all,
Come, let us go and work!

                       Is it not enough?
What, is there three, four, five?

EVE

                  Oh, guilt, guilt, guilt.

ADAM

Be comforted; muddle not your soul with doubt.
'Tis done; it was to be done; if indeed   10
Other way than this there was, I cannot say;
This was one way, and a way was needs to be found.
That which we were, we could no more remain
Than in the moist provocative vernal mould
A seed its suckers close, and rest a seed.   15
We were to grow. Necessity on us lay
This way or that to move; necessity, too,
Not to be over-careful this or that,
So only move we should.

                     Come, my wife;
We were to grow, and grow I think we may,   20
And yet bear goodly fruit.

EVE

                  Oh guilt, oh guilt!

ADAM

You weary me with your 'Oh guilt, oh guilt!'

Peace to the senseless iteration. What!
Because I plucked an apple from a twig

25   Be damned to death eterne! parted from Good,
Enchained to Ill! No, by the God of Gods,
No, by the living will within my breast,
It cannot be and shall not; and if this,
This guilt of your distracted fantasy,

30   Be our experiment's sum, thank God for guilt,
Which makes me free! —
But thou, poor wife, poor mother, shall I say?
Big with the first maternity of Man,
Draw'st from thy teeming womb thick fancies fond,

35   That with confusion mix thy delicate brain;
Fondest of which and cloudiest call the dream
(Yea, my beloved, hear me, it is a dream)
Of the serpent, and the apple and the curse:
Fondest of dreams and cloudiest of clouds.

40   Well I remember in our marriage bower
How in the dewiest balminess of rest
Inarmèd as we lay, sudden at once
Up from my side you started, screaming 'Guilt'
And 'Lost, lost, lost.' I on my elbow rose,

45   And rubbed unwilling eyes, and cried, 'Eve, Eve!
My love! my wife!' and knit anew the embrace,
And drew thee to me close, and calmed thy fear,
And woo'd thee back to sleep: In vain; for soon
I felt thee gone, and opening widest eyes

50   Beheld thee kneeling on the turf; hands now
Clenched and uplifted high; now vainly outspread
To hide a burning face and streaming eyes
And pale small lips that muttered faintly 'Death.'
And thou would'st fain depart; thou said'st the place

55   Was for the like of us too good; we left
The pleasant woodland shades, and passed abroad
Into this naked champaign, glorious soil
For digging and for delving, but indeed,
Until I killed a beast or two, and spread

60   Skins upon sticks to make our palace here,
A residence sadly exposed to wind and rain.

But I in all submit to you; and then
I turned out too; and trudged a furlong space
Till you fell tired, and fain would wait for morn.
So as our nightly journey we began,   65
Because the autumnal fruitage that had fallen
From trees whereunder we had slept, lay thick,
And we had eaten overnight, and seen
And saw again by starlight when you woke me
A sly and harmless snake glide by our couch;   70
And because some few hours before a lamb
Fell from a rock and broke its neck, and I
Had answered to your wonder, that 'twas dead,
Forsooth the molten lava of your fright
Forth from your brain, its crater, hurrying down,   75
Took the chance mould; the vapour blowing by
Caught and reflected back some random shapes;
A vague and queasy dream was obstinate
In waking thoughts to find itself renewed,
And lo, the mighty mythus of the Fall!   80
Nay, smile with me, sweet Mother!

EVE

Guilt, oh, guilt!

ADAM

Peace, woman, peace; I go.

EVE

Nay, Adam, nay;
Hear me, I am not dreaming, am not crazed.
Did not yourself confess that we are changed?
Do not you too?

ADAM

Do not I too? Well, well!   85
Listen! I too when homeward, weary of toil,
Through the dark night I have wandered in rain and wind,
Bewildered, haply, scared, — I too have lost heart,
And deemed all space with angry power replete,
Angry, almighty; and panic-stricken have cried,   90
'What have I done? What wilt thou do to me?'

Or with the coward's 'No, I did not, I will not,'
Belied my own soul's self. I too have heard,
And listened too to a Voice that in my ear
95   Hissed the temptation to curse God, or worse
And yet more frequent, curse myself, and die.
Until in fine I have begun to half-believe
Your dream *my* dream too, and the dream of both
No dream but dread reality; have shared
100 Your fright; e'en so, share thou, sweet life, my hope.
I too again when weeds with growth perverse
Have choked my corn, and marred a season's toil,
Have deemed I heard in heaven abroad a cry
'Cursed is the ground for thy sake; thou art curst,'
105 But oftener far and stronger also far,
In consonance with all things out and in,
I hear a Voice, more searching, bid me, 'On,
On, on; it is the folly of the child
To choose his path and straightway think it wrong,
110 And turn right back, or lie on the ground to weep.
Forward; go, conquer! work and live!' Withal
A Word comes, half-command, half-prophecy,
'Forgetting things behind thee, onward press
Unto the mark of your high calling.' Yea,
115 And voices, too, in woods and flowery fields
Speak confidence from budding banks and boughs,
And tell me, 'Live and grow,' and say, 'Look still
Upward, spread outward. Trust, be patient, live!'
Therefore, if weakness bid me curse and die,
120 I answer, No. I will nor curse myself
Nor aught beside; I shall not die but live.

EVE   Ah me. Alas: — Alas!

More dismally in my face stares the doubt,
More heavily on my heart weighs the world.
Methinks
125 The questionings of Ages yet to be,
The thinkings and cross-thinkings, self-contempts,
Self-horror; all despondencies, despairs,

Of multitudinous souls on souls to come
In me imprisoned fight, complain, and cry.
Alas.   130
Mystery, mystery, mystery evermore.

SCENE II
(*Adam, alone*)

Misery, o my misery; O God, God!
How could I ever, ever, could I do it?
Whither am I come? where am I? O me miserable!
My God, my God, that I were back with thee!
O fool, O fool! O irretrievable act!   5
  Irretrievable what, I should like to know.
What act, I wonder; what is it I mean? –
  O heaven! the spirit holds me; I must yield;
Up in the air he lifts me, casts me down.
I writhe in vain, with limbs convulsed in the void.   10
Well, well! go, idle words, babble your will;
I think the fit will leave me, ere I die.
  Fool, fool; where am I? O my God! Fool, fool!
Why did we do't? Eve, Eve, where are you? Quick.
His tread is in the Garden! hither it comes!   15
Hide us, O bushes, and ye thick trees, hide.
He comes, on, on; alack, and all these leaves,
These petty, quivering and illusive blinds,
Avail us nought. The light comes in and in,
Displays us to ourselves; displays, ah shame,   20
Unto the inquisitive day our nakedness.
He comes. He calls. The large eye of his truth,
His full severe all-comprehending view
Fixes itself upon our guiltiness –
O God, O God, what are we, what shall we be?   25
  What is all this about, I wonder now.
Yet I am better too – I think it will pass.
  'Tis going now, unless it comes again;
A terrible possession while it lasts;
Terrible surely; and yet indeed 'tis true   30
E'en in my utmost impotence I find
A fount of strange persistence in my soul;

Also, and that perchance is stranger still,
A wakeful, changeless touchstone in my brain,

35   Receiving, noting, testing all the while
These passing, curious, new phenomena,
Painful, and yet not painful unto it.
Though tortured in the crucible I lie,
Myself my own experiment, yet still

40   I or a something that is I indeed,
A living, central, and more inmost I
Within the scales of mere exterior me's,
I — seem eternal, O thou God, as thou;
Have knowledge of the Evil and the Good,

45   Superior in a higher Good to both.
      Well, well, well! it has gone from me; though still
Its images remain upon me whole:
And undisplaced upon my mind I view
The reflex of the total seizure past.

50   Really now, had I only time and space,
And were not troubled with this wife of mine,
And the necessity of meat and drink,
I really do believe,
With time and space and proper quietude

55   I could resolve the problem on my brain
But no: I scarce can stay one moment more
To watch the curious seething process out.
If I could only dare to let Eve see
These operations — it is like enough

60   Between us two we two could make it out.
But she would be so frightened, think it proof
Of all her own imaginings. 'Twill not do.
So as it is
I must e'en put a cheery face on it;

65   Suppress the whole; rub off the unfinished thoughts
For fear she read them. O 'tis pity indeed
But confidence is the one and main thing now.
Who loses confidence, he loses all.
A demi-grain of cowardice in me

70   Avowed were poison to the whole mankind.
When men are plentier 'twill be time to try.

At present, no.
No.
Shake it all up and go.
That is the word and that must be obeyed.
I must be off. But yet again some day   75
Again will I resume it; if not I,
I in some child of late posterity.
Yes yes, I feel it — it is here the seed,
Here in my head, but O thou power unseen   80
In whom we live and move and have our being
Let it not perish — grant unlost unhurt
In long transmission this rich atom some day
In some futurity of distant years —
How many thou intend'st to have I know not —   85
In some matured and procreant human brain may
Germinate, burst, and rise into a tree.
No, and I don't tell Eve —

SCENE III
'Now the birth of Cain was in this wise'
(*Adam and Eve*)

EVE
Oh Adam I am comforted indeed;
Where is he? O my little one.
My heart is in the garden as of old,
And Paradise come back. —

ADAM
                        My love,
Blessed be this good day to thee indeed,   5
Blessed the balm of joy unto thy soul.
A sad unskilful nurse was I to thee;
But nature teaches mothers, I perceive.

EVE
But you my husband, you meantime I feel
Join not your perfect Spirit in my joy.
No: your spirit mixes not I feel with mine.   10

ADAM
Alas sweet love for many a weary day

You and not I have borne this heavy weight.
How can I, should I, might I feel your bliss,
Now heaviness is changed to glory? Long,
In long and unparticipated pangs,
Your heart hath known its own great bitterness:
How should in this its jubilant release
A stranger intermeddle with its joy? —

EVE

My husband, there is more in it than this;
Nay, you are surely positively sad.

ADAM

What if I were (and yet I think I am not),
'Twere but the silly and contrarious mood
Of one whose sympathies refuse to mix
In aught not felt immediate from himself.

EVE

But of a truth —

ADAM

Your joy is greater, mine seems therefore none.

EVE

Nay, neither this I think nor that is true.
Evermore still you love to cheat me, Adam.
You hide from me your thoughts like evil beasts
Most foolishly; for I thus left to guess,
Catch at all hints, and where perchance one is,
People the forest with an hundred ills,
Each worse perhaps an hundred times than it.
No, you have got some fearful thoughts: no, no,
Look not in that way on my baby, Adam —
You do it harm; you shall not.

ADAM

                              Hear then, Eve,
If hear you will — and speak I think I must —
Hear me. Yet think not too much of my word.
What is it I would say? I shrink —
And yet I must — so hear me, Mother blest,

That sittest with thy nursling at thy heart.
Hope not too greatly, neither fear for him,
Feeling on thy breast his small compressing lips,
And glorying in the gift they draw from thee;   45
Hope not too greatly in thyself and him.
And hear me, O young Mother — I must speak.
This child is born of us, and therefore like us;
Is born of us, and therefore is as we;
Is born of us, and therefore is not pure;   50
Earthy as well as godlike; bound to strive —
Not doubtfully I augur from the past —
Through the same straits of anguish and of doubt,
'Mid the same storms of terror and alarm,
To the calm Ocean which he yet shall reach,   55
He or himself or in his sons hereafter,
Of consummated consciousness of self.
The selfsame stuff which wrought in us to grief
Runs in his veins; and what to work in him?
What shape of unsuspected deep disguise   60
Transcending our experience, our best cares
Baffling, evading all preventive thought,
Will the old mischief choose, I wonder, here?
O born to human trouble — also born —
Else wherefore born? —   65
Live, and may Chance treat thee no worse than us.
There, I have done — the dangerous stuff is out,
My mind is freed. And now my gentle Eve
Forgive thy foolish spouse and let me set
A father's kiss upon these budding lips,   70
A husband's on the mother's, the full flower.
There, there; and so, my own and only wife,
Believe me, my worst thought is now to count
How best and most to serve this child and thee.

EVE

This child is born of us, and therefore like us —
                                                                 75

ADAM

Most true, mine own; and if a man like me
Externally, internally I trust

Most like (his best original) to thee.

EVE

Is born of us, and therefore is not pure —

ADAM

80   Did I say that? I know not what I said,
It was a foolish humour, but indeed
Whatever you may think, I have not learnt
The trick of deft suppression, e'en the skill
To sort my thoughts and sift my words enough.
85   Not pure indeed; and if it is not pure,
What is? — Ah well, but most I look to the days
When these small arms, with pliant thewes filled out,
Shall at my side break up the fruitful glebe,
And aid the cheery labours of the year —
90   Aid, or in feebler wearier years, replace,
And leave me longer hours for home and Eve.

SCENE IV
(*Adam and Eve*)

EVE

O Adam, it was I was godless then;
But you were mournful, heavy, but composed.
At times would somewhat fiercely bite your lip
And pass your hand about your brow; but still
5   Held out, denied not God, acknowledged still
Those glories that were gone. No, I never
Felt all your worth to me before. I feel
You did not fall as I did.

ADAM

              Nay, my child,
About our falls I don't profess to know.
10   If yours indeed, as you will have it so,
Were a descent more lengthy than was mine,
It is not that your place is lower now,
But at the first your place was higher up;
It is that, I being bestial, you divine,
15   We now alike are human beings both.
About our falls I won't profess to know,

But know I do
That I was never innocent as you.
    Moping again, my love? Yes I dare swear
All the day long while I have been at work
With some religious crotchet in your head.   20

EVE

No, Adam, I am cheerful quite today;
I vary much, indeed, from hour to hour,
But since my baby's birth I am happier far,
And I have done some work as well as you.
                                                              25

ADAM

What is it though? for I will take my oath
You've got some fancy stirring now within.

EVE

Nay, but it vexes me for ever more
To find in you no credence to my thought.

ADAM

What is it then you wish me to subscribe to?   30
That in a garden we were put by God,
Allowed to eat of all the trees but one;
Somehow — I don't know how — a serpent tempted,
And eat we did, and so were doomed to die;
Whereas before we were meant to live for ever;   35
Meantime, turned out —

EVE

                        You do not think then, Adam,
We have been disobedient unto God?

ADAM

My child, how should I know, and what do you mean?
Your question's not so simple as it looks,
For if you mean that God said this or that,
As that 'You shall not touch those apples there,'   40
And that we did — why, all that I can say
Is, that I can't conceive the thing to be.
But if it were so, I should then believe
We had done right — at any rate, no harm.   45

EVE

O Adam, I can scarcely think I hear;
For if God said to us, God being God,
'You shall not,' is not His commandment His?
And are not we the Creatures He hath made?

ADAM

50 My child, God does not speak to human minds
In that unmeaning arbitrary way;
God were not God, if so, and Good not Good.
Search in your heart, and if you tell me there
You find a genuine Voice — no fancy, mind you —
55 Declaring to you this or that is Evil,
Why, this or that I daresay evil is.
Believe me, I will listen to the Word.
For not by observation of without
Cometh the Kingdom of the Voice of God:
60 It is within us — let us seek it there.

EVE

Yet I have voices surely in my heart.
Often you say I heed them overmuch.

ADAM

God's Voice is of the heart: I do not say
All voices, therefore, of the heart are God's.
65 And to discern the Voice amidst the voices
Is that hard task, my love, that we are born to.

EVE

Ah me, in me I am sure the one, one Voice
Goes somehow to the sense of what I say,
The sense of disobedience to God.
70 O Adam, some way, some time, we have done wrong,
And when I think of this, I still must think
Of Paradise and of the stately tree
Which in the middle of the garden grew
The golden fruit that hung upon its bough.
75 Of which, but once, we ate, and I must feel
That whereas once in His continual sight
We lived — in daily communing with Him —

We now are banished, and behold not Him.
Our only present communing, alas,
Is penitential mourning, and the gaze
Of the abased and prostrate prayerful Soul.
But you yourself, my Adam you at least
Acknowledge some time somehow we did wrong.

ADAM

My child, I never granted even that.

EVE

Oh but you let strange words at times fall from you.
They are to me like thunderbolts from Heaven;
I watch terrified and sick at heart,
Then haste and pick them up and treasure them.
What was it that you said when Cain was born?
'He's born of us and therefore is not pure.'
O you corrected well, my husband, then
My foolish, fond exuberance of delight.

ADAM

My child believe me, truly I was the fool;
But a first baby is a strange surprise.
I shall not say so when another comes;
And I beseech you treasure up no words.
You know me: I am loose of tongue and light.
I beg you Eve remember nought of this;
Put not at least, I pray you – nay, command –
Put not, when days come on, your own strange whim
And misconstruction of my idle words
Into the tender brains of our poor young ones.

SCENE V
(*Adam with Cain and Abel*)

ADAM

                                Cain, beware.
Strike not your brother – I have said, beware:
A heavy curse is on this thing, my son:
With Doubt and Fear,
Terror and Toil and Pain already here,

Let us not have injustice too, my son.
So Cain, beware:
And Abel too, see you provoke him not.

SCENE VI
(*Abel alone*)

            At times I could believe
My father is no better than his son;
If not as overbearing, proud, and hard,
Yet prayerless, worldly almost more than Cain.

5 Enlighten and convert him ere the end,
My God! spurn not my mother's prayer and mine.
Since I was born, was I not left to thee,
In an unspiritual and godless house
Unfathered and unbrothered; Thine and hers?

10   They think not of the Fall: e'en less they think
Of the Redemption, which God said should be,
Which, for we apprehend it by our faith,
And by our strong assurance,
Already is, is come for her and me.

15 Yea though I sin, my sin is not to death.
In my repentance I have joy, such joy
That almost I could sin to seek for it.
Yea, if I did not hate it and abhor,
And know that thou abhorr'st and hatest it,

20 And will'st for an example to the rest
That thine elect should keep themselves from it.
Alas. –
My mother calls the Fall a Mystery.
Redemption is so too. But oh, my God,

25 Thou wilt bring all things in the end to good.
Yea, though the whole Earth lie in wickedness, I
Am with thee, with thee, with thee evermore.
Ah, yet I am not satisfied with this.
Am I not feeding spiritual pride,

30 Rejoicing over sinners, inelect
And unadmitted to the fellowship
Which I unworthy, most unworthy, share?
What can I do – how can I help it then?

O God, remove it from my heart — pluck out,
Whatever pain, what [wrench] to me   35
These sinful roots and remnants, which whate'er
I do, how high soe'er I soar from earth,
Still, undestroyed, still germinate within.
Take them away in thy good time, O God.
Meantime, for that atonement's precious sake   40
Which in thy counsels predetermined works
Already to the saving of the saints,
O Father, view with Mercy, and forgive —
Nor let my vexed perception of my sin,
Nor any multitude of evil thoughts,   45
Crowding like demons in the house,
Nor life, nor death, things here or things below,
Cast out the sweet assurance of my soul
That I am thine, and thou art mine, my God.

SCENE VII
(Cain alone)

Am I or am I not this which they think me?
My mother loves me not; my brother Abel,
Spurning my heart, commends my soul to God.
My father does not spurn me; there's my comfort.
Almost I think they look askance on him —   5
Ah, but for him
I know not what might happen; for at times
Ungovernable angers take the waves
Of my deep soul and sweep them who knows whither
And a strange impulse, struggling to the truth,   10
Urges me onward to put forth my strength,
No matter how — Wild curiosity
Possesses me moreover to essay
This world of Action round me so unknown;
And to be able to do this or that   15
Seems cause enough, without a cause, for doing it —
My father he is cheerful and content
And leads me frankly forward — Yet, indeed,
His leading, — or (more truly) to be led
At all, by any one, and not myself —   20

Is mere dissatisfaction: evermore
Something I must do, individual,
To vindicate my nature, to give proof
I also am, as Adam is, a man.

SCENE VIII
(*Adam and Eve*)

ADAM

These sacrificings, O my best beloved,
These rites and forms which you have taught our boys,
Which I nor practise nor can understand,
Will turn, I trust, to good; but I much fear,
5 Besides the superstitious search of signs
In merest accidents of earth and air,
They cause, I think, a sort of jealousy –
Ill blood. Hark, now!

EVE

O God, whose cry is that?
Abel, where is my Abel?

ADAM

Cain! what, Cain!

SCENE IX
(*Cain alone with the body of Abel*)

What? fallen? so quickly down – so easily felled,
And so completely? Why, he does not move!
Will not he stir – will he not breathe again?
Still as a log, still as his own dead lamb –
5 Dead is it then? – Oh wonderful – O strange.
Dead – dead. And we can slay each other then?
If we are wronged, why we can right ourselves,
If we are plagued and pestered with a fool
That will not let us be, nor leave us room
10 To do our will and shape our path in peace,
We can be rid of him – There, he is gone;
Victory – Victory – Victory – My heaven
Methinks from infinite distances borne back

It comes to me reborn in multitude,
Echoed, re-echoed, and re-echoed again. 15
Victory – Victory – distant yet distinct,
Uncountable times repeated – O ye gods
Where am I come and whither am I borne?
    I stand upon a pinnacle of earth,
And hear the wild seas laughing all about; 20
Yet I could wish that he had struggled more –
That passiveness was disappointing. Ha!
He should have writhed and wrestled in my arms,
And all but overcome, and set his knee
Hard on my chest, till I – all faint, yet still 25
Holding my fingers at his throat – at last,
Inch after inch, had forced him to relax:
But he went down at once, without a word,
Almost without a look. –

                    Ah, hush, my God,
Who was it spoke, what is this questioner? 30
Who was it asked me where my brother is?
Ha, ha, was I his keeper? I know not!
Each for himself; he might have struck again.
Why did he not? I wished him to – was I
To strike for both at once? No! – Yet, ah 35
Where is thy brother? – Peace, thou silly Voice –
Am I my brother's keeper? – I know not,
I know not aught about it – let it be.
Henceforth I shall walk freely upon earth
And know my will and do it by my might. 40
My God – it will not be at peace –My God
It flames, it bursts to fury in my soul.
What is it I have done? – Almighty God
What is it that will come of this? –
I see it, I behold it as it is,
As it will be in all the times to come: 45
Slaughter on slaughter, blood for blood – and death
For ever ever ever evermore. –
And all for what?

                O Abel, brother mine,
Where'er thou art, more happy far than me! 50

SCENE X
(*Adam alone*)

Abel is dead, and Cain – ah, what is Cain?
Is he not even more than Abel dead?
Well, we must hope in Seth. This merest man,
This unambitious commonplace of life,
Will after all perhaps mend all – and though
Record shall tell unto the aftertime
No wondrous tales of him, in him at last –
And in his seed increased and multiplied,
Earth shall be blest and peopled and subdued,
And what was meant to be be brought to pass.
Ah but my Abel and my Cain, e'en so
You shall not be forgotten nor unknown.

SCENE XI
(*Cain and Eve*)

CAIN

I am come – Curse me;
Curse Cain, my mother, ere he goes. He waits.

EVE

Who? What is this?
Oh Abel, O my gentle, holy child,
My perfect son.
Monster! and did I bear thee too? –

CAIN

He was so good, his brother hated him,
And slew him for't. Go on, my mother, on.

EVE
★

For there are rites and holy means of grace
Of God ordained for man's eternal [weal].
With these, my son, address thyself to Him,
And seek atonement from a gracious God,
With whom is balm for every wounded heart.

CAIN

I ask not for atonement, mother mine;

I ask but one thing — never to forget.   15
I ask but — not to add to one great crime
Another, self-delusion, scarcely less.
I *could* ask more — but more I know is sin —
I could ask back again
(If sacrifices and the fat of lambs,   20
And whole burnt-offering upon piles of turf,
Will bring me this, I'd fill the heaven with smoke,
And deface earth with million fiery scars)
I could ask back (and think it but my right,
And passionately claim it as my right)   25
That precious life which one misguided blow,
Which one scarce conscious momentary [act],
One impulse blindly followed to its end
Ended — for ever — but that I know this vain.
If they shall only keep my sin in mind,   30
I shall not, be assured, neglect them either.

EVE

You ask not for Atonement — O my son,
Cain, you are proud and hard of heart e'en now.
Beware — prostrate your soul in penitential prayer,
Humble your heart beneath the mighty hand   35
Of God, whose gracious guidance oft shall lead
Through sin and crime the changed and melted heart
To sweet repentance and the sense of Him.
You ask not for Atonement, O my son!
What, to be banished from the sight of God;   40
To dwell with wicked Spirits, be a prey
To them and prey yourself on human souls;
What, to be lost in wickedness and sink
Deeper and deeper down —
What, Cain, do you choose this?

CAIN

                         Alas, my mother,   45
I know not — there are mysteries in your heart
Which I profess not knowledge of — it may be
That this is so; if so, may God reveal it.
Have faith you too in my heart's secrets, yea,

50 All I can say, alas, is that to me,
 As I now comprehend it, this were sin.
 Atonement — no not that, but punishment —
 But what avails to talk? talk as we will,
 As yet we shall not know each other's hearts;
55 Let me not talk, but act. Farewell, for ever.

SCENE XII
(*Adam and Cain conversing*)

CAIN

This is the history then, my father, is it?
This is the perfect whole.

ADAM

    My son, it is:
And whether a dream, and if it were a dream,
A transcript of an inward spiritual fact
5 (As you suggest, and I allow, might be),
Not the less true because it was a dream,
I know not, O my Cain, I cannot tell.
But in my soul I think it was a dream,
And but a dream: a thing, whence e'er it came,
10 To be forgotten and considered not.
For what is life, and what is pain, or death?
You have killed Abel: Abel killed the lamb —
An act in him prepense, in you unthought of.
One step you stirred, and lo you stood entrapped.

CAIN

15 My father, this is true: I know: but yet
There is some truth beside — I cannot say
But I have heard within my soul a Voice
Asking 'Where is thy brother?' and I said —
That is, the evil heart within me said —
20 'Am I my brother's keeper? Go ask him
Who was it that provoked me: should he rail
And I not smite? his death be on his head!'
But the voice answered in my soul again
So that the other ceased and was no more.

SCENE XIII
(Adam and Cain)

CAIN
My father, Abel is dead.

ADAM
My son, 'tis done, it was to be done; some good end
Thereby to come, or else it had not been.
Go, for it must be. Cain, I know your heart,
You cannot be with us. Go, then, depart;
But be not over-[scrupulous], my son.   5

CAIN
Curse me, my father, ere I go – your curse
Will go with me for good – your curse
Will make me not forget –
Alas I am not of that pious kind   10
Who, when the blot has fallen upon their life
Can look to heaven and think it white again –
Look up to heaven and find a something
To make what is not be, although it is.
My mother – ah, how you have spoke of this.   15
The dead – to him 'twas innocence and joy
And purity and safety from the world;
To me the thing seems sin – the worst of sin.
If it be so, why are we here? – the world,
Why is it as I find it? The dull stone   20
Cast from my hand, why comes it not again?
The broken flow'ret, why does it not live?
If it be so –
Why are we here and why is Abel dead?
                    – Shall this be true   25
Of stocks and stones and mere inanimate clay,
And not in some sort also hold for us?

ADAM
My son, Time healeth all,
Time and great Nature; heed her speech and learn.

CAIN

30   My father, you are learned in this sort:
      You read the Earth, as does my mother Heaven.
      Both books are dark to me — only I feel
      That this one thing
      And this one word in me must be declared
35   That to forget is not to be restored;
      To lose with time the sense of what we did
      Cancels not that we did: what's done remains.
      I am my brother's murderer. Woe to me,
      Abel is dead. No prayers to empty heaven,
40   No vegetative kindness of the Earth,
      Will bring back into his clay again,
      The gentleness of love into his face.
      Therefore for me farewell,
      Farewell for me the soft,
45   The balmy influences of night and sleep,
      The satisfactions of achievement done,
      The restorative pulsing of the blood
      That changes all and changes e'en the soul,
      And natural functions moving as they should,
50   The sweet good nights, the sweet delusive dreams
      That lull us out of old things into new.
      But welcome Fact, and Fact's best brother, Work;
      Welcome the conflict of the stubborn soil,
      To toil the livelong day, and at the end,
55   Instead of rest, re-carve into my brow
      The dire memorial mark of what still is.
      Welcome this worship — which I feel is mine.
      Welcome this duty —
                              — the solidarity of life
      And unity of individual soul.
60   That which I did, I did, I who am here:
      There is no safety but in this, and when
      I shall deny the thing that I have done,
      I am a dream.

ADAM
My son, what shall I say?
That which your soul in marriage with the world
Imbreeds in you, accept; – how can I say
Refuse the revelations of the soul?
Yet be not over-scrupulous, my son,
And be not over-proud to put aside
The due consolements of the circling years.
What comes, receive; be not too wise for God.   70
The Past is something, but the Present more;
Will not it too be Past? – nor fail withal
To recognise the future in our hopes.
Unite them in your manhood each and all,
Nor mutilate the perfectness of life.   75
You can remember, you can also hope;
And doubtless with the long instructive years,
Comfort will come to you, my son; to me;
Even to your Mother comfort; but to us
Knowledge at least; the certainty of things   80
Which as I think is consolation's sum.
For truly now, today, tomorrow, yes
Days many more to come alike to you
Whose earliest revelation of the world
Is, horrible indeed, this fatal fact,   85
And unto me, who knowing not much before
Look gropingly and idly into this,
And recognise no figure seen before –
Alike my son to me and to yourself
Much is dark now which one day will be light.   90
With strong assurance fortify your sense
Of this – and that you meet me here again
Promise me, Cain. So for five years farewell
To meet again.

SCENE XIV
(*Adam's Vision*)

ADAM

O Cain, the words of Adam shall be said;
Come near and hear your father's words, my son.
I have been in the spirit, as they call it,
Dreaming, as others say, which is the same.
I sat, and you were with me, Cain, and Eve
(We sat as in a picture people sit,
Great figures silent, with their place content);
And Abel came and took your hand, my son,
And wept and kissed you, saying, 'Forgive me, Cain.
Ah me, my brother, sad has been thy life,
For my sake, all through me – how foolishly;
Because we knew not both of us were right.'
And you embraced and wept, and we too wept.
Then I beheld through eyes with tears suffused,
And deemed at first 'twas blindness thence ensuing,
Abel was gone and you were gone, my son,
Gone, and yet not gone; yea, I seemed to see
The decomposing of those coloured lines
Which we called you, their fusion into one,
And therewithal their vanishing and end.
And Eve said to me, 'Adam, in the day
When in the inexistent void I heard God's Voice,
An awful whisper, bidding me to be,
How sad, how slow to come, how loth to obey,
As slow, as sad, as lingeringly loth,
I fade, I vanish, sink, and cease to be,
By the same sovereign strong compulsion borne:
Ah, if I vanish, be it into thee.'
She spoke, nor speaking ceased, I listening – but
I was alone – yet not alone – with her
And she with me, and you with us, my sons,
As at the first, and yet not wholly: – yea,
And that which I had witnessed thus in you,
This fusion and mutation and return,

Seemed in my substance working too. I slept,   35
I did not dream, my sleep was sweet to me.
Yes, in despite of all disquietudes
For Eve, for you, for Abel, which indeed
Impelled in me that gaiety of soul —
Without your fears I had listened to my own —   40
In spite of doubt, despondency and death,
Though lacking knowledge alway, lacking faith
Sometimes, and hope; with no sure trust in aught
Except a kind of impetus within
Whose sole credentials were that trust itself —   45
Yet, in despite of much, in lack of more,
Life has been beautiful to me, my Son,
And if they call me, I will come again.
But sleep is sweet, and I would sleep, my son.
O Cain, behold your father's final words are said;   50
Behold, the words of Adam have an end.

Bethesda:
A Sequel

I saw again the spirits on a day,
Where on the earth in mournful case they lay;
Five porches were there, and a pool, and round
Huddling in blankets, strewn upon the ground,
Tied-up and bandaged, weary, sore, and spent,
The maimed and halt, diseased and impotent.
For a great angel came, 'twas said, and stirred
The pool at certain seasons, and the word
Was, with this people of the sick, that they
Who in the waters here their limbs should lay
Before the motion on the surface ceased
Should of their torment straightway be released.

    So with shrunk bodies and with heads down-dropt,
Stretched on the steps and at the pillars propt,
Watching by day and listening through the night,
They filled the place, a miserable sight.

    And I beheld that on the stony floor
He too, that spoke of duty once before,
No otherwise than others here today
Fordone and sick and sadly muttering lay.
'I know not, I will do, — what is it I would say?
What was that word which once sufficed alone for all,
Which now I seek in vain, and never can recall?
I know not, I will do the work the world requires,
Asking no reason why, but serving its desires;
Will do for daily bread, for wealth, respect, good name,
The business of the day — alas, is that the same?'
And then as weary of in vain renewing
His question, thus his mournful thought pursuing,
'I know not, I must do as other men are doing.'

    But what the waters of that pool might be,
Of Lethe were they, or Philosophy;
And whether he long waiting did attain
Deliverance from the burden of his pain

There with the rest; or whether, yet before,   35
Some more diviner stanger passed the door
With his small company into that sad place,
And breathing hope into the sick man's face,
Bade him take up his bed and rise and go,
What the end were, and whether it were so,   40
Further than this I saw not, neither know. —

Resignation — To Faustus

O land of Empire, art and love
    What is it that you show me?
A sky for Gods to tread, above,
    A floor for pigs below me!
O in all place and shape and kind   5
    Beyond all thought and thinking,
The graceful with the foul combined,
    The stately with the stinking!
Was ever seen in tie so close
    With beauty dirt in union?   10
Did ever glorious things and gross
    Hold such serene communion?
For though for open bridge and street
    I will not feel compunction,
Is palace proud a place allowed   15
    For bestial-filthy function?
Must vile expectorations greet
    Angelic limbs with unction,
And marble flags attest the feat
    Of digital emunction?   20
Whilst, studying here with musings meet
    Thy mystic old injunction
Thy porch I pace or take my place
    Within thee, great Pantheon,
What sights untold of contrast bold   25
    My ranging eyes must be on! —

What though uprolled by young and old
   In slumbrous convolution
'Neath pillared shade I see displayed
   Bare limbs that scorn ablution,
Must babied hags perform with rags
   That napkin-evolution?
Though husks that swine would scarcely pick
   Bestrew the patterned paving
And sores to make a doctor sick
   Your charity come craving;
And though the meditative cur
   Account it no intrusion
Through that great gate to quit the stir
   Of market-place confusion,
True brother of the bipeds there,
   If Nature's need requireth
Lifts up his leg with tranquil air
   And quietly retireth,
Though priest from prayer stop short to spit
   Beside the altar solemn
Must therefore boys turn up to —
   By this Corinthian column? —

O richly soiled and richly sunned,
Exuberant, fervid, and fecund!
   Are these the fixed condition
On which may Northern pilgrim come
To imbibe thine ether-air, and sum
   Thy store of old tradition?
Must we be chill, if clean, and stand
Foot-deep in dirt in classic land? —

So it is: in all ages so,
And in all places man can know,
From homely roots unseen below
In forest-shade, in woodland bowers
The stem that bears the ethereal flowers
Derives that emanative power;
From mixtures fetid foul and sour

Draws juices that these petals fill.

Ah Nature, if indeed thy will   65
Thou own'st it, it shall not be ill!
And truly here in this quick clime
Where, scarcely bound by space or time,
The elements in half a day
Toss off with exquisitest play   70
What our cold seasons toil and grieve
And never quite at last achieve;
Where processes, with pain and fear,
Disgust and horror wrought, appear
The quick mutations of a dance,   75
Wherein retiring but to advance
Life in brief interpause of death,
One moment sitting, taking breath,
Forth comes again as glad as e'er
In some new figure full as fair,   80
Where what has scarcely ceased to be
Instinct with newer birth we see.
What dies already, look you, lives;
In such a clime, who thinks, forgives,
Who sees, will understand; who knows,   85
In calm of knowledge find repose,
And thoughtful as of glory gone
So too of more to come anon,
Of permanent existence sure,
Brief intermediate breaks endure.   90

O Nature, if indeed thy will
Thou ownest it, it is not ill!
And e'en as oft on heathy hill,
On moorland black and ferny fells,
Beside thy brooks and in thy dells,   95
Was welcomed erst the kindly stain
Of thy true Earth, e'en so again
With resignation fair and meet
The dirt and refuse of thy street
My philosophic foot shall greet,   100

So leave but perfect to my eye
Thy columns set against thy sky! —

Uranus

When on the primal peaceful blank profound,
Which in its still unknowing silence holds
All knowledge, ever by withholding holds —
When on that void (like footfalls in far rooms),
5   In faint pulsations from the whitening East
Articulate voices first were felt to stir,
And the great child in dreaming grown to man
Losing his dream to piece it up began,
Then Plato in me said,
10   ''Tis but the figured ceiling overhead,
With cunning diagrams bestarred that shine
In all the three dimensions, are endowed
With motion too by skill mechanical,
That thou in height, and depth, and breadth, and power,
15   Schooled unto pure Mathesis, (in thyself behold might proceed
The things of Space so disciplined),
To higher entities whereof in us
Copies are seen, existent they themselves
In the sole Kingdom of the Mind and God.
20   Mind not the stars, mind thou thy Mind and God.'
By that supremer Word
O'ermastered, deafly heard
Were hauntings dim of old astrologies,
Chaldean mumblings vast, with gossip light
25   From modern ologistic fancyings mixed,
Of suns and stars by hypothetic men
Of other frame than ours inhabited,
Of lunar seas and lunar craters huge,
And was there atmosphere or was there not,
30   And without oxygen could life subsist?
And was the world originally mist? —

Talk they as talk they list,
I in that ampler voice
Unheeding did rejoice.

O'Brien, most disconsolate of Men,
Whether thy brave delusions lap thee yet
Or the cold victor's scornful epithet
From thy blank soul come echoed to thee again,
Ah be contented! knowing no loftier rule   5
Stands in the books of Chivalry's high laws
Than this which bids one in the least good cause
Risk being thought or even being a fool.
In a great labyrinth it were not nought
Though but to show that one way error lies;   10
It should be plainer to thy country's view
Henceforward what she can and cannot do;
Ireland by thy misjudging may be taught
And by thy misadventure become wise.

From far and near
He drew the scattered ciphers,
Struck the decisive line, and with one look
Sum-totalled the experience of the World
In that Augustest Dome. —   5

As one who shoots an arrow overhead
Straining in vain to follow with his eye
Looks down and sees it by him, or like one
Who posts and hurries in his dream
Wakes suddenly and finds himself in bed —   5
So swarth Magellan through the Indian main
Pressing he knew not whither nor how far,

Faint with the sense of endless space before
For daily incurred return, one morn looked forth
10 And found himself where he had started from.
That moment
Through the ripe brain of humankind was sped
A new vibration – and in Amsterdam
Sat one who said
15 The finite also is the infinite, Man God.

Whence are ye, vague desires,
Which carry men along
However proud and strong,
And, having ruled today,
5   Tomorrow pass away?
Whence are ye, vague desires?
Whence are ye?

Which women, yielding to,
Find still so good and true;
10 So true, so good today,
Tomorrow gone away,
Whence are ye, vague desires?
Whence are ye?

From seats of bliss above,
15 Where angels sing of love;
Or from the airs around
Or from the vulgar ground,
Whence are ye, vague desires?
Whence are ye?

20 A message from the blest,
Or bodily unrest;
A call to heavenly good,
Or fever in the blood:
What are ye, vague desires?
25 What are ye?

Which men who know you best
Are proof against the least,
And rushing to today,
Tomorrow cast away.
What are ye, vague desires?   30
What are ye?

Which women, ever new,
Still warned, surrender to,
Adored with you today,
Then cast with you away: 35
What are ye, vague desires?
What are ye?

Which unto boyhood's heart
The force of man impart,
And pass, and leave it cold   40
And prematurely old:
What are ye, vague desires?
What are ye?

Which tremblingly confest
Pour in the young girl's breast   45
Joy, joy – the like is none –
And leave her then undone:
What are ye, vague desires?
What are ye?

Ah yet, though man be marred,   50
Ignoble crude and hard,
Though broken women lie
In anguish down to die,
Ah yet, ye vague desires,
Ah yet   55

By him who gave you birth,
And blended you with Earth,
For some good end designed
For man and womankind,

60 Ah yet, ye vague desires,
    Ah yet

    The petals of today,
    Tomorrow fallen away
    Shall something leave instead
65 To live when they are dead;
    When you, ye vague desires,
    When you

    Have vanished, to survive,
    Of you indeed derive
70 Its apparent earthly birth —
    But of far other worth
    Than you, ye vague desires,
    Than you.

Sa Majesté Très Chrétienne

    Papers to sign and documents to read
    Lettres de cachets, and recurrent writs,
    So many things to do I cannot do,
    To think of — to decide, my acts they say
5   And never yet they never mean that I should act
    Nor dream I should decide . . . And yet my acts
    My acts, they say — Ah you are come, my girls,
    My children dear, my flowers of Paradise,
    My darling ones, and what have you been doing?
10 Playing all day — and I, poor King, the while
    So tired, so tired. — Come round me, play with me;
    Would I had mouths as berries on a bush
    For all of you at once to pick in kisses.
    Ninon, your fingers here in mine — Fanchetta,
15 Is it not you sweet rogue behind me there?
    Come, play awhile, and then we say our prayers
    E'en as in holy Church together all
    Say prayers — and then — Which shall it be, you ask,
    Ah which — shall we draw lots? . . . the Lutheran

And Calvinistic heretics repeat   20
Hour-long thanksgivings ere they set to dinner
E'en so, prayers done – by lot? or choose in the dark?
Ah but you are not heretics, my girls.
Louise, who came from pestilent Auvergne,
You are sound, I trust, my child, – I'd have you so.   25
We will all go you know at last to heaven,
Confess our naughty deeds, repent, receive
The wafer and the Unction of the Church
And so – through Purgatory pass to heaven:
And Purgatory also is not long,   30
But much like penance upon Earth: we say
The seven penitential psalms: repeat
A course of prayers with holy meditations,
And so washed white, and clad in virgin robes
The good kind God receives us to himself.   35
You laugh, my pet ones – Ah I mean it, though.
Yes and tomorrow – I will not forget –
I'll bring with me the Catechism of Trent,
And test you in your faiths, my little ones.
Ah but you'll all be dutiful and learn   40
And docilely believe the Church's word.
Keep safely all in union blest with her,
And sinners as we are, we shall yet join
The happy Saints who in their heavenly seats
Pity us in poor sad ways below.   45
Come
The blinds are closed, the Curtains drawn; put out the lights
We'll fold each other in each other's arms,
Forget the uproarious world and dream of the day
When we shall all be mingled into Heaven.   50

                                    *

'Tis true, Monseigneur, I am much to blame;
But we must all forgive; especially
Subjects their King; would I were one to do so.
What could I do? and how was I to help it?
'Tis true it should not be so; true indeed,   55

I know I am not what I would I were.
I would I were, as God intended me,
A little quiet harmless acolyte
Clothed in long serge and linen shoulder-piece,
60 Day after day
To pace serenely through the sacred fane,
Bearing the sacred things before the priest,
Curtsey before that altar as we pass,
And place our burden reverently on this.
65 There – by his side to stand and minister,
To swing the censer and to sound the bell,
Uphold the book, the patin change and cup –
Ah me –
And why does childhood ever change to man?
70 Oh underneath the black and sacred serge
Would yet uneasy uncontented blood
Swell to revolt; beneath the tippet's white
Would harassed nerves by sacred music soothed,
By solemn sights and peaceful tasks composed,
75 Demand more potent medicine than these
Or ask from pleasure more than duty gives?

                              ★

Ah yes: but who is to blame for this? I wonder.
You found me –
Not you, but some one of your filthy kin –
80 You found me
A little foolish innocent ignorant Prince,
Awkward and sheepish, bashful and devout,
A silent, shrinking, somewhat overgrown child
Who at the coarse-tongued age of bold fifteen
85 Knew not his sister differed from himself
Save in her frock and fashion of her hair.
You found me and you told me – oh kind Saints
What was it that you told me then and how! –
But I remember that you left me weeping;
90 But I remember that from that day forth

The Wicked World was real to me and Heaven
Which had the Substance been was Shadow now.

★

    'Tis curious too
These fits of eloquence that come upon him;
He will go dozing, maundering, month on month
And if you meddle, only look distrest
And then at last if something touches him
Comes out with words like these.

★

    Ah, holy father, yes.
Without the appointed,
Without the sweet confessional relief,
Without the welcome all-absolving words,
The mystic rite, the solemn soothing forms,
Our human life were miserable indeed.
And yet methinks our holy Mother Church
Deals hardly, very, with her eldest born,
Her chosen, sacred, and most Christian Kings.
To younger pets, the blind, the halt, the sick,
The outcast child, the sinners of the street,
Her doors are open and her precinct free:
The beggar finds a nest, the slave a home,
Even thy altars, O my Mother Church —
O templa quam dilecta. We the while,
Poor Kings, must forth to action, as you say;
Action, that slaves us, drives us, fretted, worn,
To pleasure which anon enslaves us too;
Action, and what is Action, O my God?
Alas, and can it be
In this perplexing labyrinth I see,
This waste and wild infinity of ways
Where all are like, and each each other meets,
Quits, meets, and quits a many hundred times,
That this path more than that conducts to Thee?

95
100
105
110
115
120

Alas, and is it true
125 Aught I can purpose, say, or will, or do,
My fancy choose, my changeful silly heart
Resolve, my puny petty hand enact
To that great glory can in aught conduce
Which from the old eternities is Thine? —
130 Ah never, no!
If aught there be for sinful souls below
To do, 'tis rather to forbear to do;
If aught there be of Action that contains
The sense of sweet identity with God,
135 It is, methinks, it is inaction only.
To walk with God I know not; let me kneel.
Ah yes, the livelong day
To watch before the altar where they pray:
To muse and wait,
140 On sacred stones lie down and meditate.
No, through the long and dark and dismal night
We will not turn and seek the city streets,
We will not stir, we should but lose our way,
But faithful stay
145 And watch the tomb where He, our Saviour, lies
Till his great day of Resurrection rise.

Yes, the commandments you remind me, yes,
The Sacred Word has pointed out the Way,
The Priest is here for our unfailing guide,
150 Do this, not that, to right hand and to left,
A voice is with us ever at our ear.
Yes, holy father, I am thankful for it,
Most thankful I am not, as other men,
A lonely Lutheran English Heretic.
155 If I had so by God's despite been born,
Alas, methinks I had but passed my life
In sitting motionless beside the fire
Not daring to remove the once-placed chair
Nor stir my foot for fear it should be sin.
160 Thank God indeed.

Thank God for his infallible certain creed.
Yes, the commandments, precepts of good life
And counsels of perfection and the like,
'Thou knowest the commandments.' Yes indeed,
Yes, I suppose. But it is weary work,   165
For Kings I think they are not plain to read,
Ministers somehow have small faith in them.
Ah, holy father, would I were as you.
But you, no less, have trials as you say,
Inaction vexes you, and action tempts,   170
And the bad prickings of the animal heats,
As in the palace, to the cell will come.

Alas — and why
Why in that blessed and baptismal rite
When pain is small and small the sense of sin   175
Should not the holy and preventive hand
With one short act, decisive for all time,
By sharp excision pluck the unsprouted seed: the seed of ill —
There are, the Scripture tells us, who have done it.
Origen was not orthodox, you say,   180
In this at least was not his heresy:
You holy priests, who do all else for us,
What he did for himself, might do for us. —
Ah well a day,
Would I were out in quiet Paraguay   185
Mending the Jesuits' shoes! —

                         *

You drive us into Action as our duty.
Then Action persecutes and tortures us,
To pleasures and to loving soft delights
We fly for solace and for peace; and gain   190
Vexation, Persecution also here.
We hurry from the tyranny of man
Into the tyranny yet worse of woman.
No satisfaction find I any more
In the old pleasant evil ways; but less,   195

Less, I believe, of those uneasy stirs
Of discontented and rebellious will
That once with self-contempt tormented me.
Depraved, that is, degraded am I. – Sins,
200 Which yet I see not how I should have shunned,
Have in despite of all the means of grace,
Submission perfect to the appointed creed,
And absolution-plenary and prayers,
Possessed me, held, and changed – yet after all
205 Somehow I think my heart within is pure.

I dreamed a dream: I dreamt that I espied
Upon a stone that was not rolled aside
A shadow sitting by a grave – a Shade
As thin, as unsubstantial, as of old
5 Came, the Greek poet told,
To lick the life-blood in the trench Ulysses made –
As pale, as thin, and said:
'I am the resurrection of the dead.
The night is past, the morning is at hand,
10 And I must in my proper semblance stand,
Appear brief space and vanish – hear me, this is true,
I am that Jesus whom they slew.'

And shadows dim, I dreamed, the dead Apostles came,
And bent their heads for sorrow and for shame –
15 Sorrow for their great loss, and shame
For what they did in that vain name.

And in long ranges far behind there seemed
Pale vapoury angel forms; or was it cloud? that kept
Strange watch; the women also stood beside and wept.
20 And Peter spoke the word:

'O my own Lord,
What is it we must do?
Is it then all untrue?
Did we not see and hear and handle thee,
Yea for whole hours   25
Upon the Mount in Galilee,
On the lake shore, and here at Bethany,
When thou ascended to thy God and ours?'
And paler still became the distant cloud,
And all the women wept aloud.   30
And the Shade answered, 'What ye say I know not;
But it is true
I am that Jesus whom they slew,
Whom ye have preached, and in what way I know not.'

★

And the great World, it chanced, came by that way,   35
And stopped and looked and spoke to the police
And said the thing for order's sake and peace
Most certainly must be suppressed, the nuisance cease,
His wife and daughter must have where to pray,
And whom to pray to, at the least one day   40
In seven, and something definite to say.
Whether the fact so many years ago
Had, or not, happened, how was he to know?
Yet he had always heard that it was so.
As for himself, perhaps it was all one,   45
And yet he found it not unpleasant, too,
On Sunday morning in the roomy pew,
To see the thing with such decorum done.
As for himself, perhaps it was all one;
Yet on one's deathbed all men always said   50
It was a comfortable thing to think upon
The Atonement and the Resurrection of the dead.
So the great World as having said his say,

Unto his country-house pursued his way,
And on the grave the Shadow sat all day.

*

And the poor pope was sure it must be so,
Else wherefore did the People kiss his toe?
The subtle Jesuit cardinal shook his head,
And mildly looked and said
It mattered not a jot
Whether the thing indeed were so or not;
Religion must be kept up – and the Church preserved,
And for the people this best served.
And then he turned, and added most demurely,
'Whatever may befall,
We Catholics need no evidence at all,
The holy father is infallible, surely! –'

An English canon heard,
And [quietly demurred.]
Religion rests on evidence, of course,
And on inquiry we must put no force.
Difficulties still, upon whatever ground,
Are likely, almost certain, to be found.
The Theist scheme, the Pantheist, one and all,
Must with, or e'en before, the Christian fall.
And till the thing were plainer to our eyes,
To disturb faith was surely most unwise.
As for the Shade, who trusted such narrations,
Except of course in ancient revelations?

And dignitaries of the Church came by.
It had been worth to some of them, they said,
Some £100,000 a year a head.
If it fetched so much in the market, truly,
'Twas not a thing to be given up unduly.
It had been proved by Butler in one way,
By Paley better in a later day;
It had been proved in twenty ways at once,
By many a doctor, plain to any a dunce;

There was no question but it must be so.
And the Shade answered, that he did not know.   90
He had no reading, and might be deceived,
But still he was the Christ, as he believed.
And women, mild and pure,
Forth from still homes and village schools did pass,
And asked, if this indeed were thus, alas,   95
What should they teach their children and the poor?
The Shade replied, he could not know,
But it was truth, the fact was so.

*

Who had kept all commandments from his youth
Yet still found one thing lacking – even Truth: 100
And the Shade only answered, 'Go, make haste,
Enjoy thy great possessions as thou may'st.'

Easter Day
Naples, 1849

Through the great sinful streets of Naples as I past,
With fiercer heat than flamed above my head
My heart was hot within me; till at last
My brain was lightened, when my tongue had said

    Christ is not risen!   5

  Christ is not risen, no,
  He lies and moulders low;
    Christ is not risen.

What though the stone were rolled away, and though
The grave found empty there, –   10
If not there, then elsewhere,
If not where Joseph laid him first, why then
Where other men
Trans-laid him after in some humbler clay

15 Long ere today
    Corruption that sad perfect work hath done
    Which here she scarcely, lightly had begun.
    The foul engendered worm
    Feeds on the flesh of the life-giving form
20 Of our most Holy and Anointed One.

        He is not risen, no,
        He lies and moulders low;
            Christ is not risen.

        Ashes to ashes, dust to dust;
25 As of the Unjust, also of the Just —
            Christ is not risen.

    What if the women ere the dawn was grey
    Saw one or more great angels, as they say,
    Angels, or him himself? Yet neither there nor then
30 Nor afterward nor elsewhere nor at all
    Hath he appeared to Peter or the Ten,
    Nor, save in thunderous terror, to blind Saul;
    Save in an after-Gospel and late Creed
    He is not risen indeed.

35   Christ is not risen.

    Or what if e'en, as runs the tale, the Ten
    Saw, heard and touched, again and yet again?
    What if at Emmaüs' inn and by Capernaum's lake
    Came one the bread that brake,
40 Came one that spake as never mortal spake,
    And with them ate and drank and stood and walked about?
    Ah 'some' did well to 'doubt'!
    Ah the true Christ, while these things came to pass,
    Nor heard, nor spake, nor walked, nor dreamt, alas.

45   He was not risen, no,
            He lay and mouldered low,
                Christ was not risen.

    As circulates in some great city crowd

A rumour changeful, vague, importunate and loud,
From no determined centre, or of fact, 50
Or authorship exact,
Which no man can deny
Nor verify;
So spread the wondrous fame;
He all the same 55
    Lay senseless, mouldering, low.
    He was not risen, no,
        Christ was not risen.

Ashes to ashes, dust to dust;
As of the Unjust, also of the Just — 60
    Yea, of that Just One too,
This is the one sad Gospel that is true,
      Christ is not risen.

———

Is He not risen, and shall we not rise?
Oh, we unwise!
65
What did we dream, what wake we to discover?
Ye hills, fall on us, and ye mountains, cover!
In darkness and great gloom
Come ere we thought it is *our* day of doom,
From the cursed world which is one tomb, 70
      Christ is not risen.

Eat, drink and die, for we are men deceived,
Of all the creatures under heaven's wide cope
We are most hopeless who had once most hope,
We are most wretched that had most believed.
75
      Christ is not risen.

Eat, drink and play, and think that this is bliss,
There is no Heaven but this!
There is no Hell; —
Save Earth, which serves the purpose doubly well,
Seeing it visits still 80
With equallest apportionments of ill

Both good and bad alike, and brings to one same dust
The Unjust and the Just
85   With Christ, who is not risen.

Eat, drink and die, for we are souls bereaved,
Of all the creatures under this broad sky
We are most hopeless that had hoped most high,
And most beliefless that had most believed.
90 Ashes to ashes, dust to dust;
As of the Unjust, also of the Just —
Yea, of that Just One too.
It is the one sad Gospel that is true,
        Christ is not risen.

———

95 Weep not beside the Tomb,
Ye women, unto whom
He was great solace while ye tended Him;
Ye who with napkin o'er His head
And folds of linen round each wounded limb
100 Laid out the sacred dead,
And thou that bar'st Him in thy Wondering Womb.
Yea, Daughters of Jerusalem depart,
Bind up as best ye may your own sad bleeding heart;
Go to your homes, your living children tend,
105 Your earthly spouses love;
Set your affections *not* on things above,
Which moth and rust corrupt, which quickliest come to end;
Or pray, if pray ye must, and pray if pray ye can,
For Death; since dead is He whom ye loved more than man,
110   Who is not risen, no,
        But lies and moulders low,
            Who is not risen.

Ye men of Galilee!
Why stand ye looking up to heaven, where Him ye ne'er may see,
115 Neither ascending hence nor hither returning again?
Ye ignorant and idle fishermen!

Hence to your huts and boats and inland native shore,
And catch not men, but fish;
Whate'er things ye might wish,
Him neither here nor there ye e'er shall meet with more.   120
Ye poor deluded youths go home,
Mend the old nets ye left to roam;
Tie the split oar, patch the torn sail;
It was indeed 'an idle tale'.
       He was not risen.   125

And oh good men of ages yet to be,
Who shall believe *because* ye did not see,
O be ye warned! be wise!
No more with pleading eyes,
And sobs of strong desire,
Unto the empty vacant void aspire,   130
Seeking another and impossible birth
That is not of your own and only Mother Earth.
But if there is no other life for you,
Sit down and be content, since this must even do: 135
       He is not risen.

One look and then depart,
Ye humble and ye holy men of heart!
And ye! ye ministers and stewards of a word
Which ye would preach because another heard, –   140
Ye worshippers of that ye do not know,
Take these things hence and go;
       He is not risen.

Here on our Easter Day
We rise, we come, and lo we find Him not;   145
Gardener nor other on the sacred spot; –
Where they have laid Him is there none to say
No sound nor in nor out; no word
Of where to seek the dead or meet the living Lord?
There is no glistering of an angel's wings,   150
There is no voice of heavenly clear behest;
Let us go hence and think upon these things

In silence which is best.
    Is he not risen? No –
155 But lies and moulders low –
      Christ is not risen –

Easter Day II

So while the blear-eyed pimp beside me walked,
And talked,
For instance, of the beautiful danseuse
And 'Eccellenza sure must see, if he would choose'
5 Or of the lady in the green silk there,
Who passes by and bows with minx's air,
Or of the little thing not quite fifteen,
Sicilian-born who surely should be seen –
So while the blear-eyed pimp beside me walked
10 And talked, and I too with fit answer talked,
So in the sinful streets, abstracted and alone,
I with my secret self held communing of mine own.

So in the southern city spake the tongue
Of one that somewhat overwildly sung,
15 But in a later hour I sat and heard
Another voice that spake, another graver word.
    Weep not, it bade, whatever hath been said;
    Though he be dead, he is not dead.
    In the true Creed
20   He is yet risen indeed,
      Christ is yet risen.

    Weep not beside his tomb
    Ye women unto whom
He was great comfort and yet greater grief;
25 Nor ye faithful few that wont with him to roam,
Seek sadly what for him ye left, go hopeless to your home;
Nor ye despair, ye sharers yet to be of their belief;
    Though he be dead, he is not dead,

Nor gone though fled,
Not lost though vanished;   30
Though he return not, though
He lies and moulders low,
In the true Creed
He is yet risen indeed,
 Christ is yet risen.   35

Sit if ye will, sit down upon the ground,
Yet not to weep and wail, but calmly look around.
 Whate'er befell,
 Earth is not hell;
 Now too as when it first began,
 Life yet is Life and Man is Man.   40
For all that breathe beneath the heavens' high cope,
Joy with grief mixes, with despondence hope.
Hope conquers cowardice, joy grief,
Or at the least, faith unbelief.   45
 Though dead not dead;
 Not gone though fled;
 Not lost, not vanished.
 In the great Gospel and true Creed
 He is yet risen indeed,
  Christ is yet risen.   50

  What we, when face to face we see
  The Father of our souls, shall be,
  John tells us, doth not yet appear;
  Ah did he tell what we are here!

  A mind for thoughts to come into,   5
  A heart for loves to travel through,
  Five senses to detect things near, —
  Is this the whole that we are here?

Rules baffle instincts, instincts rules,
Wise men are bad and good are fools,
Facts evil, wishes vain appear, –
We cannot go, – why are we here?

O may we, for assurance-sake
Some arbitrary judgement take,
Make up our minds, and call all clear,
For this or that that we are here?

Or is it right, and will it do
To pace the dim confusion through,
And say, – It doth not yet appear
What we shall be, what we are here?

That there are powers above us I admit;
It may be true too
That while we walk the troublous tossing sea,
That when we see the o'ertopping waves advance,
And when we feel our feet beneath us sink,
There are who walk beside us; and the cry
That rises so spontaneous to the lips,
The 'Help us or we perish' is not nought,
An evanescent spectrum of disease.
It may be that in deed and not in fancy
A hand that is not ours upstays our steps,
A voice that is not ours commands the waves,
Commands the waves, and whispers in our ear
O thou of little faith, why didst thou doubt?
At any rate –
That there are beings above us I believe,
And when we lift up holy hands of prayer
I will not say they will not give us aid.

AMOURS DE VOYAGE

> Oh, you are sick of self-love, Malvolio,
> And taste with a distempered appetite! – Shakespeare
>
> Il doutait de tout, même de l'amour. – French novel
>
> Solvitur ambulando. – Solutio Sophismatum
>
> Flevit amores
> Non elaboratum ad pedem. – Horace

Canto I

Over the great windy waters, and over the clear crested summits,
  Unto the sun and the sky, and into the perfecter earth,
Come, let us go, — to a land wherein gods of the old time
      wandered,
  Where every breath even now changes to ether divine.
Come, let us go; though withal a voice whisper, 'The world that we
      live in,
  Whithersoever we turn, still is the same narrow crib;
'Tis but to prove limitation, and measure a cord, that we travel;
  Let who would 'scape and be free go to his chamber and think;
'Tis but to change idle fancies for memories wilfully falser;
  'Tis but to go and have been.' — Come, little bark, let us go!

i — CLAUDE TO EUSTACE

Dear Eustatio, I write that you may write me an answer,
Or at the least to put us again *en rapport* with each other.
Rome disappoints me much, — St Peter's, perhaps, in especial;
Only the Arch of Titus and view from the Lateran please me.
This, however, perhaps is the weather, which truly is horrid:
Greece must be better, surely; and yet I am feeling so spiteful,
That I could travel to Athens, to Delphi, and Troy, and Mount
      Sinai,
Though but to see with my eyes that these are vanity also.
  Rome disappoints me much; I hardly as yet understand, but
Rubbishy seems the word that most exactly would suit it.
All the foolish destructions, and all the sillier savings,
All the incongruous things of past incompatible ages,
Seem to be treasured up here to make fools of present and future.
Would to heaven the old Goths had made a cleaner sweep of it!
Would to heaven some new ones would come and destroy these
      churches!
However, one can live in Rome as also in London.
Rome is better than London because it is other than London.

It is a blessing, no doubt, to be rid, at least for a time, of
All one's friends and relations, yourself (forgive me) included,
30   All the *assujettissement* of having been what one has been,
What one thinks one is, or thinks that others suppose one.
Yet, in despite of all, we turn like fools to the English;
Vernon has been my fate; who is here the same that you knew
         him,
Making the tour, it seems, with friends of the name of Trevellyn.

ii — CLAUDE TO EUSTACE

35   Rome disappoints me still; but I shrink and adapt myself to it.
Somehow a tyrannous sense of a superincumbent oppression
Still, wherever I go, accompanies ever, and makes me
Feel like a tree, shall I say, buried under a ruin of brickwork.
Rome, believe me, my friend, is like its own Monte Testaceo,
40   Merely a marvellous mass of broken and castaway wine-pots.
Ye gods! what do I want with this rubbish of ages departed,
Things that Nature abhors, the experiments that she has failed in?
What do I find in the Forum? an archway and two or three
         pillars.
Well, but St Peter's? Alas, Bernini has filled it with sculpture.
45   No one can cavil, I grant, at the size of the great Coliseum.
Doubtless the notion of grand and capacious and massive
         amusement,
This the old Romans had; but tell me, is this an idea?
Yet of solidity much, but of splendour little is extant;
Brickwork I found thee, and marble I left thee, their Emperor
         vaunted;
Marble I thought thee, and brickwork I find thee, the Tourist may
50   answer.

iii — GEORGINA TREVELLYN TO LOUISA —

At last, dearest Louisa, I take up my pen to address you.
Here we are, you see; with the seven and seventy boxes,
Courier, Papa and Mamma, the children and Mary and Susan.
Here we all are at Rome, and delighted of course with St Peter's,

And very pleasantly lodged in the famous Piazza di Spagna; 55
Rome is a wonderful place, but Mary shall tell you about it;
Not very gay, however, the English are mostly at Naples,
There are the A's we hear and most of the W party,
George, however, is come; did I tell you about his mustachios?
Dear, I must really stop, for the carriage, they tell me, is waiting, 60
Mary will finish, and Susan is writing they say to Sophia,
Adieu, dearest Louise, Evermore your faithful Georgina.
Who can a Mr Claude be whom George has taken to be with?
Very stupid, I think, but George says so *very* clever.

iv – CLAUDE TO EUSTACE

No, the Christian faith, as at any rate I understood it, 65
With its humiliations and exaltations combining,
Exaltations sublime and yet diviner abasements,
Aspirations from something most shameful here upon earth and
In our poor selves to something most perfect above in the
        heavens, –
No, the Christian faith, as I, at least, understood it, 70
Is not there, O Rome, in any of these thy churches,
Is not here, but in Freiburg, or Rheims, or Westminster Abbey.
What in thy Dome I find, in all thy recenter efforts,
Is a something I think more *rational* far, more earthly,
Actual, less ideal, devout not in scorn and refusal, 75
But in a positive, calm, Stoic-Epicurean acceptance;
This I begin to detect in St Peter's and some of the churches,
Mostly in all that I see of the sixteenth-century Masters;
Overlaid of course with infinite gauds and gewgaws,
Innocent playful follies, the toys and trinkets of childhood, 80
Forced on maturer years as the serious one thing needful,
By the barbarian will of the rigid and ignorant Spaniard.
   Curious work, meantime, re-entering society: how we
Walk a live-long day, great Heaven, and watch our shadows!
What our shadows seem, forsooth we will ourselves be. 85
Do I look like that? you think me that: then I am that.

V – CLAUDE TO EUSTACE

Luther they say was unwise; like a half-taught German, he
    could not
See that old follies were passing most tranquilly out of
    remembrance.
Leo the Tenth was employing all efforts to clear out abuses;
90 Jupiter, Juno, and Venus, Fine Arts, and Fine Letters, the Poets,
Scholars, and Sculptors, and Painters, were quietly clearing
    away the
Martyrs, and Virgins, and Saints, or at any rate Thomas Aquinas:
He must forsooth make a fuss and distend his huge Wittenberg
    lungs, and
Bring back Theology once yet again in a flood upon Europe;
95 Lo you, for forty days from the windows of heaven it fell; the
Waters prevail on the earth yet more for a hundred and fifty;
Are they abating at last? the doves that are sent to explore are
Wearily fain to return, at the best with a leaflet of promise,
Fain to return as they went to the wandering wave-tost vessel,
100 Fain to re-enter the roof which covers the clean and the unclean –
Luther, they say, was unwise, he didn't see how things were going,
Luther was foolish, – but, oh great God, what call you Ignatius?
Oh, my tolerant soul, be still, but you talk of barbarians,
Alaric, Attila, Genseric, – why, they came, they killed, they
Ravaged, and went on their way! but these vile, tyrannous
105   Spaniards,
These are here still, – how long, O ye heavens, in the country of
    Dante?
These that fanaticised Europe which now can forget them,
    release not
This, their choicest of prey, this Italy; here you see them,
Here with emasculate pupils and gimcrack churches of Gesu,
110 Pseudo-learning and lies, confessional-boxes and postures,
Here with metallic beliefs and regimental devotions,
Here, overcrusting with slime, perverting, defacing, debasing
Michael Angelo's dome that had hung the Pantheon in heaven,
Raphael's Joys and Graces, and thy clear stars, Galileo!

vi — CLAUDE TO EUSTACE

Which of three Misses Trevellyn it is that Vernon shall marry,   115
Is not a thing to be known; for our friend is one of those natures
Which have their perfect delight in the general tender-domestic:
So that he trifles with Mary's shawl, ties Susan's bonnet,
Dances with all, but at home is most, they say, with Georgina,
Who is however *too* silly in my apprehension for Vernon.   120
I, as before when I wrote, continue to see them a little,
Not that I like them much or care a *bajocco* for Vernon,
But I am slow at Italian, have not many English acquaintance,
And I am asked, in short, and am not good at excuses.
Middle-class people these, bankers very likely, not wholly   125
Pure of the taint of the shop; will at table d'hôte and restaurant
Have their shilling's worth, their penny's pennyworth even;
Neither man's aristocracy this nor God's, God knoweth.
Yet they are fairly descended, they give you to know, well
        connected;
Doubtless somewhere in some neighbourhood have, and careful
        to keep, some   130
Threadbare-genteel relations, who in their turn are enchanted
Grandly among county people to introduce at assemblies
To the unpennied cadets our cousins with excellent fortunes.
Neither man's aristocracy this, nor God's, God knoweth!

vii — CLAUDE TO EUSTACE

Ah, what a shame indeed to abuse these most worthy people!   135
Ah, what a sin to have sneered at their innocent rustic
        pretensions!
Is it not laudable really this reverent worship of station,
Is it not fitting that wealth should tender this homage to culture?
Is it not touching to witness these efforts, if little availing,
Painfully made, to perform the old ritual service of manners?   140
Shall not devotion atone for the absence of knowledge, and
        fervour
Palliate, cover, the fault of a superstitious observance?
No, the Music, the cards, and the tea so genteel and insipid,

Are not, believe me, I think it, no, are not vain oblations;
145 One can endure their whist, their assemblies one can away with,
No, and it is not iniquity, even the solemn meeting.
Dear, dear, what do I say? but alas, just now, like Iago,
I can be nothing at all, if it is not critical wholly;
So in fantastic height, in coxcomb exaltation,
150 Here in the Garden I walk, can freely concede to the Maker
That the works of his hand are all very good; his creatures,
Beast of the field, and fowl, he brings them before me; I name
　　them;
That which I name them, they are, the bird, the beast, and the
　　cattle;
But for Adam, alas, poor critical coxcomb Adam,
155 But for Adam there was not found an help-meet for him.

viii — CLAUDE TO EUSTACE

No, great Dome of Agrippa, thou art not Christian, canst not,
Strip and replaster and daub and do what they will with thee,
　　be so.
Here underneath the great porch of colossal Corinthian columns,
Here as I walk, do I dream of the Christian belfries above them?
Or on a bench as I sit and abide for long hours, till thy whole
160　　vast
Round grows dim as in dreams to my eyes, I repeople thy
　　niches,
Not with the Martyrs and Saints and Confessors and Virgins and
　　children;
But with the mightier forms of an older, austerer worship;
And I recite to myself, how
165　　　　　　　　　　　　Eager for battle here
　　　Stood Vulcan, here matronal Juno,
　　　　And with the bow to his shoulder faithful
　　　He who with pure dew laveth of Castaly
　　　His flowing locks, who holdeth of Lycia

The oak forest and the wood that bore him,   170
  Delos and Patara's own Apollo.*

ix — CLAUDE TO EUSTACE

Yet it is pleasant, I own it, to be in their company; pleasant,
Whatever else it may be, to abide in the feminine presence,
Pleasant but wrong, will you say? But this happy serene
    coexistence
Is to some poor soft souls, I fear, a necessity simple,   175
Meat and drink and life, and music filling with sweetness,
Thrilling with melody sweet, with harmonies strange
    overwhelming,
All the long-silent strings of an awkward meaningless fabric.
Yet as for that, I could live, I believe, with children; to have
    those
Pure and delicate forms encompassing, moving about you,   180
This were enough, I could think; and truly with glad resignation
Could from the dream of romance, from the fever of flushed
    adolescence
Look to escape and subside into peaceful avuncular functions:
Nephews and nieces! alas, for as yet I have none, and moreover
Mothers are jealous, I fear me, too often, too rightfully; fathers   185
Think they have title exclusive to spoiling their own little
    darlings;
And by the law of the land, in despite of Malthusian doctrine,
No sort of proper provision is made for that most patriotic,
Most meritorious subject, the childless and bachelor uncle.

          * Hic avidus stetit
      Vulcanus, hic matrona Juno, et
          Nunquam humero positurus arcum,
      Qui rore puro Castaliæ lavat
      Crines solutos, qui Lyciæ tenet
      Dumeta natalemque sylvam,
          Delius et Patareus Apollo.

X — CLAUDE TO EUSTACE

190   Ye, too, marvellous Twain, that erect on the Monte Cavallo
Stand by your rearing steeds in the grace of your motionless
      movement,
Stand with your upstretched arms and tranquil regardant faces,
Stand as instinct with life in the might of immutable manhood, —
O ye mighty and strange, ye ancient divine ones of Hellas,
195   Are ye Christian too? to convert and redeem and renew you,
Will the brief form have sufficed that a Pope has set up on
      the apex
Of the Egyptian stone that o'ertops you, the Christian symbol?
And ye, silent, supreme in serene and victorious marble,
Ye that encircle the walls of the stately Vatican chambers,
200   Juno and Ceres, Minerva, Apollo, the Muses and Bacchus,
Ye unto whom far and near come posting the Christian pilgrims,
Ye that are ranged in the halls of the mystic Christian pontiff,
Are ye also baptized? are ye of the Kingdom of Heaven?
Utter, O some one, the word that shall reconcile Ancient and
      Modern;
205   Am I to turn me for this unto thee, great Chapel of Sixtus?

xi — CLAUDE TO EUSTACE

These are the facts. The uncle, the elder brother, the squire, (a
Little embarrassed, I fancy) resides in a family place in
Cornwall, of course; 'Papa is in business,' Mary informs me.
He's a good sensible man, whatever his trade is; the mother
210   Is — shall I call it fine? herself she would tell you refined, and
Greatly, I fear me, looks down on my bookish and maladroit
      manners.
Somewhat affecteth the blue, would talk to me often of poets;
Quotes, which I hate, *Childe Harold*; but also appreciates
      Wordsworth;
Sometimes adventures on Schiller; and then to religion diverges;
Questions me much about Oxford; and yet in her loftiest
215   flights still
Grates the fastidious ear with the slightly mercantile accent.

Is it contemptible, Eustace, — I'm perfectly ready to think so, —
Is it, — the horrible pleasure of pleasing inferior people?
I am ashamed my own self; and yet true it is, if disgraceful,
That for the first time in life I am living and moving with
    freedom,
I, who never could talk to the people I meet with my uncle,   220
I who have always failed, — I, trust me, can suit the Trevellyns,
I, believe me, great conquest, am liked by the country bankers.
And I am glad to be liked, and like in return very kindly.
So it proceeds, *Laissez faire, laissez aller,* such is the watchword.   225
Well I know there are thousands as pretty and hundreds as
    pleasant,
Girls by the dozen as good, and girls in abundance with polish
Higher and manners more perfect than Susan or Mary Trevellyn.
Well I know after all it is only juxtaposition;
Juxtaposition in short; and what is juxtaposition?   230

xii — CLAUDE TO EUSTACE

But I am in for it now; *laissez faire* of a truth, *laissez aller,*
Yes, I am going, I feel it, I feel and cannot recall it,
Fusing with this thing and that, entering into all sorts of
    relations,
Tying I know not what ties; which, whatever they are, I know
    one thing,
Will, and must, woe is me, be one day painfully broken,   235
Broken with painful remorses, with shrinkings of soul, and
    relentings,
Foolish delays, more foolish evasions, most foolish renewals.
But I have made the step, have quitted the ship of Ulysses,
Quitted the sea and the shore, passed into the magical island;
Yet on my lips is the *moly*, medicinal, offered of Hermes;   240
I have come into the precinct, the labyrinth closes around me,
Path into path rounding slyly; I pace slowly on, and the fancy,
Struggling awhile to sustain the long sequences, weary,
    bewildered,
Fain must collapse in despair, I yield, I am lost and know
    nothing;

245 Yet in my bosom unbroken remaineth the clue; I shall use it.
    Lo, with the rope on my loins I descend through the fissure, I
         sink, yet
    Inly secure in the strength of invisible arms up above me,
    Still, wheresoever I swing, wherever to shore or to shelf, or
    Floor of cavern untrodden, shell-sprinkled, enchanting, I know I
250 Yet shall one time feel the strong cord tighten about me,
    Feel it, relentless, upbear me from spots I would rest in, and
         though the
    Rope sway wildly, I faint, crags wound me, from crag unto crag re-
    Bounding, or, wide in the void, I die ten deaths, ere the end I
    Yet shall plant firm foot on the broad lofty spaces I quit, shall
    Feel underneath me again the great massy strengths of
255   abstraction,
    Look yet abroad from the height o'er the sea whose salt wave I
         have tasted.

xiii — GEORGINA TREVELLYN TO LOUISA —

Dearest Louisa, Enquire if you please about Mr Claude — .
He has been once at R., and remembers meeting the H's,
Harriet L. perhaps may be able to tell you about him.
260 It is an awkward youth, but still with very good manners,
Not without prospects we hear, and George says highly connected.
Georgy declares it absurd, but Mamma is alarmed and insists he has
Taken up strange opinions and may be turning a papist.
Certainly once he spoke of a daily service he went to.
Where, we asked, and he laughed and answered, At the
265   Pantheon.
This was a temple you know and now is a Catholic church, and
Though it is said that Mazzini has sold it for Protestant service,
Yet I suppose this change can hardly as yet be effected.
Adieu again, evermore my dearest, your loving Georgina.

P.S. BY MARY TREVELLYN

270 I am to tell you, you say, what I think of our last new acquaintance.
Well then I think that George has a very fair right to be jealous.

I do not like him much, though I do not dislike being with him.
He is what people call, I suppose, a superior man, and
Certainly seems so to me, but I think he is frightfully selfish.

———

Alba, thou findest me still, and, Alba, thou findest me ever,   275
   Now from the Capitol steps, now over Titus's Arch,
Here from the large grassy spaces that spread from the Lateran portal,
   Towering o'er aqueduct lines lost in perspective between,
Or from a Vatican window, or bridge, or the high Coliseum,
   Clear by the garlanded line cut of the Flavian ring.   280
Beautiful can I not call thee, and yet thou hast power to o'ermaster,
   Power of mere beauty; in dreams, Alba, thou hauntest me still.
Is it religion, I ask me, or is it a vain superstition,
   Slavery abject and gross, service, too feeble, of truth?
Is it an idol I bow to, or is it a god that I worship,
   Do I sink back on the old, or do I soar from the mean?   285
So through the city I wander and question, unsatisfied ever,
   Reverent so I accept, doubtful because I revere.

Canto II

Is it illusion? or does there a spirit from perfecter ages
   Here, even yet, amid loss, change, and corruption, abide?
Does there a spirit we know not, though seek, though we find,
     comprehend not,
   Here to entice and confuse, tempt and evade us, abide;
Lives in the exquisite grace of the column disjointed and single,   5
   Haunts the rude masses of brick garlanded gaily with vine,
E'en in the turret fantastic surviving that springs from the ruin,
   E'en in the people itself— Is it illusion or not?
Is it illusion or not that attracteth the pilgrim transalpine,
   Brings him a dullard and dunce hither to pry and to stare?   10
Is it illusion or not that allures the barbarian stranger,
   Brings him with gold to the shrine, brings him in arms to the gate?

i — CLAUDE TO EUSTACE

What do the people say, and what does the government do, you
Ask, and I know not at all. Yet fortune will favour your
    hopes; and
15 I who avoided it all am fated, it seems, to describe it.
I who nor meddle nor make in politics, I who sincerely
Put not my trust in leagues nor any suffrage by ballot,
Never predicted Parisian millenniums, never beheld a
New Jerusalem coming down dressed like a bride out of heaven
20 Right on the Place de la Concorde, I, nevertheless, let me say it,
Could in my soul of souls this day with the Gaul at the
    gates, shed
One true tear for thee, thou poor little Roman republic!
France, it is foully done; and you, my stupid old England,
You who a twelvemonth ago said nations must choose for
    themselves, you
Could not of course interfere, — you, now, when a nation has
25   chosen —
Pardon this folly; *The Times* will of course have announced the
    occasion,
Told you the news of today; and although it was slightly in error
When it proclaimed as a fact, the Apollo was sold to a Yankee,
You may believe when it tells you, the French are at Civita
    Vecchia.

ii — CLAUDE TO EUSTACE

30 *Dulce* it is, and *decorum*, no doubt, for the country to fall, to
Offer one's blood an oblation to Freedom, and die for the
    Cause; yet
Still, individual culture is also something, and no man
Finds quite distinct the assurance that he of all others is called on,
Or would be justified even in taking away from the World that
35 Precious Creature, himself: Nature sent him here to abide here,
Else why sent him at all? Nature wants him still, it is likely.
On the whole we are meant to look after ourselves, it is certain
Each has to eat for himself, digest for himself, and in general

Care for his own dear life and see to his own preservation;
Nature's intentions in most things uncertain in this are decisive;   40
These, on the whole, I conjecture the Romans will follow,
    and I shall.
  So we cling to our rocks like limpets: Ocean may bluster,
Over and under and round us; we open our shells to imbibe our
Nourishment, close them again, and are safe, fulfilling the
    purpose
Nature intended, a wise one of course, and a noble, we doubt
    not:
Sweet it may be and decorous perhaps for the country to die, but   45
On the whole we conclude the Romans won't do it, and
    I shan't.

iii — CLAUDE TO EUSTACE

Will they fight? They say so. And will the French? I can hardly,
Hardly think so; and yet — He is come, they say, to Palo,
He is passed from Monterone, at Santa Severa
He hath laid up his guns. But the Virgin, the Daughter of Roma,   50
She hath despised thee and laughed thee to scorn, — the Daughter
    of Tiber
She hath shaken her head and built barricades against thee!
Will they fight? I believe it. Alas, 'tis ephemeral folly,
Vain and ephemeral folly, of course, compared with pictures,   55
Statues, and antique gems, — Indeed: and yet indeed too,
Yet, methought, in broad day did I dream, — tell it not in
    St James's,
Whisper it not in thy courts, O Christ Church! — yet did I, waking,
Dream of a cadence that sings, *Si tombent nos jeunes héros, la*
Terre en produit de nouveaux contre vous tous prêts à se battre;   60
Dreamt of great indignations and angers transcendental,
Dreamt of a sword at my side and a battle-horse underneath me.

iv — CLAUDE TO EUSTACE

Now supposing the French or the Neapolitan soldier
Should by some evil chance come exploring the Maison Serny,

65 (Where the family English are all to assemble for safety,)
Am I prepared to lay down my life for the British female?
Really, who knows? One has bowed and talked, till, little by little,
All the natural heat has escaped of the chivalrous spirit.
Oh, one conformed, of course; but one doesn't die for good
    manners,
70 Stab or shoot, or be shot, by way of a graceful attention.
No, if it should be at all, it should be on the barricades there;
Should I incarnadine ever this inky pacifical finger,
Sooner far should it be for this vapour of Italy's freedom,
Sooner far by the side of the d—d and dirty plebeians.
75 Ah, for a child in the street I could strike; for the full-blown lady —
Somehow, Eustace, alas, I have not felt the vocation.
Yet these people of course will expect, as of course, my
    protection,
Vernon in radiant arms stand forth for the lovely Georgina,
And to appear, I suppose, were but common civility. Yes, and
80 Truly I do not desire they should either be killed or offended.
Oh, and of course you will say, 'When the time comes, you will
    be ready.'
Ah, but before it comes, am I to presume it will be so?
What I cannot feel now, am I to suppose that I shall feel?
Am I not free to attend for the ripe and indubious instinct?
85 Am I forbidden to wait for the clear and lawful perception?
Is it the calling of man to surrender his knowledge and insight,
For the mere venture of what may, perhaps, be the virtuous
    action?
Must we, walking our earth, discerning a little, and hoping
Some plain visible task shall yet for our hands be assigned us, —
90 Must we abandon the future for fear of omitting the present,
Quit our own fireside hopes at the alien call of a neighbour,
To the mere possible shadow of Deity offer the victim?
And is all this, my friend, but a weak and ignoble refining,
Wholly unworthy the head or the heart of Your Own
    Correspondent?

V — CLAUDE TO EUSTACE

Yes, we are fighting at last, it appears. This morning, as usual,   95
Murray, as usual, in hand, I enter the Café Nuovo;
Seating myself with a sense as it were of a change in the weather,
Not understanding, however, but thinking mostly of *Murray,*
And, for today is their day, of the Campidoglio Marbles,
Café-latte! I call to the waiter, — and *Non c' è latte,*   100
This is the answer he makes me, and this the sign of a battle.
So I sit; and truly they seem to think any one else more
Worthy than me of attention. I wait for my milkless *nero,*
Free to observe undistracted all sorts and sizes of persons,
Blending civilian and soldier in strangest costume, coming in, and   105
Gulping in hottest haste, still standing, their coffee, —
    withdrawing
Eagerly, jangling a sword on the steps, or jogging a musket
Slung to the shoulder behind. They are fewer moreover than
    usual,
Much, and silenter far. And so I begin to imagine
Something is really afloat. Ere I leave, the Café is empty,   110
Empty too the streets, in all its length the Corso
Empty, and empty I see to my right and left the Condotti.
    Twelve o'clock, on the Pincian Hill, with lots of English,
Germans, Americans, French, — the Frenchmen, too, are
    protected, —
So we stand in the sun, but afraid of a probable shower;   115
So we stand and stare, and see, to the left of St Peter's,
Smoke, from the cannon, white, — but that is at intervals only, —
Black, from a burning house, we suppose, by the Cavalleggieri;
And we believe we discern some lines of men descending
Down through the vineyard-slopes, and catch a bayonet
    gleaming.   120
Every ten minutes, however, — in this there is no misconception, —
Comes a great white puff from behind Michael Angelo's
    dome, and
After a space the report of a real big gun; not the Frenchman's?
That must be doing some work. And so we watch and
    conjecture.

Shortly, an Englishman comes, who says he has been to
      St Peter's,
Seen the Piazza and troops, but that is all he can tell us;
So we watch and sit, and, indeed, it begins to be tiresome. —
All this smoke is outside; when it has come to the inside,
It will be time, perhaps, to descend and retreat to our houses.
    Half-past one, or two; the report of small arms frequent,
Sharp and savage indeed; that cannot all be for nothing:
So we watch and wonder; but guessing is tiresome, very.
Weary of wondering, watching, and guessing, and gossiping idly,
Down I go, and pass through the quiet streets with the knots of
National Guards patrolling, and flags hanging out at the
      windows,
English, American, Danish, — and, after offering to help an
Irish family moving *en masse* to the Maison Serny,
After endeavouring idly to minister balm to the trembling
Quinquagenarian fears of two lone British spinsters,
Go to make sure of my dinner before the enemy enter.
But by this there are signs of stragglers returning; and voices
Talk, though you don't believe it, of guns and prisoners taken;
And on the walls you read the first bulletin of the morning.
This is all that I saw, and all I know of the battle.

vi — CLAUDE TO EUSTACE

Victory! Victory! — Yes! ah, yes, thou republican Zion,
Truly the kings of the earth are gathered and gone by together;
Doubtless they marvelled to witness such things, were astonished,
    and so forth.
Victory! Victory! Victory! — Ah, but it is, believe me,
Easier, easier far, to intone the chant of the martyr
Than to indite any paean of any victory. Death may
Sometimes be noble; but life at the best will appear an illusion.
While the great pain is upon us, it is great; when it is over,
Why, it is over. The smoke of the sacrifice rises to heaven,
Of a sweet savour, no doubt, to Somebody; but on the altar,
Lo, there is nothing remaining but ashes and dirt and ill odour.
    So it stands, you perceive; the labial muscles, that swelled with

Vehement evolution of yesterday Marseillaises,
Articulations sublime of defiance and scorning, today col-
Lapse and languidly mumble, while men and women and papers
Scream and re-scream to each other the chorus of Victory.
     Well, but   160
I am thankful they fought, and glad that the Frenchmen were
     beaten.

vii – CLAUDE TO EUSTACE

So I have seen a man killed! An experience that, among others!
Yes, I suppose I have; although I can hardly be certain,
And in a court of justice could never declare I had seen it.
But a man was killed, I am told, in a place where I saw   165
Something; a man was killed, I am told, and I saw something.
   I was returning home from St Peter's; *Murray* as usual
Under my arm, I remember; had crossed the St Angelo
     bridge; and
Moving towards the Condotti, had got to the first
     barricade, when
Gradually, thinking still of St Peter's, I became conscious   170
Of a sensation of movement opposing me, tendency this way
(Such as one fancies may be in a stream when the wave of the
     tide is
Coming and not yet come – a sort of poise and retention);
So I turned, and, before I turned, caught sight of stragglers
Heading a crowd, it is plain, that is coming behind that corner.   175
Looking up, I see windows filled with heads; the Piazza
Into which you remember the Ponte St Angelo enters,
Since I passed, has thickened with curious groups; and now the
Crowd is coming, has turned, has crossed that last barricade, is
Here at my side. In the middle they drag at something. What
     is it?
                                              180
Ha! bare swords in the air, held up! There seem to be voices
Pleading and hands putting back; official, perhaps; but the
     swords are
Many, and bare in the air. In the air? They descend; they are
     smiting,

Hewing, chopping – At what? In the air once more upstretched!
   And
185 Is it blood that's on them? Yes, certainly blood! Of whom, then?
Over whom is the cry of this furor of exultation?
      While they are skipping and screaming, and dancing their caps
         on the points of
Swords and bayonets, I to the outskirts back, and ask a
Mercantile-seeming bystander, What is it? and he, looking always
190 That way, makes me answer, A Priest, who was trying to fly to
The Neapolitan army; and thus explains the proceeding.
      You didn't see the dead man? No, I began to be doubtful,
I was in black myself, and didn't know what mightn't happen;
But a National Guard close by me, outside of the hubbub,
Broke his sword with slashing a broad hat covered with
195   dust and
Passing away from the place with *Murray* under my arm, and
Stooping, I saw through the legs of the people the legs of
         a body.
      You are the first, do you know, to whom I have mentioned
         the matter.
Whom should I tell it to, else? these girls? the Heavens forbid it.
200 Quidnuncs at Monaldini's? idlers upon the Pincian?
      If I rightly remember, it happened on that afternoon when
Word of the nearer approach of a new Neapolitan army
First was spread. I began to bethink me of Paris Septembers,
Thought I could fancy the look of the old 'Ninety-two. On that
         evening
Three or four, or it may be five, of these people were
205   slaughtered.
Some declare they had, one of them, fired on a sentinel; others
Say they were only escaping; a priest, it is currently stated,
Stabbed a National Guard on the very Piazza Colonna:
History, Rumour of Rumours, I leave it to thee to determine!
      But I am thankful to say the government seems to have
210   strength to
Put it down; it has vanished, at least; the place is most peaceful.
Through the Trastevere walking last night, at nine of the clock, I
Found no sort of disorder; I crossed by the Island-bridges,

So by the narrow streets to the Ponte Rotto, and onwards
Thence, by the Temple of Vesta, away to the great Coliseum,   215
Which at the full of the moon is an object worthy a visit.

viii — GEORGINA TREVELLYN TO LOUISA —

Only think, dearest Louisa, what fearful scenes we have witnessed —

★

George has just seen Garibaldi, dressed up in a long white
    cloak, on
Horseback, riding by, with his mounted negro behind him:
This is a man, you know, who came from America with him,   220
Out of the woods, I suppose, and uses a *lasso* in fighting,
Which is, I don't quite know, but a sort of noose, I imagine;
This he throws on the heads of the enemy's men in a battle,
Pulls them into his reach, and then most cruelly kills them:
Mary does not believe, but we heard it from an Italian.   225
Mary allows she was wrong about Mr Claude *being selfish*;
He was *most* useful and kind on the terrible thirtieth of April.
Do not write here any more; we are starting directly for
    Florence:
We should be off tomorrow, if only Papa could get horses;
All have been seized everywhere for the use of this dreadful
    Mazzini.   230

P.S.
    Mary has seen thus far. I am really so angry, Louisa,
Quite out of patience, my dearest; what can the man be
    intending?
I am quite tired; and Mary, who might bring him to in a
    moment,
Lets him go on as he likes, and neither will help nor dismiss him.

ix — CLAUDE TO EUSTACE

It is most curious to see what a power a few calm words (in   235
Merely a brief proclamation) appear to possess on the people.
Order is perfect, and peace; the City is utterly tranquil;

And one cannot conceive that this easy and *nonchalant*
    crowd, that
Flows like a quiet stream through street and market-place,
    entering
240 Shady recesses and bays of church, ostería, and café,
Could in a moment be changed to a flood as of molten lava,
Boil into deadly wrath and wild homicidal delusion.
    Ah, 'tis an excellent race, — and even in old degradation,
Under a rule that enforces to flattery, lying, and cheating,
245 E'en under Pope and Priest, a nice and natural people.
Oh, could they but be allowed this chance of redemption! —
    but clearly
That is not likely to be. Meantime, notwithstanding all journals,
Honour for once to the tongue and the pen of the eloquent
    writer,
Honour to speech, and all honour to thee, thou noble Mazzini.

x — CLAUDE TO EUSTACE

250 I am in love, meantime, you think; no doubt you would think so.
I am in love, you say; with those letters of course you would say so.
I am in love, you declare. I think not so; yet I grant you
It is a pleasure indeed to converse with this girl — O rare gift,
Rare felicity, this! she can talk in a rational way, can
255 Speak upon subjects that really are matters of mind and of thinking,
Yet in perfection retain her simplicity, never one moment,
Never however you urge it, however you tempt her, consents to
Step from ideas and fancies and loving sensations to those vain
Conscious understandings that vex the minds of man-kind.
260 No, though she talk, it is music; her fingers desert not the keys; 'tis
Song, though you hear in her song the articulate vocables sounded,
Syllabled singly and sweetly the words of melodious meaning.
    I am in love, you say; I do not think so exactly.

xi — CLAUDE TO EUSTACE

There are two different kinds, I believe, of human attraction;
265 One which simply disturbs, unsettles, and makes you uneasy,

And another that poises, retains, and fixes, and holds you.
I have no doubt, for myself, in giving my voice for the latter.
I do not wish to be moved, but growing, where I was growing,
There more truly to grow, to live where as yet I had languished.
I do not like being moved; for the will is excited; and action   270
Is a most dangerous thing; I tremble for something factitious,
Some malpractice of heart and illegitimate process;
We are so prone to these things with our terrible notions
      of duty.

xii — CLAUDE TO EUSTACE

Ah, let me look, let me watch, let me wait, unhurried,
      unprompted.
Bid me not venture on aught that could alter or end what is
      present;   275
Say not, Time flies, and occasion, that never returns, is departing.
Drive me not out, ye ill angels with fiery swords, from my Eden,
Waiting, and watching, and looking: Let love be its own
      inspiration.
Shall not a voice, if a voice there must be, from the airs that
      environ,
Yea, from the conscious heavens, without our knowledge or effort,   280
Break into audible words? And love be its own inspiration?

xiii — CLAUDE TO EUSTACE

Wherefore and how I am certain, I hardly can tell, but it *is* so.
She doesn't like me, Eustace, I think she never will like me.
Is it my fault, as it is my misfortune, my ways are not her ways?
Is it my fault, that my habits and modes are dissimilar wholly?   285
'Tis not her fault, 'tis her nature, her virtue, to misapprehend
      them:
'Tis not her fault, 'tis her beautiful nature, not ever to know me.
Hopeless it seems, yet I cannot, though hopeless, determine to
      leave it:
She goes, therefore I go; she moves, I move, not to lose her.

xiv — CLAUDE TO EUSTACE

Oh, 'tisn't manly, of course, 'tisn't manly, this method of
290   wooing;
'Tisn't the way very likely to win. For the woman, they tell you,
Ever prefers the audacious, the wilful, the vehement hero;
She has no heart for the timid, the sensitive soul; and for
    knowledge,
Knowledge, O ye gods, when did they appreciate knowledge?
295 Wherefore should they either? I'm sure I do not desire it.
    Ah, and I feel too, Eustace, she cares not a tittle about me!
(Care about me, indeed! and do I really expect it?)
But my manner offends; my ways are wholly repugnant,
Every word that I utter estranges, hurts, and repels her,
300 Every moment of bliss that I gain, in her exquisite presence,
Slowly, surely, withdraws her, removes her and severs her
    from me.
Not that I care very much! any way, I escape from the boy's own
Folly, to which I am prone, of loving where it is easy.
Not that I mind very much! why should I? I am not in love, and
305 Am prepared, I think, if not by previous habit,
Yet in the spirit beforehand for this and all that is like it.
It is an easier matter for us contemplative creatures,
Us, upon whom the pressure of action is laid so lightly:
We, discontented indeed with things in particular, idle,
310 Sickly, complaining, by faith in the vision of things in general
Manage to hold on our way without, like others around us,
Seizing the nearest arm to comfort, help, and support us.
Yet, after all, my Eustace, I know but little about it.
All I can say for myself, for present alike and for past, is
315 Mary Trevellyn, Eustace, is certainly worth your acquaintance.
You couldn't come, I suppose, as far as Florence, to see her?

xv — GEORGINA TREVELLYN TO LOUISA —

  *   *   *   Tomorrow we're starting for Florence,
Truly rejoiced, you may guess, to escape from republican terrors;
Mr C. and Papa to escort us; we by *vettura*

Through Siena, and Georgy to follow and join us by Leghorn.   320
Then – Ah, what shall I say, my dearest? I tremble in thinking.
You will imagine my feelings, the blending of hope and of
    sorrow.
How can I bear to abandon Papa and Mamma and my sisters!
Dearest Louisa, indeed it is very alarming, but trust me
Ever, whatever may change, to remain your loving Georgina.   325

P.S. BY MARY TREVELLYN

*   *   *   'Do I like Mr Claude any better?'
I am to tell you, and 'Pray, is it Susan or I that attract him?'
This he never has told, but Georgina could certainly ask him.
All I can say for myself is, alas, that he rather repels me.
There! I think him agreeable, but also a little repulsive.   330
So be content, dear Louisa; for one satisfactory marriage
Surely will do in one year for the family you would establish;
Neither Susan nor I shall afford you the joy of a second.

P.S. BY GEORGINA TREVELLYN

Mr Claude, you must know, is behaving a little bit better;
He and Papa are great friends, but he really is too *shilly-shally*,   335
So unlike George; yet I hope that the matter is going on fairly.
I shall, however, get George, before he goes, to say something.
Dearest Louise, how delightful, to bring young people together!

———

Is it to Florence we follow, or are we to tarry yet longer,
    E'en amid clamour of arms, here in the city of old,   340
Seeking from clamour of arms in the Past and the Arts to be hidden,
    Vainly 'mid Arts and the Past seeking one life to forget?
Ah, fair shadow, scarce seen, go forth, for anon he shall follow,
    He that beheld thee, anon, whither thou leadest, must go:
Go, and the wise, loving Muse, she also will follow and find thee,   345
    She, should she linger in Rome, were not dissevered from thee.

Canto III

Yet to the wondrous St Peter's, and yet to the solemn Rotonda,
*   Mingling with heroes and gods, yet to the Vatican walls,*
Yet may we go, and recline, while a whole mighty world seems
*   above us*
*   Gathered and fixed to all time into one roofing supreme;*
Yet may we, thinking on these things, exclude what is meaner
5 *   around us;*
*   Yet, at the worst of the worst, books and a chamber remain;*
Yet may we think, and forget, and possess our souls in resistance. —
*   Ah, but away from the stir, shouting, and gossip of war,*
Where, upon Apennine slope, with the chestnut the oak-trees immingle,
10 *   Where amid odorous copse bridle-paths wander and wind,*
Where under mulberry-branches the diligent rivulet sparkles,
*   Or amid cotton and maize peasants their waterworks ply,*
Where, over fig-tree and orange in tier upon tier still repeated,
*   Garden on garden upreared, balconies step to the sky, —*
15 *Ah, that I were, far away from the crowd and the streets of the city,*
*   Under the vine-trellis laid, O my beloved, with thee!*

i — MARY TREVELLYN TO MISS ROPER — *on the way to Florence*

Why doesn't Mr Claude come with us? you ask. — We don't
    know.
You should know better than we. He talked of the Vatican
    marbles;
But I can't wholly believe that this was the actual reason, —
He was so ready before, when we asked him to come and escort
20   us.
Certainly he is odd, my dear Miss Roper. To change so
Suddenly, just for a whim, was not quite fair to the party, —
Not quite right. I declare, I really almost am offended:
I, his great friend, as you say, have doubtless a title to be so.
25 Not that I greatly regret it, for dear Georgina distinctly
Wishes for nothing so much as to show her adroitness. But,
    oh, my

Pen will not write any more; — let us say nothing further
    about it.

★

Yes, my dear Miss Roper, I certainly called him repulsive;
So I think him, but cannot be sure I have used the expression
Quite as your pupil should; yet he does most truly repel me.   30
Was it to you I made use of the word? or who was it told you?
Yes, repulsive; observe, it is but when he talks of ideas,
That he is quite unaffected, and free, and expansive, and easy;
I could pronounce him simply a cold intellectual being. —
When does he make advances? — He thinks that women should
    woo him;   35
Yet, if a girl should do so, would be but alarmed and disgusted.
She that should love him must look for small love in return, —
    like the ivy
On the stone wall, must expect but a rigid and niggard support,
    and
E'en to get that must go searching all round with her humble
    embraces.

ii — CLAUDE TO EUSTACE — from Rome

Tell me, my friend, do you think that the grain would sprout in
    the furrow,   40
Did it not truly accept as its *summum* and *ultimum bonum*
That mere common and maybe indifferent soil it is set in?
Would it have force to develop and open its young cotyledons,
Could it compare, and reflect, and examine one thing with
    another?
Would it endure to accomplish the round of its natural functions,   45
Were it endowed with a sense of the general scheme of existence?
  While from Marseilles in the steamer we voyaged to Civita
    Vecchia,
Vexed in the squally seas as we lay by Capraja and Elba,
Standing uplifted, alone on the heaving poop of the vessel,
Looking around on the waste of the rushing incurious billows,   50
'This is Nature,' I said: 'we are born as it were from her waters,

Over her billows that buffet and beat us, her offspring
        uncared-for,
Casting one single regard of a painful victorious knowledge,
Into her billows that buffet and beat us we sink and are
        swallowed.'
This was the sense in my soul, as I swayed with the poop of the
55   steamer;
And as unthinking I sat in the hall of the famed Ariadne,
Lo, it looked at me there from the face of a Triton in marble.
It is the simpler thought, and I can believe it the truer.
Let us not talk of growth; we are still in our Aqueous Ages.

iii — CLAUDE TO EUSTACE

60   Farewell, Politics, utterly! What can I do? I cannot
Fight, you know; and to talk I am wholly ashamed. And
        although I
Gnash my teeth when I look in your French or your English papers,
What is the good of that? Will swearing, I wonder, mend
        matters?
Cursing and scolding repel the assailants? No, it is idle;
65   No, whatever befalls, I will hide, will ignore or forget it.
Let the tail shift for itself; I will bury my head. And what's the
Roman Republic to me, or I to the Roman Republic?
        Why not fight? — In the first place, I haven't so much as a
        musket.
In the next, if I had, I shouldn't know how I should use it.
70   In the third, just at present I'm studying ancient marbles.
In the fourth, I consider I owe my life to my country.
In the fifth, — I forget; but four good reasons are ample.
Meantime, pray, let 'em fight, and be killed. I delight in
        devotion.
So that I 'list not, hurrah for the glorious army of martyrs!
75   *Sanguis martyrum semen Ecclesiæ;* though it would seem this
Church is indeed of the purely Invisible, Kingdom-Come kind:
Militant here on earth! Triumphant, of course, then, elsewhere!
Ah, good Heaven, but I would I were out far away from the
        pother!

iv — CLAUDE TO EUSTACE

Not, as we read in the words of the olden-time inspiration,
Are there two several trees in the place we are set to abide in;   80
But on the apex most high of the Tree of Life in the Garden,
Budding, unfolding, and falling, decaying and flowering ever,
Flowering is set and decaying the transient blossom of
      Knowledge, —
Flowering alone, and decaying, the needless, unfruitful blossom.
  Or as the cypress-spires by the fair-flowing stream
      Hellespontine,   85
Which from the mythical tomb of the godlike Protesilaüs
Rose sympathetic in grief to his lovelorn Laodamia,
Evermore growing, and, when in their growth to the prospect
      attaining,
Over the low sea-banks, of the fatal Ilian city,
Withering still at the sight which still they upgrow to encounter.   90
  Ah, but ye that extrude from the ocean your helpless faces,
Ye over stormy seas leading long and dreary processions,
Ye, too, brood of the wind, whose coming is whence we discern
      not,
Making your nest on the wave, and your bed on crested billow,
Skimming rough waters, and crowding wet sands that the tide
      shall return to,   95
Cormorants, ducks, and gulls, fill ye my imagination!
Let us not talk of growth; we are still in our Aqueous Ages.

v — MARY TREVELLYN TO MISS ROPER — *from Florence*

Dearest Miss Roper, — Alas, we are all at Florence quite safe, and
You, we hear, are shut up; indeed, it is sadly distressing;
We were most lucky, they say, to get off when we did from the
      troubles.   100
Now you are really besieged; they tell us it soon will be over,
Only I hope and trust without any fight in the city.
Do you see Mr Claude? I thought he might do something
      for you.
I am quite sure on occasion he really would wish to be useful.

105 What is he doing, I wonder – still studying Vatican marbles?
Letters, I hope, pass through. We trust your brother is better.

vi – CLAUDE TO EUSTACE

Juxtaposition, in fine; and what is juxtaposition?
Look you, we travel along in the railway-carriage, or steamer,
And, *pour passer le temps*, till the tedious journey be ended,
110 Lay aside paper or book, to talk with the girl that is next one;
And, *pour passer le temps*, with the terminus all but in prospect,
Talk of eternal ties and marriages made in heaven.
      Ah, did we really accept with a perfect heart the illusion!
Ah, did we really believe that the Present indeed is the Only!
Or through all transmutation, all shock and convulsion of
115   passion,
Feel we could carry undimmed, unextinguished, the light of our
          knowledge!
    But for his funeral train which the bridegroom sees in the
          distance,
Would he so joyfully, think you, fall in with the marriage-
          procession?
But for that final discharge, would he dare to enlist in that
          service?
120 But for that certain release, ever sign to that perilous contract?
But for that exit secure, ever bend to that treacherous doorway? ·
Ah, but the bride, meantime, – do you think she sees it as
          he does?
    But for the steady fore-sense of a freer and larger existence,
Think you that man could consent to be circumscribed here
          into action?
125 But for assurance within of a limitless ocean divine, o'er
Whose great tranquil depths unconscious the wind-tost surface
Breaks into ripples of trouble that come and change and
          endure not, –
But that in this, of a truth, we have our being, and know it,
Think you we men could submit to live and move as we do here?
Ah, but the women, – God bless them! – they don't think at all
130   about it.

Yet we must eat and drink, as you say. And as limited beings
Scarcely can hope to attain upon earth to an Actual Abstract,
Leaving to God contemplation, to His hands knowledge
    confiding,
Sure that in us if it perish, in Him it abideth and dies not,
Let us in His sight accomplish our petty particular doings, —
Yes, and contented sit down to the victual that He has provided.   135
Allah is great, no doubt, and Juxtaposition his prophet.
Ah, but the women, alas, they don't look at it in that way!
  Juxtaposition is great; — but, my friend, I fear me, the maiden
Hardly would thank or acknowledge the lover that sought to
    obtain her,   140
Not as the thing he would wish, but the thing he must even put
    up with, —
Hardly would tender her hand to the wooer that candidly
    told her
That she is but for a space, an *ad-interim* solace and pleasure, —
That in the end she shall yield to a perfect and absolute
    something,
Which I then for myself shall behold, and not another, —   145
Which, amid fondest endearments, meantime I forget not,
    forsake not.
Ah, ye feminine souls, so loving and so exacting,
Since we cannot escape, must we even submit to deceive you?
Since so cruel is truth, sincerity shocks and revolts you,
Will you have us your slaves to lie to you, flatter and — leave
    you?   150

vii — CLAUDE TO EUSTACE

Juxtaposition is great, — but, you tell me, affinity greater.
Ah, my friend, there are many affinities, greater and lesser,
Stronger and weaker; and each, by the favour of juxtaposition,
Potent, efficient, in force, — for a time; but none, let me tell you,
Save by the law of the land and the ruinous force of the will, ah,   155
None, I fear me, at last quite sure to be final and perfect.
Lo, as I pace in the street, from the peasant-girl to the princess,
Homo sum, nihil humani a me alienum puto, —

Vir sum, nihil fœminei, — and e'en to the uttermost circle,
160 All that is Nature's is I, and I all things that are Nature's.
Yes, as I walk, I behold, in a luminous, large intuition,
That I can be and become anything that I meet with or look at:
I am the ox in the dray, the ass with the garden-stuff panniers;
I am the dog in the doorway, the kitten that plays in the
     window,
165 On sunny slab of the ruin the furtive and fugitive lizard,
Swallow above me that twitters, and fly that is buzzing
     about me;
Yea, and detect, as I go, by a faint, but a faithful assurance,
E'en from the stones of the street, as from rocks or trees of the
     forest,
Something of kindred, a common, though latent vitality,
     greet me,
And, to escape from our strivings, mistakings, misgrowths, and
170   perversions,
Fain could demand to return to that perfect and primitive silence,
Fain be enfolded and fixed, as of old, in their rigid embraces.

viii — CLAUDE TO EUSTACE

And as I walk on my way, I behold them consorting and
     coupling;
Faithful it seemeth, and fond, very fond, very probably faithful;
175 All as I go on my way, with a pleasure sincere and unmingled.
     Life is beautiful, Eustace, entrancing, enchanting to look at;
As are the streets of a city we pace while the carriage is
     changing,
As is a chamber filled-in with harmonious, exquisite pictures,
Even so beautiful Earth. And could we eliminate only
180 This vile hungering impulse, this demon within us of craving,
Life were beatitude, living a perfect divine satisfaction.

ix — CLAUDE TO EUSTACE

Mild monastic faces in quiet collegiate cloisters:
So let me offer a single and celibatarian phrase, a

Tribute to those whom perhaps you do not believe I can honour.
But, from the tumult escaping, 'tis pleasant, of drumming and
 shouting,   185
Hither, oblivious awhile, to withdraw, of the fact or the
 falsehood,
And amid placid regards and mildly courteous greetings
Yield to the calm and composure and gentle abstraction that
 reign o'er
Mild monastic faces in quiet collegiate cloisters.
 Terrible word, Obligation! You should not, Eustace, you
 should not,   190
No, you should not have used it. But, O great heavens, I repel it,
Oh, I cancel, reject, disavow, and repudiate wholly
Every debt in this kind, disclaim every claim, and dishonour,
Yea, my own heart's own writing, my soul's own signature.
 Ah no,
I will be free in this; you shall not, none shall, bind me.   195
No, my friend, if you wish to be told, it was this above
 all things,
This that charmed me, ah yes, even this, that she held me to
 nothing.
No, I could talk as I pleased; come close; fasten ties, as I fancied;
Bind and engage myself deep; and lo, on the following morning
It was all e'en as before; like losings in games played for nothing. 200
Yes, when I came, with mean fears in my soul, with a
 semi-performance
At the first step breaking down in its pitiful rôle of evasion,
When to shuffle I came, to compromise, not meet, engagements,
Lo, with her calm eyes there she met me and knew nothing of it;
Stood unexpecting, unconscious. *She* spoke not of obligations,   205
Knew not of debt, – ah no, I believe you, for excellent reasons.

X – CLAUDE TO EUSTACE

Hang this thinking, at last! what good is it? oh, and what evil!
Oh, what mischief and pain! like a clock in a sick man's
 chamber,
Ticking and ticking, and still through each covert of slumber
 pursuing.

What shall I do to thee, O thou Preserver of Men? Have
210   compassion;
Be favourable, and hear! Take from me this regal knowledge;
Let me, contented and mute, with the beasts of the field, my
        brothers,
Tranquilly, happily lie; — and eat grass, like Nebuchadnezzar.

xi — CLAUDE TO EUSTACE

Tibur is beautiful, too, and the orchard slopes, and the Anio
215 Falling, falling yet, to the ancient lyrical cadence;
Tibur and Anio's tide; and cool from Lucretilis ever,
With the Digentian stream, and with the Bandusian fountain —
Folded in Sabine recesses the valley and villa of Horace:
So not seeing I sung; so seeing and listening say I,
220 Here as I sit by the stream, as I gaze at the cell of the Sibyl,
Here with Albunea's home and the grove of Tiburnus
        beside me,*
Tivoli beautiful is, and musical, O Teverone,
Dashing from mountain to plain, thy parted impetuous waters.
Tivoli's waters and rocks; and fair under Monte Genaro,
(Haunt even yet, I must think, as I wander and gaze, of the
225   shadows,
Faded and pale, yet immortal, of Faunus, the Nymphs, and the
        Graces,)
Fair in itself, and yet fairer with human completing creations,
Folded in Sabine recesses the valley and villa of Horace:
So not seeing I sung; so now — Nor seeing, nor hearing,
230 Neither by waterfall lulled, nor folded in sylvan embraces,
Neither by cell of the sibyl, nor stepping the Monte Genaro,
Seated on Anio's bank, nor sipping Bandusian waters,
But on Montorio's height looking down on the tile-clad
        streets, the
Cupolas, crosses, and domes, the bushes and kitchen-gardens,

---

* — domus Albuneæ resonantis,
Et præceps Anio, et Tiburni lucus, et uda
Mobilibus pomaria rivis.

Which by the grace of the Tiber proclaim themselves Rome of
    the Romans;   235
But on Montorio's height, looking forth to the vapoury
    mountains,
Cheating the prisoner Hope with illusions of vision and fancy, —
But on Montorio's height, with these weary soldiers by me,
Waiting till Oudinot enter to reinstate Pope and Tourist.

xii — MARY TREVELLYN TO MISS ROPER

Dear Miss Roper, It seems George Vernon, before we left
    Rome, said   240
Something to Mr Claude about what they call his attentions.
Susan two nights ago for the first time heard this from Georgina.
It is *so* disagreeable and *so* annoying to think of.
If it could only be known, though we never may meet him
    again, that
It was all George's doing and we were entirely unconscious,   245
It would extremely relieve — Your ever affectionate Mary.

P.S. (1)
    Here is your letter arrived this moment, just as I wanted.
So you have seen him — indeed — and guessed — how dreadfully
    clever!
What did he really say, and what was your answer exactly?
Charming, — but wait for a moment, for I haven't read through
    the letter.   250

P.S. (2)
    Ah, my dearest Miss Roper, do just as you fancy about it.
If you think it sincerer to tell him I know of it, do so.
Though I should most extremely dislike it, I know I could
    manage.
It is the simplest thing, but surely wholly uncalled for.
Do as you please; you know I trust implicitly to you.   255
Say whatever is right and needful for ending the matter.
Only don't tell Mr Claude what I will tell you as a secret,
That I should like very well to show him myself I forget it.

P.S. (3)

I am to say that the wedding is finally settled for Tuesday.
260 Ah, my dear Miss Roper, you surely, surely can manage
Not to let it appear that I know of that odious matter.
It would be pleasanter far for myself to treat it exactly
As if it had not occurred, and I do not think he would like it.
I must remember to add, that as soon as the wedding is over
265 We shall be off, I believe, in a hurry, and travel to Milan.
There to meet friends of Papa's, I am told, at the Croce di Malta.
Then I cannot say whither, but not at present to England.

xiii — CLAUDE TO EUSTACE

Yes, on Montorio's height for a last farewell of the city,
So it appears; though then I was quite uncertain about it.
270 So however it was. And now to explain the proceeding.

I was to go, as I told you I think, with the people to Florence,
Only, the day before, the foolish family Vernon
Made some uneasy remarks, as we walked to our lodging
          together,
As to intentions forsooth, and so forth. I was astounded;
275 Horrified quite; and obtaining just then, as it happened, an offer
(No common favour) of seeing the great Ludovisi collection,
Why, I made this a pretence, and wrote that they must
          excuse me.
How could I go? Great Heaven! to conduct a permitted flirtation
Under those vulgar eyes, the observed of such observers.
280 Well, but I now, by a series of fine diplomatic inquiries,
Find from a sort of relation, a good and sensible woman,
Who is remaining at Rome with a brother too ill for removal,
That it was wholly unsanctioned, unknown: not, I think, by
          Georgina.
She however ere this, and that is the best of the story,
She and the Vernon, thank Heaven, are wedded and gone —
285   honeymooning.
So — on Montorio's height for a last farewell of the city.
Tibur I have not seen, nor the lakes that of old I had dreamt of;
Tibur I shall not see, nor Anio's waters, nor deep en-

Folded in Sabine recesses the valley and villa of Horace;
Tibur I shall not see; but something better I shall see.   290
  Twice I have tried before, and failed in getting the horses,
Twice I have tried and failed, this time it shall not be a failure.

————

Therefore farewell, ye hills, and ye, ye envineyarded ruins,
  Therefore farewell, ye walls, palaces, pillars, and domes;
Therefore farewell, far seen, ye peaks of the mythic Albano,   295
  Seen from Montorio's height, Tibur and Æsula's hills.
Ah, could we once, ere we go, could we stand, while, to ocean
    descending,
  Sinks o'er the yellow dark plain slowly the yellow broad sun,
Stand, from the forest emerging at sunset, at once in the champaign,
  Open but studded with trees, chestnuts umbrageous and old,
E'en in those fair open fields that incurve to thy beautiful hollow,   300
  Nemi imbedded in wood, Nemi inurned in the hill! —
Therefore farewell, ye plains, and ye hills, and the City Eternal,
  Therefore farewell, we depart, but to behold you again.

Canto IV

Eastward, or Northward, or West? I wander, and ask as I wander,
  Weary, yet eager and sure, Where shall I come to my love?
Whitherward hasten to seek her? Ye daughters of Italy, tell me,
  Graceful and tender and dark, is she consorting with you?
Thou that out-climbest the torrent, that tendest thy goats to the summit,   5
  Call to me, child of the Alp, has she been seen on the heights?
Italy, farewell I bid thee! for, whither she leads me, I follow.
  Farewell the vineyard! for I, where I but guess her, must go.
Weariness welcome, and labour, wherever it be, if at last it
  Bring me in mountain or plain into the sight of my love.   10

i — CLAUDE TO EUSTACE — *from Florence*

Gone from Florence; indeed, and this is truly provoking; —
Gone to Milan, it seems; then I go also to Milan.

Five days now departed; but they can travel but slowly; —
I quicker far; and I know, as it happens, the house they will go to. —
15 Why, what else should I do? Stay here and look at the pictures,
Statues, and churches? Alack, I am sick of the statues and
        pictures! —
No, to Bologna, Parma, Piacenza, Lodi, and Milan,
Off go we tonight — and the Venus go to the Devil!

ii — CLAUDE TO EUSTACE — *from Bellaggio*

Gone to Como, they said; and I have posted to Como.
20 There was a letter left, but the *cameriere* had lost it.
Could it have been for me? They came, however, to Como,
And from Como went by the boat, — perhaps to the Splügen, —
Or to the Stelvio, say, and the Tyrol; also it might be
By Porlezza across to Lugano, and so to the Simplon
25 Possibly, or the St Gothard, — or possibly, too, to Baveno,
Orta, Turin, and elsewhere. Indeed, I am greatly bewildered.

iii — CLAUDE TO EUSTACE — *from Bellaggio*

I have been up the Splügen, and on the Stelvio also:
Neither of these can I find they have followed; in no one
        inn, and
This would be odd, have they written their names. I have been
        to Porlezza;
30 There they have not been seen, and therefore not at Lugano.
What shall I do? Go on through the Tyrol, Switzerland,
        Deutschland,
Seeking, an inverse Saul, a kingdom, to find only asses?
    There is a tide, at least in the *love* affairs of mortals,
Which, when taken at flood, leads on to the happiest fortune, —
35 Leads to the marriage-morn and the orange-flowers and the altar,
And the long lawful line of crowned joys to crowned joys
        succeeding. —
Ah, it has ebbed with me! Ye gods, and when it was flowing,
Pitiful fool that I was, to stand fiddle-faddling in that way!

iv – CLAUDE TO EUSTACE – *from Bellaggio*

I have returned and found their names in the book at Como.
Certain it is I was right, and yet I am also in error.
Added in feminine hand, I read, *By the boat to Bellaggio.* –
So to Bellaggio again, with the words of her writing, to aid me.
Yet at Bellaggio I find no trace, no sort of remembrance.
So I am here, and wait, and know every hour will remove them.

v – CLAUDE TO EUSTACE – *from Bellaggio*

I have but one chance left, – and that is, going to Florence.
But it is cruel to turn. The mountains seem to demand me, –
Peak and valley from far to beckon and motion me onward.
Somewhere amid their folds she passes whom fain I would
    follow;
Somewhere among those heights she haply calls me to seek her.
Ah, could I hear her call! could I catch the glimpse of her
    raiment!
Turn, however, I must, though it seem I turn to desert her;
For the sense of the thing is simply to hurry to Florence,
Where the certainty yet may be learnt, I suppose, from
    the Ropers.

vi – MARY TREVELLYN, *from Lucerne*, TO MISS ROPER, *at Florence*

Dear Miss Roper, – By this you are safely away, we are hoping,
Many a league from Rome; ere long we trust we shall see you.
How have you travelled? I wonder; – was Mr Claude your
    companion?
As for ourselves, we went from Como straight to Lugano;
So by the Mount St Gothard; – we meant to go by Porlezza,
Taking the steamer, and stopping, as you had advised, at
    Bellaggio,
Two or three days or more; but this was suddenly altered,
After we left the hotel, on the very way to the steamer.
So we have seen, I fear, not one of the lakes in perfection.
  Well, he is not come; and now, I suppose, he will not come.

What will you think, meantime? – and yet I must really
    confess it; –
65 What will you say? I wrote him a note. We left in a hurry,
Went from Milan to Como three days before we expected.
But I thought, if he came all the way to Milan, he really
Ought not to be disappointed; and so I wrote three lines to
Say I had heard he was coming, desirous of joining our party; –
70 If so, then I said, we had started for Como, and meant to
Cross the St Gothard, and stay, we believed, at Lucerne, for the
    summer.
Was it wrong? and why, if it was, has it failed to bring him?
Did he not think it worth while to come to Milan? He knew (you
Told him) the house we should go to. Or may it, perhaps, have
    miscarried?
75 Any way, now, I repent, and am heartily vexed that I wrote it.

––––––

There is a home on the shore of the Alpine sea, that upswelling
   High up the mountain-sides spreads in the hollow between;
Wilderness, mountain, and snow from the land of the olive conceal it;
   Under Pilatus's hill low by its river it lies:
80 *Italy, utter the word, and the olive and vine will allure not, –*
   Wilderness, forest, and snow will not the passage impede;
Italy, unto thy cities receding, the clue to recover,
   Hither, recovered the clue, shall not the traveller haste?

Canto V

There is a city, upbuilt on the quays of the turbulent Arno,
   Under Fiesole's heights, – thither are we to return?
There is a city that fringes the curve of the inflowing waters,
   Under the perilous hill fringes the beautiful bay, –
5 *Parthenope do they call thee? – the Siren, Neapolis, seated*
   Under Vesevus's Hill, – thither are we to recede?
Sicily, Greece, will invite, and the Orient; – or are we to turn to
   England, which may after all be for its children the best?

i — MARY TREVELLYN, *at Lucerne*, TO MISS ROPER, *at Florence*

So you are really free, and living in quiet at Florence;
That is delightful news; — you travelled slowly and safely;   10
Mr Claude got you out; took rooms at Florence before you;
Wrote from Milan to say so; had left directly for Milan,
Hoping to find us soon; — *if he could, he would, you are certain.* —
Dear Miss Roper, your letter has made me exceedingly happy.
    You are quite sure, you say, he asked you about our
      intentions;   15
You had not heard as yet of Lucerne, but told him of Como. —
Well, perhaps he will come; — however, I will not expect it.
Though you say you are sure, — *if he can, he will, you are certain.*
O my dear, many thanks from your ever affectionate Mary.

ii — CLAUDE TO EUSTACE

                                           Florence.

Action will furnish belief, — but will that belief be the true one?   20
This is the point, you know. However, it doesn't much matter.
What one wants, I suppose, is to predetermine the action,
So as to make it entail, not a chance-belief, but the true one.
Out of the question, you say; *if a thing isn't wrong, we may do it.*
Ah! but this *wrong*, you see — but I do not know that it matters.   25
    Eustace, the Ropers are gone, and no one can tell me about
      them.

                                           Pisa.

Pisa, they say they think; and so I follow to Pisa,
Hither and thither inquiring. I weary of making inquiries;
I am ashamed, I declare, of asking people about it. —
Who are your friends? You said you had friends who would   30
    certainly know them.

                                         Florence.

But it is idle, moping, and thinking, and trying to fix her
Image more and more in, to write the old perfect inscription
Over and over again upon every page of remembrance.
    I have settled to stay at Florence to wait for your answer.
Who are your friends? Write quickly and tell me. I wait for your
    answer.   35

iii — MARY TREVELLYN TO MISS ROPER, *at Lucca Baths*

You are at Lucca Baths, you tell me, to stay for the summer;
Florence was quite too hot; you can't move further at present.
Will you not come, do you think, before the summer is over?
    Mr C. got you out with very considerable trouble;
40 And he was useful and kind, and seemed so happy to serve you;
Didn't stay with you long, but talked very openly to you;
Made you almost his confessor, without appearing to know it, —
What about? — and you say you didn't need his confessions.
O my dear Miss Roper, I dare not trust what you tell me!
45   Will he come, do you think? I am really so sorry for him!
They didn't give him my letter at Milan, I feel pretty certain.
You had told him Bellaggio. We didn't go to Bellaggio;
So he would miss our track, and perhaps never come to Lugano,
Where we were written in full, *To Lucerne, across the St Gothard,*
But he could write to you; — you would tell him where you
50   were going.

iv — CLAUDE TO EUSTACE

Let me, then, bear to forget her. I will not cling to her falsely;
Nothing factitious or forced shall impair the old happy relation.
I will let myself go, forget, not try to remember;
I will walk on my way, accept the chances that meet me;
55 Freely encounter the world, imbibe these alien airs, and
Never ask if new feelings and thoughts are of her or of others.
Is she not changing, herself? — the old image would only
    delude me.
I will be bold, too, and change, — if it must be. Yet if in all
    things,
Yet if I do but aspire evermore to the Absolute only,
60 I shall be doing, I think, somehow, what she will be doing; —
I shall be thine, O my child, some way, though I know not in
    what way.
Let me submit to forget her; I must; I already forget her.

v — CLAUDE TO EUSTACE

Utterly vain is, alas, this attempt at the Absolute, — wholly!
I, who believed not in her, because I would fain believe nothing,
Have to believe as I may, with a wilful, unmeaning acceptance.   65
I, who refused to enfasten the roots of my floating existence
In the rich earth, cling now to the hard, naked rock that is
          left me. —
Ah! she was worthy, Eustace, — and that, indeed, is my comfort, —
Worthy a nobler heart than a fool such as I could have given.

————

Yes, it relieves me to write, though I do not send, and the
          chance that   70
Takes may destroy my fragments. But as men pray, without
          asking
Whether One really exist to hear or do anything for them, —
Simply impelled by the need of the moment to turn to a Being
In a conception of whom there is freedom from all limitation, —
So in your image I turn to an *ens rationis* of friendship.   75
Even so write in your name I know not to whom nor in
          what wise.

————

There was a time, methought it was but lately departed,
When, if a thing was denied me, I felt I was bound to attempt it;
Choice alone should take, and choice alone should surrender.
There was a time, indeed, when I had not retired thus early,   80
Languidly thus, from pursuit of a purpose I once had adopted.
But it is over, all that! I have slunk from the perilous field in
Whose wild struggle of forces the prizes of life are contested,
It is over, all that! I am a coward, and know it.
Courage in me could be only factitious, unnatural, useless.   85

————

Comfort has come to me here in the dreary streets of the city,
Comfort — how do you think? — with a barrel-organ to bring it.
Moping along the streets, and cursing my day, as I wandered,

All of a sudden my ear met the sound of an English psalm tune.
90 Comfort me it did, till indeed I was very near crying.
Ah there is some great truth, partial very likely, but needful,
Lodged, I am strangely sure, in the tones of the English
        psalm tune.
Comfort it was at least; and I must take without question
Comfort however it come in the dreary streets of the city.

        ———

95 What with trusting myself and seeking support from within me
Almost I could believe I had gained a religious assurance,
Found in my own poor soul a great moral basis to rest on.
Ah, but indeed I see, I feel it factitious entirely;
I refuse, reject, and put it utterly from me;
100 I will look straight out, see things, not try to evade them:
Fact shall be fact for me; and the Truth the Truth as ever
Flexible, changeable, vague, and multiform, and doubtful —
Off, and depart to the void, thou subtle fanatical tempter!

        ———

I shall behold thee again (is it so?) at a new visitation,
105 O ill genius thou! I shall, at my life's dissolution,
(When the pulses are weak, and the feeble light of the reason
Flickers an unfed flame retiring slow from the socket)
Low on a sick bed laid, hear one, as it were, at the doorway,
And looking up see thee, standing by, looking emptily at me.
110 I shall entreat thee then, though I now dare to refuse thee, —
Pale and pitiful now, but terrible then to the dying —
Well, I will see thee again: and while I can, will repel thee.

        vi — CLAUDE TO EUSTACE

Rome is fallen, I hear, the gallant Medici taken,
Noble Manara slain, and Garibaldi has lost *il Moro*; —
115 Rome is fallen; and fallen, or falling, heroical Venice.
I, meanwhile, for the loss of a single small chit of a girl, sit
Moping and mourning here, — for her, and myself much smaller.

Whither depart the souls of the brave that die in the battle,
Die in the lost, lost fight, for the cause that perishes with them?
Are they upborne from the field on the slumberous pinions of
    angels   120
Unto a far-off home, where the weary rest from their labour,
And the deep wounds are healed, and the bitter and burning
    moisture
Wiped from the generous eyes? or do they linger, unhappy,
Pining, and haunting the grave of their by-gone hope and
    endeavour?
    All declamation, alas! though I talk, I care not for Rome, nor   125
Italy; feebly and faintly, and but with the lips, can lament the
Wreck of the Lombard youth and the victory of the oppressor.
Whither depart the brave? – God knows; I certainly do not.

vii – MARY TREVELLYN TO MISS ROPER

He has not come as yet; and now I must not expect it.
You have written, you say, to friends at Florence, to see him,   130
If he perhaps should return; – but that is surely unlikely.
Has he not written to you? – he did not know your direction.
Oh, how strange never once to have told him where you were
    going!
Yet if he only wrote to Florence, that would have reached you.
If what you say he said was true, why has he not done so?   135
Is he gone back to Rome, do you think, to his Vatican marbles? –
O my dear Miss Roper, forgive me! do not be angry! –
You have written to Florence; – your friends would certainly
    find him.
Might you not write to him? – but yet it is so little likely!
I shall expect nothing more. – Ever yours, your affectionate
    Mary.   140

viii – CLAUDE TO EUSTACE

I cannot stay at Florence, not even to wait for a letter.
Galleries only oppress me. Remembrance of hope I had cherished

(Almost more than as hope, when I passed through Florence the
    first time)
Lies like a sword in my soul. I am more a coward than ever,
145 Chicken-hearted, past thought. The cafés and waiters distress me
All is unkind, and, alas, I am ready for anyone's kindness.
Oh, I knew it of old, and knew it, I thought, to perfection,
If there is any one thing in the world to preclude all kindness,
It is the need of it, — it is this sad self-defeating dependence.
Why is this, Eustace? Myself, were I stronger, I think I could tell
150   you.
But it is odd when it comes. So plumb I the deeps of
    depression,
Daily in deeper, and find no support, no will, no purpose.
All my old strengths are gone. And yet I shall have to do
    something.
Ah, the key of our life, that passes all wards, opens all locks,
155 Is not *I will*, but *I must*. I must, — I must, — and I do it.

———

After all do I know that I really cared so about her?
Do whatever I will, I cannot call up her image.
For when I close my eyes, I see very likely St Peter's,
Or the Pantheon façade, or Michael Angelo's figures,
160 Or at a wish, when I please, the Alban hills and the Forum, —
But that face, those eyes — ah no, never anything like them;
Only, try as I will, a sort of featureless outline,
And a pale blank orb, which no recollection will add to.
After all, perhaps there was something factitious about it;
165 I have had pain, it is true; have wept; and so have the actors.

———

At the last moment I have your letter, for which I was
    waiting.
I have taken my place, and see no good in inquiries.
Do nothing more, good Eustace, I pray you. It only will
    vex me.
Take no measures. Indeed, should we meet, I could not be
    certain;

All might be changed, you know. Or perhaps there was
    nothing to be changed. .   170
It is a curious history, this; and yet I foresaw it;
I could have told it before. The Fates, it is clear, are
    against us;
For it is certain enough that I met with the people you
    mention;
They were at Florence the day I returned there, and spoke to
    me even;
Stayed a week, saw me often; departed, and whither I
    know not.   175
Great is Fate, and is best. I believe in Providence, partly.
What is ordained is right, and all that happens is ordered.
Ah, no, that isn't it. But yet I retain my conclusion:
I will go where I am led, and will not dictate to the chances.
Do nothing more, I beg. If you love me, forbear interfering.   180

ix — CLAUDE TO EUSTACE

Shall we come out of it all, some day, as one does from a
    tunnel?
Will it be all at once, without our doing or asking,
We shall behold clear day, the trees and meadows about us,
And the faces of friends, and the eyes we loved looking at us?
Who knows? Who can say? It will not do to suppose it.   185

x — CLAUDE TO EUSTACE — *from Rome*

Rome will not suit me, Eustace; the priests and soldiers
    possess it;
Priests and soldiers; — and, ah! which is worst, the priest or the
    soldier?
  Politics farewell, however! For what could I do? with
    inquiring,
Talking, collating the journals, go fever my brain about things
    o'er
Which I can have no control. No, happen whatever may
    happen,   190

Time, I suppose, will subsist; the earth will revolve on its axis;
People will travel; the stranger will wander as now in the city;
Rome will be here, and the Pope the *custode* of Vatican
    marbles.
    I have no heart, however, for any marble or fresco;
195 I have essayed it in vain; 'tis vain as yet to essay it:
But I may haply resume some day my studies in this kind.
Not as the Scripture says, is, I think, the fact. Ere our
    death-day,
Faith, I think, does pass, and Love; but Knowledge abideth.
Let us seek Knowledge; — the rest must come and go as it
    happens.
200 Knowledge is hard to seek, and harder yet to adhere to.
Knowledge is painful often; and yet when we know, we are
    happy.
Seek it, and leave mere Faith and Love to come with the
    chances.
As for Hope, — tomorrow I hope to be starting for Naples.
Rome will not do, I see, for many very good reasons.
    Eastward, then, I suppose, with the coming of winter,
205   to Egypt.

xi — MARY TREVELLYN TO MISS ROPER

You have heard nothing; of course, I know you can have
    heard nothing.
Ah, well, more than once I have broken my purpose, and
    sometimes,
Only too often, have looked for the little lake-steamer to bring
    him.
But it is only fancy, — I do not really expect it.
210 Oh, and you see I know so exactly how he would take it:
Finding the chances prevail against meeting again, he would
    banish
Forthwith every thought of the poor little possible hope, which
I myself could not help, perhaps, thinking only too much of;
He would resign himself, and go. I see it exactly.

So I also submit, although in a different manner.
215
    Can you not really come? We go very shortly to England.

———

So go forth to the world, to the good report and the evil!
    Go, little book! thy tale, is it not evil and good?
Go, and if strangers revile, pass quietly by without answer.
    Go, and if curious friends ask of thy rearing and age,
220
Say, 'I am flitting about many years from brain unto brain of
    Feeble and restless youths born to inglorious days;
But', so finish the word, 'I was writ in a Roman chamber,
    When from Janiculan heights thundered the cannon of France.'

Say not the struggle nought availeth,
　　The labour and the wounds are vain,
The enemy faints not, nor faileth,
　　And as things have been, things remain.

5　If hopes were dupes, fears may be liars;
　　It may be in yon smoke concealed
Your comrades chase e'en now the fliers,
　　And but for you possess the field.

For while the tired waves vainly breaking
10　Seem here no painful inch to gain,
Far back through creeks and inlets making
　　Came, silent, flooding-in, the main.

And not by eastern windows only,
　　When daylight comes, comes-in the light,
15　In front the sun climbs slow, how slowly,
　　But westward, look, the land is bright.

In controversial foul impureness
　　The peace that is thy light to thee
Quench not; in faith and inner sureness
　　Possess thy soul and let it be.

5　No violence – perverse, persistent –
　　What cannot be can bring to be,
No zeal what is makes more existent,
　　And strife but blinds the eyes that see.

What though in blood their souls embruing,
10　The [great,] the good, and wise they curse,
Still sinning, what they know not doing;
　　Stand still, forbear, nor make it worse.

By cursing, by denunciation,
  By [   ] they cannot stay;
Nor thou by fiery indignation,   15
  Though just, accelerate the day.

While circling, chasing, unescaping,
  The waters here these eddies tease,
Unconscious, far its free course shaping,
  The great stream silent seeks the seas.   20

While here, to nooks and shallows drifted,
  Leaf, stick, and foam dispute the shore,
The boatman there his sail has lifted
  Or plies his unimpeded oar.

The Latest Decalogue

Thou shalt have one God only; who
Would be at the expense of two?
No graven images may be
Worshipped, except the currency:
Swear not at all; for for thy curse   5
Thine enemy is none the worse:
At church on Sunday to attend
Will serve to keep the world thy friend:
Honour thy parents; that is, all
From whom advancement may befall: 10
Thou shalt not kill; but needst not strive
Officiously to keep alive:
Do not adultery commit;
Advantage rarely comes of it:
Thou shalt not steal; an empty feat,   15
When it's so lucrative to cheat:
Bear not false witness; let the lie
Have time on its own wings to fly:
Thou shalt not covet; but tradition
Approves all forms of competition.   20

The sum of all is, thou shalt love,
If any body, God above:
At any rate shalt never labour
More than thyself to love thy neighbour.

From *DIPSYCHUS AND THE SPIRIT*

SCENE II
(*Venice: The Public Garden*)

DIPSYCHUS

Assuredly a lively scene:
And ah, how pleasant, something green,
With circling heavens, one perfect rose,
Each smoother patch of water glows
Hence to where, o'er the full tide's face,   5
We see the Palace and the Place
And the white dome. Beauteous but hot.
Where in the meantime is the spot,
My favourite, where by masses blue
And white cloud-folds, I follow true   10
The great Alps, rounding grandly o'er,
Huge arc, to the Dalmatian shore?

SPIRIT

This rather stupid place today,
'Tis true, is most extremely gay,
And rightly – the Assunzione   15
Was always a *gran' funzione*.

DIPSYCHUS

What is this persecuting voice that haunts me?
What, whence, of whom? How am I to discover?
Myself or not myself? My own bad thoughts
Or some external agency at work   20
To lead me who knows whither?

SPIRIT

What lots of boats beside us plying,
What lots of pretty girls, too, hieing
Hither and thither; coming, going;
And with what satisfaction showing   25
To our male eyes unveiled and bare
The exuberant blackness of their hair,

Dark eyes, rich tints, and sundry graces
Of classic pure Italian faces.

DIPSYCHUS

30 Off, off; oh heaven, depart, depart, depart.
Oh heaven! the toad that whispered in Eve's ear
Whispered no dream so dangerous as this.

SPIRIT

A perfect show of girls I see it is;
Ah, what a charming leg; ye deities!
35 In that attraction as one fancies
Italy's not so rich as France is;
In Paris —

DIPSYCHUS

Cease, cease, cease,
I will not hear this. Go. —

SPIRIT

Eh?
What do the pretty verses say?

40 *Ah comme je regrette*
mon bras si dodu,
Ma jambe bien faite
et le temps perdu
et le temps perdu.

45 'Tis here, I see, the practice too
For damsels eager to be lovered
To go about with arms uncovered.
And doubtless there's a special charm
In the full round voluptuous arm.
At Paris, I was saying —

DIPSYCHUS

Ah me, me,
50 Clear stars above, thou roseate westward sky,
Take up my being into yours; assume

My sense to know you only; steep my brain
In your essential purity; or, great Alps
That wrapping round your heads in solemn clouds   55
Seem sternly to sweep past our vanities,
Lead me with you – take me away, preserve me.
– Ah, if it must be, look then, foolish eyes;
Listen, fond ears; but oh poor mind stand fast!

SPIRIT

   At Paris, at the Opera, –   60
   In the *Coulisses* – but ah, aha!
   There was a glance: – I saw you spy it –
   So! shall we follow suit and try it?
   Pooh! what a goose you are! quick, quick.
   This hesitation makes me sick.   65
   You simpleton! what's your alarm?
   She'd merely thank you for your arm.

DIPSYCHUS

Sweet thing! ah well! but yet I am not sure.
Ah no. I think she did not mean it. No.

SPIRIT

   Plainly, unless I much mistake,   70
   She likes a something in your make:
   She turned her head, another glance;
   She really gives you every chance.

DIPSYCHUS

Ah pretty thing – well well. Yet should I go?
Alas, I cannot say! What should I do?   75

SPIRIT

   What should you do? well, that is funny!
   I think you are supplied with money.

DIPSYCHUS

No, no; it may not be. I could, I would
And yet I would not, cannot. To what end?

SPIRIT

80 Trust her for teaching – go but you,
She'll quickly show you what to do.
Well, well! it's too late now – they're gone;
Some wiser youth is coming on.
Really I could be in a passion
85 To see you treat in that odd fashion,
As sweet a little thing as e'er
I saw since first I learnt to stare.

DIPSYCHUS

Ah me –
O hateful, hateful, hateful! to the Hotel!

SCENE III
(*The Quays*)

DIPSYCHUS

O hateful, hateful, hateful! to the Hotel.

SPIRIT

Pooh, what the devil! what's the harm?
I only bid you take her arm.

DIPSYCHUS

And I half yielded! O unthinking I!
5 O weak weak fool! O God how quietly
Out of our better into our worse selves
Out of a true world which our reason knew
Into a false world which our fancy makes
We pass and never know – O weak weak fool.

SPIRIT

10 Well, if you don't wish, why, you don't.
Leave it! but that's just what you won't.
There is nothing that your fancy tickles so

As this at which your conscience stickles so;
Come now! How many times per diem
Are you not hankering to try 'em?   15
How often are you not pursuing
The thought of how 'twould feel in doing?

DIPSYCHUS

O moon and stars forgive! And thou clear heaven
Look pureness back into me. Oh great God,
Why, why in wisdom and in grace's name,   20
And in the name of saints and saintly thoughts
Of mothers and of sisters and chaste wives,
And angel woman-faces we have seen
And angel woman-spirits we have guessed,
And innocent sweet children, and pure love,   25
Why did I ever one brief moment's space
To this insidious lewdness lend chaste ears
Or parley with this filthy Belial?
O were it that vile questioner that loves
To thrust his fingers into right and wrong   30
And before proof knows nothing – or the fear
Of being behind the world – which is, the wicked.

SPIRIT

Oh yes, mere ignorance must mis-state it
Now this, now that way overrate it,
First canonise, then reprobate it,
And in all kinds exaggerate it.   35
Yes! dream of raptures whelmed in shame
Voluptuous joys, whose very name
Is curst by after keen self-blame. –
O yes, you dream of sin and shame –   40
Trust me – it leaves one much the same.
– 'Tisn't Elysium any more
Than what comes after or before:
But heavens! as innocent a thing
As picking strawberries in spring.
You think I'm anxious to allure you –   45
My object is much more to cure you.

With the high amatory-poetic
My temper's no way sympathetic;
To play your pretty woman's fool
I hold but fit for boys from school.
Come now it's mainly your temptation
To think the thing a revelation,
A mystic mouthful that will give
Knowledge and death, – none know and live;
I tell you plainly that it brings
Some ease, but the emptiness of things
(That one old sermon Earth still preaches
Until we practise what she teaches)
Is the sole lesson that you'll learn by it –
Still you undoubtedly should try it.
'Try all things', bad and good, no matter,
You can't till then hold fast the latter.
If not, this itch will stick and vex you
Your live-long days till death unsex you –
Hide in your bones for aught I know
And with you to the next world go:
Briefly – you cannot rest, I'm certain,
Until your hand has drawn the curtain:
Once known the little lies behind it,
You'll go your way, and never mind it.
Ill's only cure is, never doubt it,
To do – and think no more about it. –

DIPSYCHUS

Strange talk, strange words. Ah me, I cannot say.
Could I believe it even of us men
That once the young exuberance drawn off
The liquor would run clear; that once appeased
The vile inquisitive wish, brute appetite fed,
The very void that ebbing flood had left
From purer sources would be now refilled;
That to rank weeds of rainy spring mowed off
Would a green wholesome aftermath succeed;
That the empty garnished tenement of the soul

Would not behold the seven replace the one:
Could I indeed as of some men I might   85
Think this of maidens also. But I know;
Not as the male is, is the female, Eve
Was moulded not as Adam.

SPIRIT
                    Stuff!
The women like it; that's enough:
The pretty creatures come and proffer
The treasures of their privy coffer   90
And I refuse not a good offer.
Sold in the shambles without question.
I eat, and vex not my digestion. —
O, yes, a pretty height, par bleu   95
Your chivalry you've brought to
You'd have 'em like not what they do
But what you think they ought to.

DIPSYCHUS
Could I believe, as of a man I might,
So a good girl from weary workday hours   100
And from the long monotony of toil
Might safely purchase these wild intervals,
And from that banquet rise refreshed, and wake
And shake her locks and as before go forth
Invigorated, unvitiate to the task —   105
But no, it is not so.

SPIRIT
                    That may be true;
It is uncommon, though some do.
The temperaments of women vary
And Jane is not the same as Mary
Yet single women, ah, mon Dieu   110
Being women, must have much ado
Not to o'erstep the *juste milieu*.

In married life you sometimes find
Proceedings something of the kind.

DIPSYCHUS

115 No no, apart from pressure of the world
And yearning sensibilities of Soul,
The swallowed dram entails the drunkard's curse
Of burnings ever new; and the coy girl
Turns to the flagrant woman of the street,
120 Ogling for hirers, horrible to see.

SPIRIT

That is the high moral way of talking;
I'm well aware about street-walking.

DIPSYCHUS

Hungering but without appetite; athirst
From impotence; no humblest feeling left
125 Of all that once too rank exuberance.
No kindly longing, no sly coyness now
Not e'en the elastic appetence of lust
No not a poor petal hanging to that stalk
Where thousands once were redolent and rich.
130 Look, she would fain allure; but she is cold,
The ripe lips paled, the frolick pulses stilled,
The quick eye dead, the once fair flushing cheek
Flaccid under its paint; the once heaving bosom –
Ask not! – for oh, the sweet bloom of desire
135 In hot fruition's pawey fingers turns
To dullness and the deadly spreading spot
Of rottenness inevitably soon
That while we hold, we hate – Sweet Peace! no more!

SPIRIT

Fiddle di diddle, fal lal lal!
140 By candlelight they are *pas mal*;
Better and worse of course there are;
Star differs (with the price) from star.

I found it hard I must confess
To a small Frenchman to say yes
Who told me, in a steamer talking,   145
That one can pick up in one's walking
In the Strand Street in London town
Something quite nice for half-a-crown.
But — in the dark what comes amiss
Except bad breath and syphilis?   150

DIPSYCHUS

Could I believe that any child of Eve
Were formed and fashioned, raised and reared for nought
But to be swilled with animal delight
And yield five minutes' pleasure to the male,
Could I think cherry lips and chubby cheeks   155
That seem to exist express for such fond play,
Hold in suppression nought to come; o'ershell
No lurking virtuality of more —
Could I think this, I could, perhaps, join in it.

SPIRIT

It was a lover and his lass,   160
    With a hey and a ho, and a hey nonino!
Betwixt the acres of the rye,
    With a hey and a ho, and a hey nonino!
These pretty country folks would lie —
    In the spring time, the pretty spring time.   165

DIPSYCHUS

And could I think I owed it not to her,
In virtue of our manhood's stronger sight,
Ever against entreaty to forbear —

SPIRIT

O Joseph and Don Quixote! This
A chivalry of chasteness is,
That turns to nothing all that story   170
Has made out of your ancient glory!
Still I must urge, that though 'tis sad

'Tis sure, once gone, for good or bad
175 The prize whose loss we are deploring
Is physically past restoring:
C'en est fait. Nor can God's own self,
As Coleridge on the dusty shelf
Says in his wicked *Omniana*,
180 Renew to Ina frail or Ana
Her once rent hymenis membrana.
So that it needs consideration
By what more moral occupation
To support this vast population?

DIPSYCHUS

185 Could I believe that purity were not
Lodged somewhere, precious pearl, e'en underneath
The hardest coarsest outside: could I think
That any heart in woman's bosom set
By tenderness o'ermastering mean desire,
190 Faithfulness, love, were unredeemable,
Or could I think it sufferable in me
For my poor pleasure's sake to superadd
One possible finger's pressure to the weight
That turns, and grinds as in a fierce machine
195 This hapless kind, these pariahs of the sex —

SPIRIT

Well; people talk — their sentimentality.
Meantime, as by some sad fatality
Mortality is still mortality,
Nor has corruption, spite of facility,
200 And doctrines of perfectibility
Yet put on incorruptibility,
As women are and the world goes
They're not so badly off — who knows?
They die, as we do in the end;
205 They marry; or they — *superintend*:
Or Sidney Herberts sometimes rise,
And send them out to colonise.

DIPSYCHUS

Or could I think that it had been for nought,
That from my boyhood until now, in spite
Of most misguiding theories, at the moment   210
Somewhat has ever stepped in to arrest
My ingress at the fatal-closing door,
That many and many a time my foolish foot
O'ertreading the dim sill, spite of itself
And spite of me, instinctively fell back.   215

SPIRIT

Like Balaam's ass, in spite of thwacking,
Against the wall his master backing,
Because of something hazy stalking
Just in the way they should be walking;
Soon after too he took to talking!   220

DIPSYCHUS

Backed, and refused my bidding – Could I think,
In spite of carnal understanding's sneers,
All this fortuitous only – all a chance?

SPIRIT

Ah, just what I was going to say;
An Angel met you in the way.   225
Cry mercy of his heavenly highness,
I took him for that cunning shyness.

DIPSYCHUS

Shyness. 'Tis but another word for Shame;
And that for Sacred Instinct. Off ill thoughts!
'Tis holy ground your foot has stepped upon.   230

SPIRIT

Ho, Virtue quotha! trust who knows;
There's not a girl that by us goes
But mightn't have you if she chose:
No doubt but you would give her trouble;

235   But then you'd pay her for it double.
          By Jove – if I were but a lass,
          I'd soon see what I'd bring to pass.

DIPSYCHUS

        O welcome then, the sweet domestic bonds,
        The matrimonial sanctities; the hopes
240   And cares of wedded life; parental thoughts,
        The prattle of young children, the good word
        Of fellow men, the sanction of the law,
        And permanence and habit, that transmute
        Grossness itself to crystal. O why why
245   Why ever let this speculating brain
        Rest upon other objects than on this?

SPIRIT

        Well well – if you must stick perforce
        Unto the ancient holy course,
        And map your life out on the plan
250   Of the connubial puritan,
        For God's sake carry out your creed,
        Go home, and marry and be d—d;
        I'll help you.

DIPSYCHUS
        You!

SPIRIT
                O never scout me;
        I know you'll ne'er propose without me.

DIPSYCHUS
255   I have talked o'ermuch. The Spirit passes from me.
        O folly folly, what have I done? Ah me!

SPIRIT
        You'd like another turn, I see.
        Yes yes, a little quiet turn.

By all means let us live and learn.
Here's many a lady still waylaying,   260
And sundry gentlemen purveying.
And if 'twere only just to see
The room of an Italian *fille*,
'Twere worth the trouble and the money.
You'll like to find — I found it funny —   265
The chamber *où vous faites vôtre affaire*
Stand nicely fitted up for prayer;
While dim you trace along one end
The Sacred Supper's length extend,
The calm Madonna o'er your head   270
Smiles, *col bambino*, on the bed
Where — but your chaste ears I must spare —
Where, as we said, *vous faites vôtre affaire*.
They'll suit you, these Venetian pets,
So natural, not the least coquettes,   275
Really at times one quite forgets —

DIPSYCHUS

Oh heaven, to yield a treasured innocence
To frosty fondlings and a forced caress,
To heavy kisses and the plastery speech
Of a would-be but can't-be sentiment —   280

SPIRIT

You don't like sentiment? he he!
'T should have been you instead of me,
When t'other day just after noon
Having got up a little soon
Tiring of cafés, quays, and barks   285
I turned for shade into St Mark's.
I sit a while — studying mosaics
Which we untheorising laics
Have leave to like — a girl slips by,
And gives the signal with her eye.   290
She takes the door; I follow out:
Curious, amused, but scarce in doubt

While street on street she winds about,
Heedful at corners, but *du reste*
295 Assured, and grandly self-possessed,
Trips up a stair at last, and lands me;
Up with her petticoats, and hands me
Much as one might a *pot de chambre*
The vessel that relieves *le membre*.
300 No would-be-pretty hesitation
No farce of female expectation
Most business-like in her vocation
She but the brief half instant lingers
That strikes her bargain with five fingers.
305 'Twas well enough – I do not mean
Voluptuous, but plain and clean;
Doctors perhaps might recommend it,
You step and do the thing and end it.

DIPSYCHUS

Ah well, I like a mild infusion
310 Of something bordering on illusion,
To dream and dreaming know one knows
That as the dream comes, so it goes –
You know that feeling, I suppose.
Foolish it may be, but it serves
315 One's purpose better for one's nerves.

SPIRIT

Well! the Piazza? *mio carino*
A better place than the Giardino,
Or would you like perhaps to arrive at
A pretty creature's home in private?
320 We can look in, just say goodnight,
And, if you like to stay, all right.
Just as you fancy – is it well?

DIPSYCHUS

O folly folly folly! To the Hotel.

SCENE IV
(*The Hotel*)

DIPSYCHUS

O hateful, hateful – let me shudder it off.
Thank God, thank God we are here – that's well at least.

SPIRIT

Well it is somewhat coarse it's true
For such a modest youth as you
To couple here in public view.
Well, well – I may have been a little strong;   5
Of course, I wouldn't have you do what's wrong.
But we who've lived much in the World, you know,
Don't see these little things precisely so.
You feel yourself, to loathe and yet be fain,   10
And still to move and still draw back again,
Is a proceeding wholly without end.
So if you really hate the street, my friend,
Why one must try the drawing room, one fancies:
Say, will you run to concerts and to dances   15
And with my help go into good society?
The World don't love, 'tis true, this peevish piety:
E'en they with whom it thinks to be securest –
Your most religious, delicatest, purest –
Discern, and show as well-bred people can,   20
Their feeling that you are not quite a man.
Still the thing has its place; and with sagacity,
Much might be done by one of your capacity.
A virtuous attachment formed judiciously
Would come, one sees, uncommonly propitiously: 25
Turn you but your affections the right way,
And what mayn't happen none of us can say;
For in despite of devils and of mothers,
Your good young men make catches, too, like others.
Oh yes; into society we go: 30
At worst, 'twill teach you much you ought to know.

DIPSYCHUS

To herd with people one can feel no care for,
To drain the heart with empty complaisance,
To warp the unfashioned diction on the lips,
And twist one's mouth to counterfeit; enforce
35   The laggard cheeks to falsehood; base-alloy
The ingenuous golden frankness of the past;
To calculate, to plot; be rough and smooth,
Forward and silent; deferential, cool,
40   Not by one's humour, which is the true truth,
But on consideration —

SPIRIT

    That is, act
On a dispassionate judgement of the fact;
Look all the data fairly in the face
And rule your conduct simply by the case.

DIPSYCHUS

45   On vile consideration. At the best
With pallid hotbed courtesies to forestall
One's native vernal spontaneities
And waste the priceless moments of the man
In softening down grimace to grace. Whether these things
50   Be right, I do not know; I only know 'tis
To lose one's youth too early. Oh not yet,
Not yet I make this sacrifice!

SPIRIT

    Du tout!
To give up nature's just what wouldn't do.
By all means keep your sweet ingenuous graces
And bring them in at proper times and places!
55   For work, for play, for business, talk, and love,
I own as wisdom truly from above
That scripture of the serpent and the dove;
Nor's aught so perfect for the world's affairs
60   As the old parable of wheat and tares;

What we all love is good touched up with evil —
Religion's self must have a spice of devil.

DIPSYCHUS

Let it be enough
That in our needful mixture with the world,
On each new morning with the rising sun
Our rising heart, fresh from the seas of sleep,   65
Scarce o'er the level lifts his purer orb
Ere lost and mingled with polluting smoke,
At noon a coppery disk. Lo, scarce come forth,
Some vagrant miscreant meets, and with a look   70
Transmutes me his, and for a whole sick day
Lepers me.

SPIRIT

       Just the one thing, I assure you,
From which good company can't but secure you.
About the individuals 't'ain't so clear,
But who can doubt the general atmosphere?   75

DIPSYCHUS

Aye truly, who? at first. But in a while —

SPIRIT

O dear, this o'er-discernment makes me smile —
You don't pretend to tell me you can see
Without one touch of melting sympathy
Those lovely, stately flowers, that fill with bloom   80
The brilliant season's gay parterre-like room,
Moving serene yet swiftly through the dances,
Those graceful forms and perfect countenances,
Whose every fold and line in all their dresses
Something refined and exquisite expresses?   85
To see them smile and hear them talk so sweetly
In me destroys all grosser thoughts completely.
I really seem without exaggeration
To experience the True Regeneration;

90 One's own dress too, one's manner, what one's doing
And saying, all assist to one's renewing.
I love to see in these their fitting places
The bows and forms and all you call grimaces.
I heartily could wish we'd kept some more of them,
95 However much they talk about the bore of them.
Fact is, your awkward parvenus are shy at it,
Afraid to look like waiters if they try at it.
'Tis sad, to what democracy is leading;
Give me your Eighteenth Century for high breeding.
100 Though I can put up gladly with the present,
And quite can think our modern parties pleasant.
One shouldn't analyse the thing too nearly;
The main effect is admirable clearly.
Good manners, said our great aunts, next to piety;
105 And so, my friend, hurrah for good society.
For, mind you, if you don't do this, you still
Have got to tell me what it is you will.

SCENE V
(*In a Gondola*)

SPIRIT
Per ora. To the Grand Canal.
And after that as fancy shall.

DIPSYCHUS
Afloat; we move. Delicious. Ah,
What else is like the gondola?
5 This level floor of liquid glass
Begins beneath us swift to pass.
It goes as though it went alone
By some impulsion of its own.
How light it moves, how softly. Ah,
10 Were all things like the gondola!

How light it moves, how softly. Ah,
Could life, as does our gondola,
Unvexed with quarrels, aims and cares
And moral duties and affairs,
Unswaying noiseless swift and strong 15
For ever thus, thus glide along!
How light we move, how softly! Ah,
Were life but as the gondola.

With no more motion than should bear
A freshness to the languid air; 20
With no more effort than exprest
The need and naturalness of rest,
Which we beneath a grateful shade
Should take on peaceful pillows laid; —
How light we move, how softly! Ah, 25
Were life but as the gondola! —

In one unbroken passage borne
To closing night from opening morn,
Uplift at whiles slow eyes to mark
Some palace front, some passing bark; 30
Through windows catch the varying shore,
And hear the soft turns of the oar —
How light we move, how softly! Ah,
Were life but as the gondola!

So live, nor need to call to mind 35
Our slaving brother set behind!

SPIRIT

Pooh, Nature meant him for nothing better
Than our most humble menial debtor.
He thanks us for his day's employment,
As we our purse for our enjoyment. 40

DIPSYCHUS

To make one's fellow man an instrument —

SPIRIT

Is just the thing that makes him most content.
See: he is wedded to his trade;
He loves, he all but is his blade.
His life is in his function! look,
How perfectly that turn he took:
His sum has found without one fraction
Its integer in this small action.
A pleasant day – a lovely day
Come sing your sweet songs and be gay!

DIPSYCHUS

Yes, it is beautiful ever, let foolish men rail at it never;
Life it is beautiful truly, my brothers, I grant it you duly,
Wise are ye others that choose it, and happy are all that can
use it.
Life it is beautiful wholly, and could we eliminate only
This interfering, enslaving, o'ermastering demon of craving,
This wicked tempter inside us to ruin still eager to guide us,
Life were beatitude, Action a possible pure satisfaction.

Ah but it will not, it may not, its nature and law is to
stay not,
This semi-vision enchanting with but actuality wanting,
And as a picture or book at, this life that is lovely to
look at,
When that it comes as we go on to th'eating and drinking
and so on
Is not beatitude, Action in no way a pure satisfaction.

SPIRIT

Hexameters, by all that's odious,
Beshod with rhyme to run melodious.

DIPSYCHUS

All as I go on my way I behold them consorting and
coupling;
Faithful it seemeth and fond, very fond, very possibly faithful;

All as I go on my way with a pleasure sincere and unmingled.
Life it is beautiful truly, my brothers, I grant it you duly.
But for perfection attaining is one method only, abstaining;
Let us abstain, for we should so, if only we thought that we
           could so.   70

SPIRIT

Bravo, bravissimo! – this time, though,
  You rather were run short for rhyme though;
Not that on that account your verse
  Could be much better – or much worse.   75

This world is bad enough, maybe;
    We little comprehend it;
But in one fact can all agree,
    God won't and we can't mend it.

Being common sense it can't be sin
    To take it as we find it,   80
The pleasure to take pleasure in,
    The pain, try not to mind it.

DIPSYCHUS

Yet it is noble I doubt not the slaving and striving
    and straining;
Earning and spending; and seeking and finding; and losing and
    gaining;
Weeping and laughing and scolding, consulting, exulting,
    complaining,   85
Angers, relentings, repentings, fond pleading, and lofty
    disdaining –
Ah – for perfection attaining, alack, there is only abstaining!
Let us abstain; for we should so, we could so, if only we would so.

Better it were, thou sayest, to consent,
Feast while we may, and live ere life be spent;   90
Close up clear eyes, and call the unstable sure,

The unlovely lovely and the filthy pure;
In self-belyings, self-deceivings roll,
And lose in Action, Passion, Talk, the soul.
95 Ah better far to mark off so much air
And call it heaven, place bliss and glory there,
Fix perfect homes in the unsubstantial sky
And say what is not shall be by and by,
What here exists not, must exist elsewhere.
100 Play thou not tricks upon thyself, O man;
Let fact be fact, and life the thing it can.

SPIRIT

So! stand you up, my friend, for fact?
    And I am for confusion?
Bare thought is common sense; an act
105   The acme of illusion?

Worthy of Malebranche or Berkeley,
    So philosophical and clerkly.
I trust it won't be thought a sin
    Should I too 'answer with grin'.

110 These juicy meats, this flashing wine
    May be an unreal mere appearance;
Only – for my inside, in fine,
    They have a singular coherence.

This lovely creature's glowing charms
115   Are gross illusion, I don't doubt that,
But folded in each other's arms
    We didn't somehow think about that.

Oh yes, my pensive youth, abstain:
    And any empty sick sensation,
120 Remember, anything like pain
    Is only your imagination.

Trust me, I've read your German sage
    To far more purpose e'er than you did;
You find it in his wisest page,
125   Whom God deludes is well deluded.

St Giorgio and the Redemptore!
This Gothic is a worn-out story;
No building, trivial, gay or solemn
Can spare the shapely Grecian column:
'Tis not these centuries four for nought   130
Our European world of thought
Has made familiar to its home
The Classic mind of Greece and Rome;
In all new work that dare look forth
To more than antiquarian worth   135
Palladio's pediments and bases
Or something such will find their places:
Maturer optics don't delight
In childish dim religious light,
In evanescent vague effects   140
That shirk, not face, one's intellects;
They love not fancies fast betrayed,
And artful tricks of light and shade,
But pure form nakedly displayed,
And all things absolutely made.   145

The Doge's palace, though, from hence,
In spite of Ruskin's d—d pretence,
The tide now level with the quay,
Is certainly a thing to see.
We'll turn to the Rialto soon;   150
They say it looks well by the moon.

DIPSYCHUS

Where are the great whom thou would'st wish should praise
    thee?
Where are the pure whom thou would'st choose to love thee?
Where are the brave to stand supreme above thee,
Whose high commands would cheer, whose chiding raise thee? 155
Seek, seeker, in thyself; submit to find
In the stones bread, and life in the blank mind.

(Written in London, standing in the Park,
An evening last June, just before dark.)

SPIRIT

160   As I sat at the café, I thought to myself
They may talk as they please about what they call pelf,
They may jeer if they like about eating and drinking,
But help it I cannot, I cannot help thinking
    How pleasant it is to have money, heigh ho,
165   How pleasant it is to have money.

I sit at my table *en grand seigneur*,
And when I have done, toss a crust to the poor;
Not only the pleasure, oneself, of good living,
But also the pleasure of now and then giving.
170   So pleasant it is to have money, heigh ho,
     So pleasant it is to have money.

The horses are brought, and the horses they stay,
I haven't quite settled on riding today,
The servants they wait, and they mustn't look sour,
175   Though we change our intention ten times in an hour
    So pleasant it is to have money, heigh ho,
     So pleasant it is to have money.

I drive through the streets, and I care not a d—mn,
The people they stare, and inquire who I am,
180   And if I should chance to run over a cad,
I can pay for the damage, if ever so bad.
    So pleasant it is to have money, heigh ho,
     So pleasant it is to have money.

We stroll to our box, and look down on the pit,
185   If it weren't rather low should be tempted to spit;
We loll and we talk until people look up,
And when it's half over we go out and sup.
    So pleasant it is to have money, heigh ho,
     So pleasant it is to have money.

190   The best of the rooms and best of the fare,
And as for all others, the devil may care;

It isn't our fault, if they dare not afford
To sup like a prince and be drunk as a lord.
  So pleasant it is to have money, heigh ho,
  So pleasant it is to have money.   195

We sit at our table, and tipple champagne,
Ere one bottle goes, comes another again;
The waiters they skip and they scuttle about,
And the landlord attends us so civilly out.
  So pleasant it is to have money, heigh ho,   200
  So pleasant it is to have money.

It was but last Winter I came up to town,
But I'm getting already a little renown;
I get to good houses without much ado,
Am beginning to see the nobility too,   205
  So pleasant it is to have money, heigh ho,
  So pleasant it is to have money.

O dear! what a pity they ever should lose it,
For they are the gentry that know how to use it,
So grand and so graceful, such manners, such dinners,
But yet, after all, it is we shall be winners.   210
  So pleasant it is to have money, heigh ho,
  So pleasant it is to have money.

So I sat at my table *en grand seigneur*,
And when I had done threw a crust to the poor;   215
Not only the pleasure, oneself, of good eating,
But also the pleasure of now and then treating.
  So pleasant it is to have money, heigh ho,
  So pleasant it is to have money.

They may talk as they please about what they call pelf, 220
Declare one ought never to think of oneself,
Say that pleasures of thought surpass eating and drinking;
My pleasure of thought is the pleasure of thinking
  How pleasant it is to have money, heigh ho,
  How pleasant it is to have money.   225

Written in Venice, somewhere about two;
'Twas not a crust I gave him, but a sou.
And now it is time I think, my men
We try the Grand Canal again.

230   A gondola here and a gondola there,
'Tis the pleasantest fashion of taking the air.
To right and to left; stop, turn, and go yonder,
And let us repeat o'er the tide as we wander,
        How pleasant it is to have money, heigh ho,
235   How pleasant it is to have money.

DIPSYCHUS

Nor ever think to call to mind
Our brother slaving hard behind
Nor ever need, so light we go,
Whether he lives or not, to know.

240   How light we go, how soft we skim,
And all in moonlight seem to swim.
The south side rises o'er our bark,
A wall impenetrably dark;
The north is seen profusely bright;
245   The water — is it shade or light?
Say gentle moon, which conquers now,
The flood, those bulky hulls, or thou?
How light we go, how softly! Ah
Were life but as the gondola!

250   How light we go, how soft we skim
And all in moonlight seem to swim.
In moonlight is it now or shade?
In planes of clear division made
By angles sharp of palace walls
255   The clear light and the shadow falls:
O sight of glory, sight of wonder,
Seen, a pictorial portent under,
O great Rialto, the clear round
Of thy vast solid arch profound.

How light we go, how softly! Ah
Life should be as the gondola!   260

How light we go, how softly —

SPIRIT
                              Stay,
Enough, I think of that today.
I'm deadly weary of your tune,
And half-*ennuyé* with the moon;   265
The shadows lie, the glories fall,
And are but moonshine after all;
It goes against my conscience really
To let myself feel so ideally:
Make me repose no power of man shall   270
In things so deuced unsubstantial.
Come, to the Piazzetta steer,
'Tis nine by this, or very near.
These airy blisses, skiey joys
Of vague romantic girls and boys,   275
Which melt the heart (and the brain soften)
When not affected, as too often
They are, remind me I protest
Of nothing better at the best
Than Timon's feast to his ancient lovers,   280
Warm water under silver covers;
'Lap, dogs', I think I hear him say,
And lap who will, so I'm away.

DIPSYCHUS
How light we go, how soft we skim,
And all in open moonlight swim: 285
Bright clouds against, reclined I mark
The white dome now projected dark,
And by o'er-brilliant lamps displayed,
The Doge's columns and arcade;
Over smooth waters mildly come   290
The distant laughter and the hum.

How light we go, how softly! ah,
Life should be as the gondola!

SPIRIT

By Jove we've had enough of you,
295 Quote us a little Wordsworth, do;
Those lines which are so true, they say:
'A something far more deeply' eh?
'Interfused' — what is it they tell us?
Which and the sunset are bedfellows.

DIPSYCHUS

300 How light we go, how soft we skim,
And all in open moonlight swim.
Oh, gondolier, slow, slow, more slow!
We go; but wherefore thus should go?
O let not muscles all too strong
305 Beguile, betray thee to our wrong.
On to the landing, onward. Nay,
Sweet dream, a little longer stay!
On to the landing. Here. And, ah,
Life is not as the gondola.

SPIRIT

310 *Tre ore*. So. The Parthenone,
Is it, you haunt for your *limone*?
Let me induce you to join me
In *gramolata persici*.

There is no God, the wicked saith,
  And truly it's a blessing,
For what he might have done with us
  It's better only guessing.

There is no God, a youngster thinks,
  Or really, if there may be,
He surely didn't mean a man
  Always to be a baby.

There is no God, or if there is,
  The tradesman thinks, 'twere funny
If he should take it ill in me
  To make a little money.

Whether there be, the rich man says,
  It matters very little,
For I and mine, thank somebody,
  Are not in want of victual.

Some others also to themselves
  Who scarce so much as doubt it,
Think there is none, when they are well,
  And do not think about it.

But country folks who live beneath
  The shadow of the steeple,
The parson and the parson's wife,
  And mostly married people,

Youths green and happy in first love,
  So thankful for illusion,
And men caught out in what the world
  Calls guilt, in first confusion,

And almost every one when age,
  Disease or sorrows strike him,
Inclines to think there is a God,
  Or something very like him.

From the contamination
Of laudation,
From weak alliances, base compliances,
From Condescensions and attentions
5   And would-be grace that is grimace,
And Complaisance that brings Conceit
And from the baffling and defeat
Of a soul that strives in vain
By a self worship to maintain
10   Its ebbing Purity,
And from that wealth that is not health
But insecurity
And from self will that is not sanity
And from the thousandfold inanity
15   Of worldly kindliness that turns to vanity,
From worldly help bequeathing imbecility
And praise corrupting incorruptibility,
From worldly joys that weaken, waste and wither us
O Thou! deliver us —

In stratis viarum I

Each for himself is still the rule,
We learn it when we go to school —
    The devil take the hindmost, o.

And when the schoolboys grow to men,
5   In life they learn it o'er again —
    The devil take the hindmost, o.

For in the church, and at the bar,
On change, at court, where'er they are,
    The devil takes the hindmost, o.

Husband for husband, wife for wife,   10
Are careful that in married life
    The devil take the hindmost, o.

From youth to age, whate'er the game,
The unvarying practice is the same –
    The devil take the hindmost, o.   15

And after death, we do not know,
But scarce can doubt, where'er we go,
    The devil takes the hindmost, o.

Tol rol de rol, tol rol de ro,
The devil take the hindmost, o!   20

In stratis viarum II

Our gaieties, our luxuries
    Our pleasures and our glee,
Mere insolence and wantonries
    Alas, they feel to me.

How shall I laugh and sing and dance?   5
    My very heart recoils
While here to give my mirth a chance
    A hungry brother toils.

The joy that does not spring from joy
    Which I in others see   10
How can I venture to employ
    Or find it joy for me?

In stratis viarum III

Blessed are those who have not seen,
    And who have yet believed;
The witness, here that has not been,
    From heaven they have received.

5   Blessed are those who have not known
        The things that stand before them,
And for a vision of their own
        Can piously ignore them.

So let me think, whate'er befall,
10   That in the city duly,
Some men there are who love at all,
        Some women who love truly;

And that upon two million odd
        Transgressors in sad plenty,
15   Mercy will of a gracious God
        Be shown – because of twenty.

In stratis viarum IV

Put forth thy leaf, thou lofty plane,
        East wind and frost are safely gone;
With zephyrs mild and balmy rain
        The summer comes serenely on;
5   Earth, air, and sun and skies combine
        To promise all that's kind and fair. –
But thou, O human heart of mine,
        Be still, contain thyself and bear.

December days were brief and chill,
10   The winds of March were wild and drear,
And nearing, and receding still
        Spring never would, we thought, be here;
The leaves that burst, the suns that shine
        Had, not the less, their certain date. –
15   But thou, O human heart of mine,
        Be still, refrain thyself and wait.

Peschiera

What voice did on my spirit fall,
Peschiera, when thy bridge I crost?
' 'Tis better to have fought and lost,
Than never to have fought at all.'

The tricolor a trampled rag   5
Lies, dirt and dust: the lines I track
By sentry boxes yellow-black
Lead up to no Italian flag.

I see the Croat soldier stand
Upon the grass of your redoubts;   10
The Eagle with his black wing flouts
The breadth and beauty of your land.

Yet not in vain, although in vain,
O men of Brescia, on the day
Of loss past hope, I heard you say   15
Your welcome to the noble pain.

You said, 'Since so it is, goodbye
Sweet life, high hope; but whatsoe'er
May be or must, no tongue shall dare
To tell, "the Lombard feared to die." '   20

You said (there shall be answer fit)
'And if our children must obey,
They must; but thinking on this day
'Twill less debase them to submit.'

You said (Oh not in vain you said)   25
'Haste, brothers, haste: while yet we may:
The hours ebb fast of this one day
When blood may yet be nobly shed.'

Ah not for idle hatred, not
For honour, fame, nor self-applause,   30
But for the glory of the cause
You did, what will not be forgot.

And though the Stranger stand, 'tis true,
By force and fortune's right he stands,
35   By fortune which is in God's hands,
And strength which yet shall spring in you.

This voice did on my spirit fall,
Peschiera, when thy bridge I crost,
' 'Tis better to have fought and lost,
40   Than never to have fought at all.'

Alteram partem

Or must I say, Vain Word, false thought!
Since Prudence hath her martyrs too,
And Wisdom dictates not to do
Till doing shall be not for nought?

5   Ah blood is blood and life is life:
Will Nature then, when brave ones fall
Remake her work, and songs recall
Death's victim lost in useless strife?

That rivers run into the sea
10   Is loss and waste, the foolish say,
Nor know that back they find their way
Unseen to where they wont to be.

Upon the hills showers fall; streams flow,
The river runneth still at hand;
15   Brave men are born into the land
And whence, the foolish never know.

No. No vain voice did on me fall,
Peschiera, as thy bridge I crost:
''*Tis* better to have fought and lost,
20   Than never once have fought at all.'

These vulgar ways that round me be,
These faces shabby, sordid, mean,
Shall they be daily, hourly seen
And not affect the eyes that see?

Long months to play the censor's part,   5
Lie down at night and rise at morn
In mere defiance and stern scorn
Is scarcely well for human heart.

Accept, O soul, not in disdain,
But patience, faith and simple sooth;   10
Poise all things in the scales of truth,
And one day they shall pay thy pain.

It fortifies my soul to know
That though I perish, Truth is so:
That howsoe'er I stray and range,
Whate'er I do, Thou dost not change:
I steadier step, when I recall   5
That if I slip, Thou dost not fall.

July's Farewell

Yet once again, ye banks and bowery nooks,
And once again, ye dells and flowing brooks,
I come to list the plashing of your fountains
And lie within the foldings of your mountains.
Yet once again, ye mossy flowery plots,   5
And once again, ye leaf-enguarded grots,
And breathing fields and soft enclosing shades,
And once again, ye fair and loving maids,
I come to twist my fingers in your tresses,
And watch your eyes and laugh in your caresses,   10

And beg or steal or seize your pouting kisses
And live and die in your oblivious blisses;
Yet once again, ye banks and bowers, I hie to you,
And once again, ye loves and graces, fly to you.

15 I come, I come, upon the heart's wings fly to you,
Ye dreary lengths of brick and flag, goodbye to you,
Ambitious hopes and money's mean anxieties,
And worldly-wise decorum's false proprieties,
And politics and news and fates of nations too,
20 And philanthropic sick investigations too,
And company, and jests, and feeble witticisms
And talk of talk, and criticism of criticisms;
I come, I come, ye banks and bowers, to hide in you,
And once again, ye loves and joys, confide in you.

25 Yet once again, and why not once again?
The leaves they tumbled, but the boughs remain;
Cold winds they blew, and biting frosts they dried them,
But didn't wholly kill the old life inside them;
What Winter numbed, sweet Spring anon revisiteth,
30 And vernal airs to vernal stir soliciteth,
No scruples fond, no sly fastidious tarrying here,
Sweet air and earth forthwith are intermarrying here;
To intermixtures subtle, strange, mysterious
A voice, an impulse soft, sublime, imperious,
35 Calls all around us; shall we deaf remain?
Yet once again, and why not once again,
Yet once again, ye leafy bowers, I hide in you
And once again, ye tender loves, confide in you.

I come, I come, upon the soul's wings hie to you,
40 Ye weary lines of printer's ink, goodbye to you,
With all the tomes of all the hundred pages there,
The mighty books of all the World's great sages there,
Grammarians old, and modern fine Philologists,
And Poets gone, and going Ideologists,
45 From old solemnities, new trivialities,
Philosophies, economies, moralities,

I come, I come, ye banks and bowers, I hie to you,
And once again, ye loves and graces, fly to you.

Yet once again – how often once again?
The days die fast, old age comes on amain: 50
Age, loss, decay. Ah come, if come they will,
The leaf shall fall, the tree subsisteth still.
Age, weakness, death. Ah come, if come they must,
Age, weakness, death; and over our cold dust
The joyous spring shall lead, as erst, her flowers   55
To deck as erst our fresh reviving bowers,
And with the Spring and flowers the youth and maid
Shall laugh and kiss and play as we have played,
Shall part and meet and kiss old kisses o'er
And sing old verses we had sung before,   60
'Yet once again, ye banks and bowers, we hie to you,
And once again, ye loves and graces, fly to you.'

Go foolish thoughts, and join the throng
    Of myriads gone before
To flutter and flap and flit along
    The airy limbo shore.

Go, words of sport and words of wit,   5
    Sarcastic points and fine,
And words of wisdom wholly fit
    With folly's to combine.

Go, words of wisdom, words of sense,
    Which while the heart belied,   10
The tongue still uttered for pretence
    The inner blank to hide.

Go, words of wit, so gay, so light,
    That still were meant express
To soothe the smart of fancied slight   15
    By fancies of success.

Go, broodings vain o'er fancied wrong;
    Go, love-dreams vainer still,
And scorn that's not, but would be, strong,
20   And Pride without a Will.

Go, foolish thoughts, and find your way
    Where myriads went before,
To linger, languish and decay
    Upon the limbo shore.

ὕμνος ἄυμνος *

O thou whose image in the shrine
Of human spirits dwells divine,
Which from that precinct once conveyed
To be to outer day displayed
5   Doth vanish, part, and leave behind
Mere blank and void of empty mind,
Which wilful fancy seeks in vain
With casual shapes to fill again —

O thou that in our bosoms' shrine
10 Dost dwell because unknown divine,
I thought to speak, I thought to say
'The light is here', 'behold the way',
'The voice was thus', and 'thus the word',
And 'thus I saw', and 'that I heard', —
15 But from the lips but half essayed
The imperfect utterance fell unmade.

O thou in that mysterious shrine
Enthroned, as we must say, divine,
I will not frame one thought of what
20 Thou mayest either be or not.
I will not prate of 'thus' and 'so',
And be profane with 'yes' and 'no';
Enough that in our soul and heart
Thou, whatsoe'er thou may'st be, art.

* A hymn, yet not a hymn.

Unseen, secure in that high shrine   25
Acknowledged present and divine,
I will not ask some upper air,
Some future day, to place thee there;
Nor say, nor yet deny, Such men
Or women saw thee thus and then;   30
Thy name was such, and there or here
To him or her thou didst appear.

Do only thou in that dim shrine
Unknown or known remain divine.
There, or if not, at least in eyes   35
That scan the world that round them lies.
The hand to sway, the judgement guide,
In sight and sense thyself divide:
Be thou but there, – in soul and heart
I will not ask to feel thou art.   40

'Old things need not be therefore true,'
O brother men, nor yet the new;
Ah still awhile the old thought retain,
And yet consider it again!

The Souls of now two thousand years   5
Have laid up here their toils and tears,
And all the earnings of their pain –
Ah yet consider that again!

We! what do *we* see? each a space
Of some few yards before his face;   10
Does that the whole wide plan explain?
Ah yet consider it again!

Alas, the great World goes its way,
And takes its truth from each new day.
They do not quit, nor can retain,   15
Far less consider it again.

To spend unsolaced years of pain
Again again and yet again
In turning o'er in heart and brain
   The riddle of our being here;
To gather facts from far and near,
Upon the mind to keep them clear,
And thinking more may yet appear,
Unto one's latest breath to fear
The premature result to draw –
Is this the purpose and high law
   And object of our being here?

To doubt not if it's good or not
But cheerfully accept our lot
And get whatever may be got
   And gained out of our being here;
To get our pleasures while we may
We must set us to obey
And while today is called today,
Be it work or play where'er we're found,
To join in what goes on around, –
What else, in sense and reason's mind,
   Can be the good of being here?

Ah one is sad, and one is vain
Poor pleasure one and one much pain –
Both ways there seems but little gain
   Or benefit in being here;
If go we might and go we could,
I think we ought and think we should,
Yet as we can't whate'er we would
We can't but think there is some good
However little understood
   In having been and being here.

Dance on, dance on, we see, we see.
Youth goes, alack, and with it glee,
A boy the grown man ne'er can be;
Maternal thirty scarce shall find
The sweet sixteen long left behind;   5
Old folks must toil and scrape and strain
That boys and girls may once again
Be that for them they cannot be
But which it gives them joy to see.
Youth goes and glee, but not in vain,   10
Young folks, if only you remain.
Dance on, dance on, 'tis joy to see.

Dance on, dance on, 'tis joy to see.
The dry red leaves on winter's tree
Enjoy the new sap rising free: 15
On, on, young folks; so you survive,
The dead themselves are still alive,
The blood in dull parental veins
Long numbed a tingling life regains,
For deep in earth the tough old root   20
Is conscious still of flower and fruit.
Spring goes and glee, but were not vain,
They're come in you young folks again.
On, on, dance on, 'tis joy to see.

Dance on, dance on, we see, we feel: 25
Wind, wind your waltzes, wind and wheel,
Our senses too with music reel;
Nor let your pairs neglect to fill
The old ancestral scorned quadrille.
Let hand the hand uplifted seek,   30
And pleasure fly from cheek to cheek;
Love too – but gently; nor astray;
And yet, deluder, yet in play.
Dance on; youth goes, but 'tis not vain,
Young folks, if only you remain.   35
Dance on, dance on, 'tis joy to see.

Dance on, dance on, 'tis joy to see:
We once were nimble e'en as ye,
And danced to give the oldest glee;
O wherefore add, as we you too
Once gone your prime cannot renew;
You too like us at last shall stand
To watch and not to join the band,
Content some day (a far-off day)
To your supplanters soft to say,
'Youth goes and glee, but not in vain,
Young folks, so only you remain.'
Dance on, dance on, 'tis joy to see.

Because a Lady chose to say
I know not what long months away
A Lady charming fair and young,
En passant, in the crowd, one night,
She'd read my verse with such delight –
For this is it and not for more
My brain I ransack o'er and o'er
And consecrate, to make and mend
Each busy workday's scanty end,
With labour long and service hard
To win some future word's reward?
                    Ah folly, folly, folly.

Fair words of friends they come perforce
A thing of kindness and of course,
And author's compliments alack
Are only given to be given back.
The public's favour – the Vulgar – these
It were pollution did we please,
But oh to cause one feeling's stir
To make one moment sweet to her

That is so lovely and so young
And speaks with oh so true a tongue –
With sweet musings blend the word
And to her confidence be heard,
                    Oh folly, folly, folly.   25

I wondered much what once I spurned
To pleasure all at once was turned,
Content here found, I knew not why,
Long hours of vext correction ply,
To turn, to twist, reject, replace   30
And win the rebel rhymes to grace.
In joy I slaved nor had one thought
I was but fooled in all I wrought
By one that lovely was and young
And spoke with such a flattering tongue.   35
I had my joy nor had a doubt;
Oh that I found my folly out,
                    Oh folly, folly, folly.

If to write, rewrite, and write again,
Bite now the lip and now the pen,
Gnash in a fury the teeth, and tear
Innocent paper or it may be hair,
In eager endless chases to pursue   5
That swift escaping word that would do,
Inside and out turn a phrase, o'er and o'er,
Till all the little sense goes, it had before, –
If it be these things make one a poet,
I am one – Come and all the world may know it.   10

If to look over old poems and detest
What one once hugged as a child to one's breast,
Find the things nothing that once had been so much,
The old noble forms gone into dust at a touch:
If to see oneself of one's fancied plumage stript,   15
If by one's faults as by furies to be whipt;

If to become cool and, casting for good away
All the old implements, take 'em up the next day;
If to be sane tonight and insane again tomorrow,
20 And salve up past pains with the cause of future sorrow, –
If to do these things make a man a poet,
I am one – Come and all the world may know it.

If nevertheless no other peace of mind,
No inward unity ever to find,
25 No calm, well-being, no sureness or rest
Save when by that one curious temper possest,
Out of whose kind sources in pure rhythm flow
The easy melodious verse-currents go;
If to sit still while the world goes by,
30 Find old friends dull and new friends dry,
Dinners a bore and dancing worse,
Compared to the tagging of verse unto verse, –
If it be these things make one a poet,
I am one – Come and all the world may know it.

But that from slow dissolving pomps of dawn
No verity of slowly strengthening light
Early or late hath issued; but that the day,
Scarce-shown, relapses rather, self-withdrawn,
5 Back to the glooms of antenatal night,
    For this, O human beings, mourn we may.

To think that men of former days
In naked truth deserved the praise
Which, fain to have in flesh and blood
An image of the imagined good,
5 Poets have sung and men received
And all too glad to be deceived

Most plastic and most inexact
Posterity has told for fact –
To say what was, was not as we,
This also is a vanity.   10

Ere Agamemnon, warriors were,
Ere Helen, beauties equalling her,
Heroes and graces whom no one knows;
And brave or fair as these or those
The commonplace, whom daily we   15
In our dull streets and houses see.
To think of other mould than these
Were Solon, Cato, Socrates,
Or Mahomet or Confutzee,
This also a vanity.   20

Hannibal, Cæsar, Charlemain
And he, before, who back on Spain
Repelled the fierce inundant Moor;
Godfrey, St Louis wise and pure,
Washington, Cromwell, John and Paul,   25
Columbus, Luther, one and all,
Go mix them up, the false and true,
With Sinbad, Crusoe, or St Preux,
And say as he was, so was he,
This also is a vanity.   30

It is not here, it is not there,
Nor in the earth, nor in the air,
That better thing than can be seen
Is neither now nor e'er has been;
It is, not in this land or that,   35
But in a place we soon are at,
Where all can seek and some can find,
Where hope is liberal, fancy kind,
And what we wish for we can see –
Which also is a vanity.   40

Seven Sonnets

I

That children in their loveliness should die
Before the dawning beauty, which we know
Cannot remain, has yet begun to go;
That when a certain period has passed by,
5   People of genius and of faculty,
Leaving behind them some result to show,
Having performed some function, should forego
A task which younger hands can better ply
Appears entirely natural. But that one
10   Whose perfectness did not at all consist
In things towards framing which time could have done
Anything – whose sole office was to exist –
Should suddenly dissolve and cease to be
Calls up the hardest questions and perplexity.

II

That there are better things within the womb
Of Nature than to our unworthy view
She condescends to publish may be true:
The cycle of the birthplace and the tomb
5   Fulfils at least the order and the doom
Of her that has not ordinance to do
More than to withdraw and to renew,
To show one moment and the next resume.
The law that we return from whence we came
10   May for the flowers, beasts, and most men remain;
If for ourselves we nor question nor complain.
But for a being that demands the name
We highest deem – a Person and a Soul –
It troubles us if this should be the whole.

III

To see the rich autumnal tints depart
And view the fading of the roseate glow
That veils some Alpine altitude of snow,
To hear some mighty masterpiece of art
Lost or destroyed, may to the adult heart,   5
Impatient of the transitory show
Of lovelinesses that but come and go,
A positive strange eager thankfulness impart.
When human pure perfections disappear,
Not at the first but at some later day   10
The buoyancy of such reaction may
With strong assurance conquer blank dismay,
Make Hope triumphant over Doubt and fear
To Prove that spiritual victory clear.

IV

If it is thou whose casual hand withdraws
What it at first as casually did make,
Say what amount of ages it will take
With tardy rare concurrences of laws,
And subtle multiplicities of cause   5
The thing they once had made us to remake?
May hopes dead-slumbering dare to reawake
E'en after utmost interval of pause?
What revolutions must have passed, before
The great celestial cycles shall restore   10
The starry [sign] whose present hour is gone;
What worse than dubious chances interpose,
With cloud and sunny gleam to recompose
The skiey picture we had gazed upon?

V

But if as (not by that the soul desired
Swayed in the judgement) wisest men have thought,
And (furnishing the evidence it sought)
Man's heart hath ever fervently required,

5   And story, for that reason deemed inspired,
     To every clime in every age hath taught;
     If in this human complex there be aught
     Not lost in death as not in birth acquired,
     O then though cold the lips that did convey
10   Rich freights of meaning, dead each living sphere
     Where thought abode and fancy loved to play,
     Thou, yet we think, somewhere somehow still art,
     And satisfied with that the patient heart
     The where and how doth not desire to hear.

VI

     But whether in the uncoloured light of truth
     This inward strong assurance be indeed
     More than the self-willed arbitrary creed,
     Manhood's inheritor to the dream of youth;
5   Whether to shut out fact because forsooth
     To live were unsupportable, unfreed,
     [   ]
     Be not or be the service of untruth:
     Whether this vital confidence be more
10   Than his, who upon death's immediate brink
     Knowing, perforce determines to ignore,
     Or than the bird's, that with the hunters near
     Burying her eyesight can forget her fear —
     Who about this shall tell us what to think?

VII

     Shall I decide it by a random shot?
     Our happy hopes, so happy and so good,
     Are not mere idle motions of the blood
     And when they seem most baseless, most are not.
5   A seed there must have been upon the spot
     Where the flowers grow; without it ne'er they could.
     The confidence of growth least understood
     Of some deep intuition was begot.

What if despair and hope alike be true?
The heart, 'tis manifest, is free to do   10
Which ever Nature and itself suggest;
And always 'tis a fact that we are here;
And with being here, doth palsy-giving fear —
Whoe'er can ask? — or hope accord the best?

Thesis and Antithesis

θέσις

If that we thus are guilty doth appear,
Ah guilty though we are, grave judges, hear,
Ah yes, if ever you in your sweet youth
'Midst pleasure's borders missed the track of truth,
Made love on benches underneath green trees,   5
Stuffed tender rhymes with old new similes,
Whispered soft anythings and in the blood
Felt all you said not, most was understood —
Ah if you have — as which of you has not? —
Nor what you were have utterly forgot,   10
[Then be not stern] to faults yourselves have known,
To others harsh, kind to yourselves alone.

ἀντίθεσις

That we, young sir, beneath our youth's green trees
Once did not what should profit but should please,
In foolish longing and in lovesick play   15
Forgot the truth and lost the flying day —
That we went wrong we say not is not true,
But if we erred were we not punished too?
If not — if no one checked our wandering feet —
Shall we our parents' negligence repeat?   20
For future times that ancient loss renew,
If none saved *us*, forbear from saving you,
Nor let that justice in your faults be seen
Which in our own or was or should have been?

θέσις

25 Yet yet recall the mind that you had then,
And so recalling, listen yet again;
If you escaped, 'tis plainly understood
Impunity may leave a culprit good;
If you were punished, did you then as now
30 The justice of that punishment allow?
Did what your age consents to now, appear
Expedient then and needfully severe?
In youth's indulgence think there yet might be
A truth forgot by grey severity;
35 That strictness and that laxity between,
Be yours the wisdom to detect the mean.

ἀντίθεσις

'Tis possible, young sir, that some excess
Mars youthful judgement and old men's no less,
Yet we must take our [counsel] as we may
40 For (flying years this lesson still convey),
'Tis worst unwisdom to be overwise,
And not to use but still correct one's eyes.

Sectantem levia nervi deficiunt

O tell me, friends, while yet we part
And heart can yet be heard of heart,
O tell me, friends, for what is it
Our early hopes so soon we quit,
5 So easily so far have ranged,
And why is it that all has changed?
O tell me, friends, while yet we part.

O tell me, friends, while yet ye hear,
May it not be some coming year,
10 These ancient paths that here divide
Shall yet again run side by side,

And you from there and I from here
All on a sudden reappear?
O tell me, friends, while yet ye hear.

O tell me, friends, ere words are o'er,   15
There's something in me sad and sore
Repines, and underneath my eyes
I feel a somewhat that would rise, –
O tell me, O my friends, and you,
Do you feel nothing like it too?   20
O tell me, friends – Ye hear no more. –

O happy they whose hearts receive
The implanted word with faith; believe
Because their fathers did before,
Because they learnt, and ask no more

High triumphs of convictions sought   5
And won by individual thought,
The joy, delusive oft, but keen,
Of having with our own eyes seen.

What if they have not felt nor known?
An amplitude instead they own   10
Of [   ]; above their head
The glory of the Unseen is spread.

Their happy heart is free to range
Through largest tracts of pleasant change;
Their intellects encradled lie   15
In boundless possibility.

By no self-binding ordinance prest
To toil in labour they detest,
By no deceiving reasoning tied
Or this or that way to decide.   20

For impulses of strangest kinds
The Ancient Home a lodging finds;
Each appetite our nature breeds,
It meets with viands for its needs.

25   Oh happy they – nor need they fear
The wordy strife that rages near;
All reason wastes by day, and more,
Will Instinct in a night restore.

O happy, so their state but give
30   A clue by which a man can live;
O blest, unless 'tis proved by fact
A dream impossible to act.

Come home, come home! and where an home hath he
Whose ship is driving o'er the driving sea?
To the frail bark here plunging on its way
To the wild waters shall I turn and say
5   Ye are my home?

Fields once I walked in, faces once I knew,
Familiar things my heart had grown unto,
Far away hence behind me lie; before
The dark clouds mutter and the deep seas roar
10   Not words of home.

Beyond the clouds, beyond the waves that roar
There may indeed, or may not be, a shore,
Where fields as green and friendly hearts as true
The old foregone appearance may renew
15   As of an home.

But toil and care must add day on to day,
And weeks bear months and months bear years away,
Ere, if at all, the way-worn traveller hear
A voice he dare believe say in his ear
20   Come to thy home.

Come home, come home! and where an home hath he
Whose ship is driving o'er the driving sea?
Through clouds that mutter and o'er seas that roar
Is there indeed, or is there not a shore
         That is our home?   25

     Ye flags of Piccadilly,
       Where I posted up and down,
   And wished myself so often
       Well away from you and Town, –

   Are the people walking quietly   5
       And steady on their feet,
   Cabs and omnibuses plying
       Just as usual in the street?

   Do the houses look as upright
       As of old they used to be,   10
   And does nothing seem affected
       By the pitching of the sea?

   Through the Green Park iron railings
       Do the quick pedestrians pass?
   Are the little children playing   15
       Round the plane tree in the grass?

   This squally wild Northwester
       With which our vessel fights,
   Does it merely serve with you to
       Carry up some paper kites?   20

   Ye flags of Piccadilly,
       Which I hated so, I vow
   I could wish with all my heart
       You were underneath me now! –

Mari Magno I

Some future day, when what is now is not,
When all old faults and follies are forgot,
And thoughts of difference passed like dreams away,
We'll meet again – upon some future day.

5 When all that hindered, all that vexed our love,
The tall rank weeds that clomb the blade above,
And all but It has yielded to decay,
We'll meet again, upon some future day.

When we have proved, each on his course alone,
10 The wider world and learnt what's now unknown,
Have made life clear and worked out each a way,
We'll meet again, – we shall have much to say.

With happier mood and feelings born anew,
Our boyhood's bygone fancies we'll review,
15 Talk o'er old talks, play as we used to play,
And meet again on many a future day.

Some day, which oft our hearts shall yearn to see,
In some far year, though distant, yet to be,
Shall we indeed – Ye winds and water, say! –
20 Meet yet again upon some future day?

Mari Magno II

Where lies the land to which the ship would go?
Far, far ahead, is all her sailors know,
And where the land she travels from? Away,
Far, far behind, is all that they can say.

5 On sunny noons upon the deck's smooth face
Linked arm in arm, how pleasant here to pace;
Or o'er the poop reclining, watch below
The foaming wake far widening as we go.

On stormy nights when wild Northwesters rave,
How proud a thing to fight with wind and wave;   10
The shivering sailor on the reeling mast
Exults to bear and scarce would wish it past.

Where lies the land to which the ship would go?
Far, far ahead, is all her sailors know.
And where the land she travels from? Away,   15
Far, far behind, is all that they can say.

Come pleasant thoughts; sweet thoughts, at will
Of hope and love, recurring still;
And while the preacher, much perplext,
To pieces pulls the weary text, –

O pleasant thoughts – around the home   5
Of happy memories free to roam
Let me, there, underneath the trees
That grow for me beyond the seas,

Among far-distant English flowers
Compose the blessed Sunday hours;   10
And see before and by me move
The darling figure of my love.

The purple silk I see, – I hear
Its rustle as she passes near, –
As 'twere the shadow of sweet sound   15
Her voice upon my heart is found.

An halo of a loving grace
Hangs interposed before her face;
My eyes are dim, and do not see,
I only feel that it is she.   20

Come, happy fancies, come, and go,
And come again, forever so;
I shall be blest, whate'er my lot
So you, – and she, – forsake me not.

Were I with you or you with me
My love, how happy should we be.
Day after day it is sad cheer
To have you there, while I am here.

5   My darling's face I cannot see,
My darling's voice is mute for me,
My fingers vainly seek the hair
Of her that is not here, but there.

In a strange land to her unknown
10   I sit and think of her alone,
And in that happy chamber where
We sat, she sits, nor has me there.

Yet still the happy thought recurs
That she is mine, as I am hers,
15   That she is there, as I am here,
And loves me, whether far or near.

The mere assurance that she lives
And loves me, full contentment gives;
I need not doubt, despond, nor fear
20   *For*, she is there and I am here.

How in all wonder Columbus got over,
    That is a marvel to me I protest;
Cabot; and Raleigh too, that well-read rover;
    Frobisher, Dampier, Drake and the rest:
        Bad enough all the same,   5
        For them that after came,
        But in great heaven's name,
        How *he* should ever think
        That on the other brink
Of this huge waste terra firma should be,   10
Is a pure wonder, I must say, to me,
Is a pure wonder, I must say, to me.

How a man ever should hope to get thither
    E'en if he knew of there being another side!
But to suppose he should come any whither,   15
    Sailing right on into chaos untried,
        Across the whole Ocean,
        In spite of the motion,
        To stick to the notion
        That in some nook or bend   20
        Of a sea without end
He should find North and South Amerikee
Was a pure madness, as it seems to me,
Was a pure madness, as it seems to me.

What if wise men had as far back as Ptolemy   25
    Judged that the Earth like an orange was round,
None of them ever said, 'Come along, follow me,
    Sail to the West and the East will be found.'
        Many a day before
        Ever they'd touched the shore   30
        Of the San Salvador,
        Sadder and wiser men,
        They'd have turned back again,
And that he did not, but did cross the sea,
Is a pure wonder, I must say, to me.   35
And that he crossed and that we cross the sea
Is a pure wonder, I must say to me.

That out of sight is out of mind
Is true of most we leave behind;
It is not, sure, nor can be true,
My own and dearest love, of you.

5 They were my friends, 'twas sad to part,
Almost a tear began to start,
But yet as things run on, they find
That out of sight is out of mind.

For men that will not idlers be
10 Must lend their hearts to things they see;
And friends who leave them far behind,
Being out of sight are out of mind.

I do not blame. I think that when
The cold and silent see again,
15 Kind hearts will yet as erst be kind;
'Twas out of sight was out of mind.

I knew it, when we parted, well,
I knew it, though was loth to tell;
I knew before, what now I find,
20 That out of sight was out of mind.

That friends, however friends they were,
Still deal with things as things occur,
And that, excepting for the blind,
What's out of sight is out of mind.

25 But love *is*, as they tell us, blind;
So out of sight and out of mind
Need not, nor will I think be true,
My own and dearest love, of you.

O qui me – !

Amid these crowded pews must I sit and seem to pray,
All the blessed Sunday-morning while I wish to be away,
While in the fields I long to be or on the hill-tops high,
The air of heaven about me, above, the sacred sky?

Why stay and form my features to a 'foolish face of' prayer,   5
Play postures with the body, while the Spirit is not there?
Not there, but wandering off to woods, or pining to adore
Where mountains rise or where the waves are breaking on
        the shore.

In a calm sabbatic chamber when I could sit alone,
And feed upon pure thoughts to workday hours unknown,
Amidst a crowd of lookers-on why come, and sham to pray,   10
While the blessed Sunday-morning wastes uselessly away?

Upon the sacred morning that comes but once a week,
Where'er the Voice addresses me, there let me hear it speak;
Await it in the chamber, abroad to seek it roam,   15
The Worship of the heavens attend, the Services of home.

Pent-up in crowded pews am I really bound to stay,
And to edify my neighbours make a sad pretence to pray,
And where the Truth indeed speaks, neglect to hear it speak,
On the blessed Sunday morning that comes but once a week?   20

                Upon the water in the boat,
                I sit and sketch as down I float:
                The stream is wide, the view is fair,
                I sketch it looking backward there.

                The stream is strong, and as I sit   5
                And view the picture that we quit,
                It flows and flows and bears the boat,
                And I sit sketching as we float.

Still as we go the things I see
E'en as I see them, cease to be;
Their angles swerve, and with the boat
The whole perspective seems to float.

Still as I sit with something new
The foreground intercepts my view;
Even the towering mountain range
From the first moments suffers change;

Each pointed height, each wavy line
To wholly other forms combine,
Proportions vary, colours fade,
And all the landscape is remade.

Depicted neither far nor near
And larger there and smaller here,
And varying down from old to new,
E'en I can hardly think it true

Yet still I look, and still I sit,
Adjusting, shaping, altering it,
And still the current bears the boat,
And me, still sketching as I float.

Veni

While labouring thousands ply their task
And scarcely what it tends to ask,
While trembling thinkers on the brink
Pause sad and see not what to think,
Ere all believe that all is vain,
Come to express and to explain.
Come Thou, for whom all hearts are fain.

In faultless outline to portray
The substance of each shadowy day,
The deeds within us to rehearse
And give our meanings life in Verse,

To tell the purport of our pain
And what our silly joys contain,
Come Poet – for whom all hearts are fain.

Come, Poet, come! to give the dumb
A voice, to still vain talkers, come;
By hope allured, and caught by glare
Ten thousand dupes seek here and there;
While sages half have learnt to doubt,
And think we may be best without;
Come thou! for both but wait to see
Their error proved to them by thee.

Come Poet come, for but in vain
We do the work and feel the pain
And gather up the seeming gain
Unless while yet 'tis time, Thou come
And ere we lose it, tell their sum.

In vain I seem to call. And yet
Think not the living Times forget:
Ages of heroes fought and fell,
That Homer in the end might tell;
O'er grovelling generations past
Upstood the Doric fane at last;
And countless hearts on countless years
Had wasted wishes, hopes, and fears,
Rude laughters and unmeaning tears,
Ere England Shakespeare saw, or Rome
The pure perfection of her Dome.
Others I doubt not, if not we,
The issue of our toils shall see;
Young children gather as their own
The harvests that the dead have sown
(The dead, forgotten and unknown):

Nay draw not yet the cork, my friend,
    Draw not at least for me
Nor let into the alien airs
    The priceless essence flee –
Draw not yet the cork, as yet, as yet,
    Ah no, no, no, not yet.

A time shall come that is not now,
    We wait for and shall see;
What now is kept shall then be spent
    And will not wasted be
Upon a time that is not yet
    Ah no, no, no, not yet.

The joy, the rich exuberance,
    The glory, the belief
Were not upon the soul bestowed
    To part with for relief –
Ah part with them not yet, not yet,
    Ah no, no, no, not yet.

For they shall come that are not now,
    We know, though do not see;
On them the treasure shall be spent
    And spent, renewed shall be –
On them that are not yet, not yet,
    Ah no, no, no, not yet.

O stream, descending to the sea,
    Thy mossy banks between,
The flowrets blow, the grasses grow,
    The leafy trees are green,

In garden plots the children play,
    The fields the labourers till,
And houses stand on either hand, –
    And thou descendest still.

O life, descending unto death,
   Our waking eyes behold   10
Parent and friend thy lapse attend,
   Companions young and old;

Strong purposes our minds possess,
   Our hearts affections fill,
We toil and earn, we seek and learn, –   15
   And thou descendest still.

O end, to which our currents tend,
   Inevitable sea,
To which we flow, what do we know,
   What shall we guess of thee?   20

A roar we hear upon thy shore
   As we our course fulfil;
Scarce we divine a sun will shine
   And be above us still.

From thy far sources 'mid mountains airily climbing,
   Pass to the rich lowland, thou busy sunny river;
Murmuring once, dimpling, pellucid, limpid, abundant,
   Deepening now, widening, swelling, a lordly river.
Through woodlands steering, with branches waving above thee,   5
   Through the meadows sinuous, wandering irriguous;
Farms, hamlets leaving, towns by thee, bridges across thee,
   Pass to palace-gardens, pass to cities populous.
Murmuring once, dimpling, 'mid woodlands wandering idly,
   Now with mighty vessels loaded, a mighty river.   10
Pass to the great waters, though tides may seem to resist thee,
   Tides to resist seeming, quickly will lend thee passage,
Pass to the dark waters that roaring wait to receive thee;
   Pass them thou wilt not, thou busy sunny river.

From *MARI MAGNO*
or
TALES ON BOARD

The Clergyman's Second Tale

Edward and Jane a married couple were,
And fonder she of him or he of her
Were hard to say; their wedlock had begun
When in one year they both were twenty-one,
And friends who would not sanction, left them free.   5
He gentle born, nor his inferior she,
And neither rich; to the new-wedded boy
A great Insurance Office found employ.
Strong in their loves and hopes, with joy they took
This narrow lot and the world's altered look;   10
Nothing beyond their home they sought or craved,
And even from the narrow income saved;
Their busy days for no ennui had place,
Neither grew weary of the other's face.
Nine happy years had crowned their married state   15
With children — one a little girl of eight.
With nine industrious years his income grew,
With his employers rose his favour too;
Nine years complete had passed when something ailed,
Friends and the doctor said his health had failed,   20
He must recruit or worse would come to pass;
And though to rest was hard for him, alas,
Three months of leave he found he could obtain,
And go, they said, get well and work again.
Just at this juncture of their married life,   25
Her mother, sickening, begged to have his wife.
Her house among the hills in Surrey stood,
And to be there, said Jane, would do the children good.
They let their own, and to her mother's she
Went with the children, he beyond the sea;   30
Far to the south his orders were to go.
A watering-place, whose name we need not know,
For climate and for change of scene was best:
There he was bid, laborious task, to rest. —
   A dismal thing in foreign lands to roam   35

To one accustomed to an English home,
Dismal yet more, in health if feeble grown,
To live a boarder, helpless and alone
In foreign town: and worse yet worse is made,
40 If 'tis a town of pleasure and parade.
Dispiriting the public walks and seats,
The alien faces that the alien meets,
The caterers for amusement in the streets
Fresh accosting still, whom he must still refuse;
45 Drearily every day this old routine renews.
Yet here this alien prospered, change of air
Or change of scene did more than tenderest care.
Three weeks were scarce completed — to his home
He wrote to say he thought he now could come,
50 His usual work was sure he could resume,
And something said about the place's gloom,
And how he loathed idling his time away.
O, but they wrote, his wife and all, to say
He must not think of it, 'twas quite too quick,
55 Let was their house, her mother still was sick,
Three months were given, and three he ought to take,
For his and hers and for his children's sake. —
    He wrote again, 'twas weariness to wait,
This doing nothing was a thing to hate.
60 He'd cast his nine laborious years away,
And was as fresh as on his wedding-day;
Yielded at last, supposed he must obey.
    And now, his health repaired, his spirits grown
Less feeble, less he cared to live alone.
65 'Twas easier now to walk the crowded shore,
The table d'hôte less tedious than before.
His ancient silence sometimes he would break,
And the mute Englishman was heard to speak.
His youthful colour soon, his youthful air
70 Came back; amongst the busy idlers there,
With whom good looks entitle to good name,
For his good looks he gained a sort of fame;
People would watch him as he went and came.

Explain the tragic mystery who can,
Something there is — we know not what — in man,   75
With all established happiness at strife,
And bent on revolution in his life.
Explain the plan of Providence who dare,
And tell us wherefore in his world there are
Beings who seem for this alone to live,   80
Temptation to another soul to give.
A beauteous woman at the table d'hôte,
To try this English heart, at least to note
This English countenance, conceived the whim;
She sat exactly opposite to him.   85
Ere long he noticed with a vague surprise
How every day she bent on him her eyes;
Soft and inquiring now they looked; and then
Wholly withdrawn, unnoticed came again.
His shrunk aside: and yet there came a day,   90
Alas, they did not wholly turn away.
Turned, but like hers returned; and yet and yet
The days drew on, and conscious glances met.
So beautiful her beauty was, so strange,
And to his Northern feeling such a change.   95
Her throat and neck Junonian in their grace,
The blood just mantled in her Southern face.
Dark hair, dark eyes; and all the arts she had
With which some dreadful power adorns the bad —
Bad women in their youth — and young was she,   100
Twenty perhaps, or at the utmost twenty-three,
And timid seemed, and innocent of ill
Her feelings went and came without her will.
Her youthful feelings overcame her still
Timid at first, a little thing might daunt   105
And a harsh look be taken as a taunt.
Changing anon — but simply I should fail
Should I attempt her changes to detail,
Nor will you wish minutely to know all
His efforts in the prospect of the fall.   110
He oscillated to and fro, he took

High courage oft, temptation from him shook,
Compelled himself to virtuous acts and just,
And as it were in ashes and in dust
115 Abhorred his thought. But living thus alone,
Of solitary tedium weary grown,
From sweet society so long debarred,
And fearful in his judgement to be hard
On her – that he was sometimes off his guard
120 What wonder? She relentless still pursued
Unmarked, and tracked him in his solitude. –
    Going to his room, one day, upon the stair
Above him he perceived her lingering there;
Upon the stair she lingered; at the top,
125 As though till he should follow, seemed to stop,
And when he followed moved – and yet looked round
And seeming as if waiting to be found
At her half-open chamber door she stood;
A sudden madness mounted in his blood
130 And took him in a moment to the place;
He stooped, and spying swift the half-hiding face,
There with the exultation of a boy
Read in her liquid eyes the passion of her joy,
And went in with her at the fatal door
135 Whence he reissued innocent no more.
    Two days elapsed and found him in this flame
And left him; on the third a letter came
From home; indeed it had been long delayed,
The mother's illness had the occasion made:
140 It came from his wife, the little daughter too
In a large hand – the exercise was new –
To her papa her love and kisses sent: –
Into his very heart and soul it went.
Forth on the high and dusty road he sought
145 Some issue for the vortex of his thought.
Returned, packed up his things, and ere the day
Descended was a hundred miles away.
    There are, I know, of course, who lightly treat
Such slips; we stumble, we regain our feet;

What can we do, they say, but hasten on   150
And disregard it as a thing that's gone?
Many there are who in a case like this
Would calm re-seek their sweet domestic bliss,
Accept unshamed the wifely tender kiss
And lift their little children on their knees   155
And take their kisses too; with hearts at ease
Will read the household prayers, to Church will go,
And Sacrament – nor care if people know.
Such men, so minded, do exist, God knows,
And God be thanked this was not one of those. –   160
   Late in the night at a provincial town
In France a passing traveller was put down;
Haggard he looked, his hair was turning grey,
His hair, his clothes, were much in disarray.
In a bedchamber here one day he stayed,   165
Wrote letters, posted them, his reckoning paid,
And went. 'Twas Edward four days from his fall;
Here to his wife he wrote and told her all. –
Forgiveness – yes, perhaps she might forgive:
For her and for the children he must live   170
At any rate; but their old home to share
As yet was something that he could not bear.
She with her mother still her home should make,
A lodging near the office he should take,
And once a quarter he would bring his pay,   175
And he would see her on the quarter-day.
But her alone, – e'en this would dreadful be:
The children 'twas not possible to see.
   Back to the office at this early day
To see him come, old-looking thus and grey,   180
His comrades wondered, wondered too to see
How dire a passion for his work had he,
And seldom spoke, and scarcely showed his face,
And was the worst companion in the place,
How in a garret too he lived alone,   185
So cold a husband, cold a father grown.
   In a green lane beside her mother's home,

Where in old days they had been used to roam,
His wife had met him on the appointed day,
190   Fell on his neck, said all that love could say
And wept; he put the loving arms away.
At dusk they met, for so was his desire.
She felt his cheeks and forehead all on fire;
The kisses which she gave he could not brook.
195   Once in her face he gave a sidelong look,
Said, but for them he wished that he were dead,
And put the money in her hand and fled.

    Sometimes in easy and familiar tone
Of sins resembling more or less his own
200   He heard his comrades in the office speak,
And felt the colour tingling in his cheek;
Lightly they spoke as of a thing of nought;
He of their judgement ne'er so much as thought.

    I know not in his solitary pains
205   Whether he seemed to feel as in his veins
The moral mischief circulating still,
Writhed with the torture of a double will;
And like a frontier land where armies wage
The mighty wars, engage and yet engage
210   All through the summer in the fierce campaign,
March, counter-march, gain, lose, and yet regain;
With battle reeks the desolated plain –
So felt his nature yielded to the strife
Of the contending good and ill of life.

215   But a whole year this penance he endured,
Nor even then would think that he was cured.
Once in the quarter in the country lane
He met his wife and paid his quarter's gain.
To bring the children she besought in vain.

220   He has a life small happiness that gives,
Who friendless in a London lodging lives,
Dines in a dingy chophouse, and returns
To a lone room, while all within him yearns
For sympathy, and his whole nature burns
225   With a fierce thirst for someone – is there none? –

To expend his human tenderness upon.
So blank and hard and stony is the way
To walk, I wonder not men go astray.
Unhappy he who in such temper meets
(Sisters in pain) the unhappy of the streets.   230
    Edward, whom still a sense that never slept
On the strict path undeviating kept,
One winter evening found himself pursued
Amidst the dusky thronging multitude
By a poor flaunting creature of the town   235
In crumpled bonnet and in faded gown
With tarnished flowers and ribbons hanging down.
Quickly he walked, but strangely swift was she
And pertinacious, and would make him see.
He saw at last, and recognising slow   240
Discovered in this hapless thing of woe
The occasion of his shame twelve wretched months ago.
She gaily laughed, she cried, and sought his hand
And spoke sweet phrases of her native land;
Exiled, she said, her lovely home had left   245
Not to forsake a friend of all but her bereft,
She was — still limpid eyes she turned above —
Exiled, she cried, for liberty, for love.
So beauteous once, and now this misery in,
Pity had all but softened him to sin,   250
But while she talked, and still in his despite
Called to his mind the dreadful past delight,
And wildly laughed and miserably cried
And plucked the hand which sadly he denied,
A stranger came and swept her from his side.   255
He watched them in the gaslit darkness go,
While a voice said within him, Even so,
So 'midst the gloomy mansions where they dwell
The lost souls walk the flaming streets of hell.
The lamps appeared to fling a baleful glare,   260
A brazen heat was heavy in the air,
And it was hell, and he some unblest wanderer there.
For a long hour he stayed the streets to roam,

Late, gathering sense, he gained his garret home,
265   There found a telegraph that bade him come
Straight to the country, where his daughter, still
His darling child, lay dangerously ill.
The doctor would he bring? Away he went,
And found the doctor; to the office sent
270   A letter, asking leave; and went again,
And with a wild confusion in his brain,
Joining the doctor, caught the latest train.
The train swift whirled them from the city light
Into the shadows of the natural night.
275   'Twas silent starry midnight on the down,
Silent and chill, when they, straight come from town,
Leaving the station, walked a mile to gain
The lonely house amid the hills where Jane,
Her mother, and her children should be found.
280   Waked by their entrance out of sleep unsound,
The child not yet her altered father knew,
Yet talked of her papa in her delirium too.
Danger there was, yet hope there was; and he,
To attend the crisis, and the changes see,
285   And take the steps, at hand should surely be.
Said Jane the following day, Edward, you know,
Over and over I have told you so,
As in a better world I seek to live,
As I desire forgiveness, I forgive;
290   Forgiveness does not feel the word to say.
As I believe in one who takes away
Our sin and gives us righteousness instead,
You to this sin, I do believe, are dead.
'Twas I you know who let you leave your home
295   And bid you stay when you so wished to come.
My fault was that — I've told you so before,
And vainly told, but now it's something more.
Say, is it right, without a single friend,
Without advice, to leave me to attend
300   Children and mother both? Indeed I've thought
Through want of you the child her fever caught.

Chances of mischief come with every hour;
And 'tis not in a single woman's power,
Alone and ever haunted more or less
With anxious thoughts of you and your distress, — 305
'Tis not indeed, I'm sure of it, in me,
All things with perfect judgement to foresee.
This weight has grown too heavy to endure;
And you, I tell you now, and I am sure,
Neglect your duty both to God and man 310
Persisting thus in your unnatural plan.
This feeling you must conquer, for you can.
And after all, you know we are but dust,
What are we, in ourselves that we should trust?

    He scarcely answered her; but he obtained 315
A longer leave and quietly remained.
Slowly the child recovered, long was ill,
Long delicate; and he must watch her still;
To give up seeing her he could not bear,
To leave her less attended, did not dare. 320
The child recovered slowly, slowly too
Recovered he, and more familiar drew
Home's happy breath. All apprehension o'er,
Their former life he yielded to restore,
And to his mournful garret went no more. 325

Currente calamo

    Quick, painter, quick the moment seize
Amid the snowy Pyrenees:
More evanescent than the snow
The pictures come, are seen, and go:
Quick, quick, *currente calamo*.
    I do not ask the tints that fill 5
The gate of day 'twixt hill and hill,
I ask not for the hues that fleet

Above the distant peaks, my feet
Are on a poplar-bordered road
Where with a saddle and a load
A donkey, old and ashen grey,
Reluctant works his dusty way.
Before him, still with might and main
Pulling his rope, the rustic rein,
A girl: before both him and me,
Frequent she turns and lets me see,
Unconscious, lets me scan and trace
The sunny darkness of her face
And outlines full of southern grace.
 Following, I notice yet and yet
Her olive skin, dark eyes deep set,
And black, and blacker e'en than jet,
The escaping hair, that scantly showed,
Since o'er it in the country mode,
For winter warmth and summer shade,
The lap of scarlet cloth is laid.
And then back-falling from the head
A crimson kerchief overspread
Her jacket blue, thence passing down
A skirt of darkest yellow brown,
Coarse stuff, allowing to the view
The smooth limbs to the woollen shoe.
But who –? here's someone following too, –
A priest, and reading at his book!
Read on, O priest, and do not look,
Consider – she is but a child,
Yet might your fancy be beguiled.
Read on, O priest, and pass and go!
But see, succeeding in a row,
Two, three, and four, a motley train,
Musicians wandering back to Spain;
With fiddle and with tambourine,
A man with women following seen;
What dresses! ribbon-ends, and flowers,
And, sight to wonder at for hours,

The man, – to Phillip has he sat? –
With butterfly-like velvet hat;
One dame his big bassoon conveys,
On one his gentle arm he lays;   50
They stop, and look, and something say,
And to 'España' ask the way.
But while I speak, and point them on,
Alas, my dearer friends are gone;
The dark-eyed maiden and the ass   55
Have had the time the bridge to pass.
Vainly beyond it far descried,
Adieu, and peace with you abide,
Grey donkey, and your beauteous guide.
    The pictures come, the pictures go,   60
Quick, quick, *currente calamo*.

NOTES

p. 1 'O Heaven, and thou most loving family' (1835). Like the following three poems, this sonnet was printed in the school journal *Rugby Magazine* (1835–7), founded by Thomas Burbidge and subsequently edited by Clough.

p. 1 'I watched them from the window' (1835–6). Written when Clough was ill and had been watching the Arnold children playing. Although the family moved to a house by the sea at Charleston, South Carolina, in 1822, the children – Charles, Anne Jemima, Arthur Hugh and George – were taught to regard England as home.

p. 2 An Incident (1836). James Insley Osborne compares this poem to Wordsworth's 'We are Seven' (*Arthur Hugh Clough*, 1920, p. 31).

p. 3 The Effusions of a School-Patriarch (1837). Much of the school lore described here is amplified in Thomas Hughes's *Tom Brown's Schooldays* (1857). Of 'new boys on the pump' (l. 9), Hughes writes 'Each new boy was placed on the table in turn and made to sing a solo' (*Tom Brown*, I, vi). The duties of 'night-fags' (l. 15) included tending fishing lines in the middle of the night. 'Chaired' (l. 18), cf. 'Tom . . . was chaired round the quadrangle, on one of the hall benches borne aloft by the eleven' (*Tom Brown*, II, viii). Being 'cobbed' (l. 20) consisted of running a gauntlet of boys armed with knotted handkerchiefs, possibly containing stones. The 'Island' (l. 47), a mound on the corner of the Close at Rugby, was originally moated and complete with drawbridge. At Easter it was dressed with flowers 'bagged' or acquired by fags from wherever they could be found (*Tom Brown*, II, viii). 'The good old dirty shambles' (l. 26) was an area which included a butcher's. The 'tree of Treen' (l. 52) was an elm tree on the site of an old farm owned by the Treen family. The 'National School-room' (l. 53) was built after public money was first granted for education in England in 1833.

Clough's priggish evangelism within the school and his excessive loyalty to Dr Arnold are evident in letters such as that to J. P. Gell of 24 October 1835: 'I sometimes think that the last two years were given me to make me strong and discipline me for this time, and it is very painful to think how neglected they have been – more particularly if through that neglect the balance will be decided in favour of evil' (*Corr* I, p. 24).

p. 5 'He sate, no stiller stands a rock' (1838?). Published in *Poems Longer and Shorter* by Thomas Burbidge (1838) but ascribed in a manuscript note to 'A.H.C.' in a volume described by Simon Nowell-Smith (*TLS*, 8 March 1974).

p. 6 'Truth is a golden thread' (1838). The text is taken from the manuscript, which is reproduced in facsimile in Clough's *Diaries* (whereas *1974* follows *1865*).

p. 6 'Thou bidd'st me mark how swells with rage' (1839). 'Against the Evangelical emphasis on the universal Fall and the innate depravity of children, [Clough] places Platonic–Wordsworthian remembrance, the innate knowledge of the One, and out of this opposition he builds the synthesis of his belief, which, typically, rejects neither view outright' (Robindra Kumar Biswas, *Arthur Hugh Clough: Towards a Reconsideration*, 1972, p. 97).
  'Of more the heart is ware . . .' (ll. 45–6), cf. *Hamlet* (I, v, 166–7).

p. 8 'Oh, I have done those things that my Soul fears' (1839).

p. 8 'Enough, small Room, – though all too true' (1839). 'I must take care not to seek to be brilliant in conversation, nor yet again to be lazy & indolently self-indulgent to my own dulness' (11 April 1838, *Diaries*, p. 43).
  Matthew Arnold wrote to Clough in December 1847, '[This poem] I do not think – valuable – worthy of you – what is the word?' (*Letters to Clough*, p. 61).

p. 9 'Here have I been these one and twenty years' (1840). Although there is only one manuscript, the reading given here is quite different from that in *1974*.

p. 9 To the Great Metropolis (1841). Clough's sonnet replies to that of Wordsworth 'Composed Upon Westminster Bridge, September 3, 1802' ('Earth has not anything to show more fair', published 1807), in which Wordsworth refers to London as 'that mighty heart'.

p. 10 'About what sort of thing'. From a letter to Thomas Burbidge, 28 July 1841 (*CAKL* 120). 'Todo' (l. 11) was Theodore Walrond, head boy at Rugby, whom Clough was tutoring in the Lake District for a Balliol scholarship.

p. 11 'Do duty feeling nought and truth believe' (1841).

p. 11 'Like one that in a dream would fain arise' (1841).

p. 11 'If help there is not, but the Muse' (1841).

p. 11 'To be, be thine' (1842).

p. 11 'Irritability unnatural' (1839–42).

p. 12 'See! the faint green tinge' (1844?). Composed as part of Clough's 'Illustrations of Latin Lyrical Metres': 'The following quasi-nonsense verses do their utmost to preserve in their strongest character Horace's favourite central molossi [metrical feet consisting of three long syllables]' (*Classical Museum*, vol. IV, 1847).

p. 12 Epi-Strauss-ium [A little poem about Strauss] (1847). In *Das Leben Jesu Kritisch Bearbeit* (1835–6) the German theologian David Friedrich Strauss (1808–74) questioned the historical reliability of the supernatural elements of the New Testament. The book was translated into English by George Eliot under the title *The Life of Jesus* in 1846. Strauss's teacher Ferdinand Christian Baur (1792–1860) assigned most of the New Testament to the second century AD, which meant that the Gospels could not have been written by the Apostles.

In 1838 Clough took the Gospel literally as history: 'On this day that I have spent so ill, on this day, as it were, – 1800 Years ago, – our Lord was in Bethany, just arrived; – this His last sabbath day ... This is the first day of the Nine successive ones we can distinguish. Found historically only in St John's Gospel' (7 April, *Diaries*, p. 38). But in May 1847 he wrote to his sister Anne, 'I do not think that doubts respecting the facts related in the Gospels need give us much trouble. Believing that in one way or other the thing is of God, we shall in the end know perhaps in what way and how far it was so. Trust in God's Justice and Love, and belief in his Commands as written in our Conscience stand unshaken, though Matthew, Mark, Luke, and John, or even St Paul, were to fall' (4–23 May, *Corr* I, p. 182).

The reason for Clough's change of mind is clear from a letter to Edward Hawkins, Provost of Oriel. 'Again books like Strauss's life of Jesus have disturbed the historical foundations of Christianity ... I don't think young men are at all inclined to part with Christianity, absolutely: but they have no Christian ideal, which they feel sure is really Christian, except the Roman Catholic. And middle term is felt to be a sort of mixed Christianity; and whence that admixture comes they are not careful to inquire, nor in what quantity it may be admitted: – but they have a growing sense of discrepancy' (3 March 1849, *Corr* I, p. 249).

p. 12 Homo sum, nihil humani – (1847/8). The title, from Terence, *Heauton*

Timorumenos (I, 25), means 'I am a man; nothing that is human [is foreign to me]'. Cf. *Amours de Voyage*, III, 158–9. The poem was deleted by Clough from the proofs of *Ambarvalia*.

p. 15 AMBARVALIA

This book of poems by Clough and by Thomas Burbidge was published in 1849. It is named after an annual festival of purification of fields, at which animals were led around the boundaries of old Rome. The title may imply that the poems are offered for slaughter like the ritual sacrifices by two brothers said to have been made at the festival. As explained in the Introduction (pp. xiii–xiv), the original published text is followed here, although Clough later annotated three copies of his part of the book: *Poems A* and *Poems B*, which are both in the Bodleian, and a presentation copy to Charles Eliot Norton, *Poems (Norton)*, which is now in the Yale University Library.

The friendship of Clough and Matthew Arnold was strained by their different conceptions of poetry. In response to this volume Arnold wrote expressing doubts as to whether Clough should persevere in writing poems: '–You succeed best you see, in fact, in the hymn, where man, his deepest personal feelings being in play, finds poetical expression as *man* only, not as artist: – but consider whether you attain the *beautiful*, and whether your product gives PLEASURE, not excites curiosity and reflexion. Forgive me all this: but I am always prepared myself to give up the attempt, on conviction: and so, I know, are you: and I only urge you to reflect whether you are advancing' (February 1849, *Letters to Clough*, p. 99).

p. 17 'The human spirits saw I on a day' (1844). In *Poems A* Clough added the title 'Through a Glass Darkly' (1 Corinthians 13:12), and in a letter of 28 December 1858 to Charles Eliot Norton he asked for the poem to be titled 'The Questioning Spirit' (*Corr* II, pp. 560–62). Cf. Keats's 'Ode on a Grecian Urn', especially the final lines:

> 'Beauty is truth, truth beauty,' – that is all
> Ye know on earth, and all ye need to know.

In a very rough manuscript the first line reads 'Seven human spirits saw I on a day'. Anthony Kenny suggests that the seven allegorical spirits are sensibility, sensuality, science, valour, love, tradition and duty (*God and Two Poets*, 1988, pp. 27–31).

p. 18 'Ah, what is love, our love, she said' (1845). In *Poems A* Clough added the title '*Flet noctem*', meaning 'She weeps all night' (of a nightingale whose nestlings have been stolen; Virgil, *Georgics*, IV, 514).

p. 19 'When panting sighs the bosom fill' (1844). Clough's attitude to marriage in 1846 can be judged from the postscript to a letter to his sister Anne: 'to fall in love without knowledge is foolery – to obtain knowledge without time and opportunity and something like an intimate acquaintance is for the most part impossible – and to obtain time, opportunity, etc., is just the thing which somehow or other has never duly befallen me, at least in the cases where I could have wished it most. Then again there comes the question of reconciling marriage with one's work, which for me is a problem of considerable difficulty. It is not everyone who would like to be an helpmate in the business I am likely to have' (3 May 1846, *Corr* I, p. 170).

p. 21 'As, at a railway junction' (1844–5). First published in the *Balance* with the title 'Differ to Agree' (13 February 1846). In *Poems A* Clough added the title '*Sic itur*' (Virgil, *Aeneid*, IX, 641; Apollo to Iulus: 'Sic itur ad astra', meaning 'So does man ascend to the stars').

A scarcely legible note in Clough's hand in *Poems B* reads 'Ins[ert?] the two ships [i.e., *Qua cursum ventus*, p. 40] better and partly the same'.

The subject is probably Clough's difficult relationship with the Balliol tutor and Newmanite, W. G. Ward, who became emotionally dependent upon Clough (see *Diaries*, pp. 85–90). Ward's arguments severely strained Clough's belief in Dr Arnold's brand of Christianity. On 16 July 1838 Ward wrote to Clough '[Vaughan of Oriel] is perfectly certain of this, that there is no mean between Newmanism on the one side and extremes *FAR* beyond anything of Arnold's on the other . . . Well I do hope dearest that nothing may happen to make me split from you decidedly in any opinion on these matters' (*Corr* I, pp. 81–3). But as Ward moved towards Rome, becoming a Catholic in 1845, Clough became an agnostic. 'It struck me today that perhaps the worst this may come to will be that for some years W[ard] & I shall not be able to see much of ea[ch] other: but then a good deal' (21 October 1838, *Diaries*, p. 90).

p. 22 'When soft September brings again' (1840).

p. 23 'Oh, ask not what is love, she said'. Sending this poem to Burbidge on 2 November 1845, Clough called it a 'Jeu d'esprit' (for other extracts from this letter, see *Corr* I, pp. 159–60).

p. 23 'Light words they were' (1839–40?).

p. 24 Qui laborat, orat [Who labours, prays] (1845). The title is adapted from the ancient maxim 'Laborare est orare' or from St Bernard's 'Qui orat et laborat'. Rugby School's motto is 'Orando laborando' ('Praying at work'). Clough worked over the poem in both *Poems B* and *Poems (Norton)*.

p. 25 When Israel came out of Egypt (1845). The title is taken from Psalm 114: 1–2:

'When Israel came out of Egypt: and the house of Jacob from among the strange people; Judah was his sanctuary: and Israel his dominion' (Book of Common Prayer, attributed to Coverdale, 1786 edition). The title phrase is used metaphorically for a passage to enlightenment.

Among other revisions, in the letter to Norton of 28 December 1858 Clough supplied the title 'The New Sinai' and asked for the omission of ll. 83–104 (which he also deleted in *Poems B*).

While Moses was on Mount Sinai, the 'clouded hill' from which he brought the testimony of God, the Israelites turned to Aaron, 'the Prophet's brother-Priest', and began to worship a golden calf (Exodus 32).

'Dusky air' (l. 78), cf. *Paradise Lost*, I, 226.

p. 29 'Sweet streamlet bason!' (1840). In the letter to Norton, Clough added the title 'The Clouded Hill' (cf. 'When Israel came out of Egypt', l. 117).

p. 29 'Away, haunt not thou me' (1840). Clough annotated *Poems* (Norton) 'in a lecture at Balliol College', and in the letter to Norton of 28 December 1858 he directed that this poem and the one following be printed successively under the title 'In a Lecture Room'.

In 1853 Clough recalled his Oxford studies: 'Had I not read pretty nearly all the books? Was I to go on, keeping up my Latin prose writers, for three years more? . . . The daily lectures now, and the weary re-examination in Classics three years ahead! An infinite lassitude and impatience, which I saw reflected in the faces of others, quickly began to infect me' (*North American Review*, April 1853; *Prose Remains*, p. 406).

'For my people have committed two evils; they have forsaken me the fountain of living waters, and hewed them out cisterns, broken cisterns, that can hold no water' (Jeremiah 2:13).

p. 30 'My wind is turned to bitter north' (1847?).

p. 30 'Look you, my simple friend' (1840). In *Poems A* Clough added the title '*THE POET!*'

'The fresh ore' (l. 13), cf. 'Truth is a golden thread', ll. 4–6.

p. 31 'Thought may well be ever ranging' (1841). In *Poems A* Clough added the title 'DUTY-LOVE'. For his attitude to love and marriage, see note to 'When panting sighs the bosom fill' (p. 19).

p. 32 'Duty – that's to say complying' (1840).

p. 33 '*Blank Misgivings of a Creature moving about in Worlds not realised*' (1840–42). The title is from Wordsworth's ode of 1807, 'Intimations of Immortality from Recollections of Early Childhood', IX:

Blank misgivings of a Creature
Moving about in worlds not realised,
High instincts before which our mortal Nature
Did tremble like a guilty Thing surprised:
But for those first affections,
Those shadowy recollections,
Which, be they what they may,
Are yet the fountain-light of all our day

Clough's line 'Carrying on the child into the man' (I, 3) recalls Wordsworth's phrase 'The Child is father of the Man', used in the epigraph to 'Intimations of Immortality'.

In the letter to Norton of 28 December 1858 Clough directed that only sections II and VIII be reprinted and these as separate poems, the first with the title 'Sonnet'. Paul McGrane notes the existence of a manuscript not listed in 1974 ('Unpublished Poetic Fragments and Manuscripts of Arthur Hugh Clough', *Victorian Poetry*, vol. 14, no. 4, 1976, p. 363).

During his undergraduate years Clough struggled against a sense of sin and deliberately isolated himself. For the biographical background, see Kenny, *God and Two Poets*, pp. 14–23.

p. 40 Qua cursum ventus (1845). The title, from Virgil (*Aeneid*, III, 269), means 'Where the wind [called] our course'.

In *Poems A* Clough altered 'year by year' (l. 10) to 'through long years'.

p. 41 Alcaics. Date unknown. The title means verses in the style of the Greek lyric poet Alcaeus.

p. 41 Natura naturans (1846/7). The title means 'The creating nature', that which underlines phenomena (as opposed by Spinoza to *natura naturata*, 'the created nature'). Cf. Coleridge's 'On Poesy or Art': 'If the artist copies the mere nature, the *natura naturata*, what idle rivalry! . . . Believe me, you must master the essence, the *natura naturans*, which presupposes a bond between nature in the higher sense and the soul of man' (collected in *Biographia Literaria*, ed. J. Shawcross, 1907, vol. II, p. 257).

Clough revised l. 41 in *Poems B* to read 'Touched not, nor looked – Yet owned in one', and in the letter to Norton of 28 December 1858 he added the instruction 'omit stanzas 3 & 4 and in stanza 6 line 1 read Touched not, nor looked; yet owned we both'. His widow excluded the poem from *1862*, writing to Norton, 'The only thing I particularly desire is to leave out Natura Naturans which is abhorrent to me' (25 April 1862, *CAKL* 1129).

p. 44 ὁ θεὸς μετὰ σοῦ [God be with you] (1847). Three longer manuscript drafts exist. It is possible that the Highland Lassie was the sister of Clough's friend Theodore Walrond, Agnes, whom he met in Scotland in 1845 (see *New Zealand Letters of Thomas Arnold the Younger*, ed. James Bertram, 1966, pp. 222–3; Biswas, *Reconsideration*, pp. 183–4; and *Diaries*, pp. lxiii–lxiv).

p. 45 ADAM AND EVE

(1848–50). Preparing this poem for publication in *1869*, Clough's widow wrote, 'The MS of Adam and Eve is singularly fragmentary. The poem must have lain long in the author's mind – how long is impossible to say, but certainly during several years'. Subsequent editions have followed her ordering and conflation of scenes from different notebooks, and these are followed here, although the punctuation is generally that of the manuscripts.

'Wrench' (VI, 35), 'weal' (XI, 10), 'act' (XI, 27) and 'scrupulous' (XIII, 6) were supplied in *1869* to fill lacunae in the manuscripts. The manuscript reading 'distant yet distant' (IX, 16) was amended in *1869*. Seth (X, 3) was the third son of Adam and Eve (Genesis 4:25).

As well as *Paradise Lost*, the poem is indebted to Byron's *Cain*.

Walter E. Houghton reads the conflict between Eve's 'Christian orthodoxy' and Adam's 'liberal ethical philosophy' as parallel to that between Oxford University's requirement that fellows subscribe to the Thirty-nine Articles and Clough's conscientious scepticism, which led him to resign his fellowship in October 1848. Houghton suggests that the poem is 'an *apologia pro abdicatione sua*' (*Revaluation*, pp. 80–91). For Clough's religious difficulties, see his correspondence with Edward Hawkins (1789–1882), the orthodox Provost of Oriel (*Corr* I, pp. 191–8, 219–27, 247–9).

———

p. 72 Bethesda: A Sequel

(1849). A sequel to 'The human spirits' (p. 17). The poem recounts the story of Christ's healing given in John 5:

Now there is at Jerusalem by the sheep market a pool, which is called in the Hebrew tongue Bethesda, having five porches. In these lay a great multitude of impotent folk, of blind, halt, withered, waiting for the moving of the water. For an angel went down at a certain season into the pool, and troubled the water: whosoever then first after the troubling of the water stepped in was made whole of whatsoever disease he had. And a certain man was there, which had an infirmity thirty and eight years. When Jesus saw him lie, and knew that he had been now a long time in that case, he saith unto him, Wilt thou be made whole? The impotent man answered him, Sir, I have no man, when the water is troubled, to put me into the pool: but while I am coming, another

steppeth down before me. Jesus saith unto him, Rise, take up thy bed, and
walk.

And immediately the man was made whole, and took up his bed, and
walked: and on the same day was the sabbath.

p. 73 Resignation – To Faustus. Probably written in Rome, 1849. The first
forty-eight lines are taken from an incomplete manuscript (clearly part of a
letter), headed 'Now you shall have some sweet pretty verses in *your* style'; the
rest of the poem is from a toned-down fair copy. (*1974* follows the fair copy
throughout.) The title 'Resignation – To Faustus' appears on the fair copy but
may not be in Clough's hand. Matthew Arnold's 'Resignation – To Fausta'
was published in February 1849.

Clough wrote to F. T. Palgrave on 23 April 1849: 'In my way I saw Genoa
again, and visited the Doria Palace, which had just been quitted by the
victorious Piedmontese soldiery, who had not I am glad to say damaged the
frescoes on the ceilings – at least so far as I saw; the battle of the Titans which I
suppose is the finest was quite uninjured – but in other respects had played all
sort of furious and beastly pranks. The balcony with the fresco figures of
Andrea Doria and his family is a good deal damaged, one or two cannon balls
have passed through; and the soldiers have scratched comme ça [flourish] with
their bayonets. The furniture is all destroyed . . . gilded cupboards and tables,
japonned cabinets, and chessboards, porcelain vases and french clocks mingled
their precious fragments on the floors with relics of bread, & other unmention-
able deposits – empty bottles also should be mentioned' (*Prose Remains*, pp.
141–2).

In his 1849 *Roma* notebook he wrote: 'What used to disgust me so was the
sight of a man looking up in this way into . . . Vacuum, seeking and claiming
spiritual *en-rapportité* with Angels and Archangels and all the company of
heaven at the same time that his nether parts were not in *en-rapportité* only but
in actual active combination with Elementa Terrestria *vel pudendissima*. This is
the hypocrisy of hated men' (*Roma* notebook, cit. Scott's edition of *Amours de
Voyage*, p. 82).

p. 76 Uranus (1849). The title refers not to the planet but to the Greek
personification of the heavens. 'This thought is taken from a passage on astronomy
in Plato's *Republic*, in which the following sentence occurs, VII.529, D: "We must
use the fretwork of the sky as patterns, with a view to the study which aims at these
higher realities, just as if we chanced to meet with diagrams cunningly drawn and
devised by Daedalus or some other craftsman or painter"' (footnote, *1869*).

p. 77 'O'Brien, most disconsolate of Men' (1848–9). At the foot of MS2,
which is followed here as in *1974*, is written 'Rome'.

Printing this sonnet for the first time in her book *Arthur Hugh Clough: The Growth of a Poet's Mind* (1970, pp. 201–2), Evelyn Greenberger took it to refer to the Chartist James (Bronterre) O'Brien (1805–64). It is more likely, however, to refer to the Irish nationalist MP, William Smith O'Brien (1803–64), who led an abortive insurrection near Ballingarry in 1848, for which he was condemned to death, although the sentence was commuted to transportation for life and in 1856 he received a free pardon. In a mocking report, which claimed that O'Brien had 'not relinquished one iota of his Royal pretensions', *The Times* of 7 August 1848 referred to him as 'The Celtic Pluto', which may be what Clough means by 'the cold victor's scornful epithet' (l. 3).

p. 77 'From far and near' (1849). The Dome is that of St Peter's at Rome, designed by Michelangelo.

L. 2 originally read 'He drew the scattered ciphers, magnet like'.

'To sum up the large experience of ages, to lay the finger on yet unobserved, or undiscovered phenomena of the Inner Universe, something we can detect of these in the spheric architecture of St Peter's, in the creative touches of the Tempest' ('Letters of Parepidemus I', *Putnam's Magazine*, July 1853; *Prose Remains*, p. 394).

p. 77 'As one who shoots an arrow overhead' (1849). Although Benedict de Spinoza (1632–77) was not a contemporary of Magellan (d. 1521), the last lines of the poem apparently refer to his *Ethica*, specifically to Pt I, Prop. VIII, Schol. 1 and to the development of the argument in Prop. XXII and XXIII.

In the *Roma* notebook of 1849 Clough wrote, 'A divinely *ordained* (example of the) *conquest over Evil* – (in the Temptation and in the Passion) *effected by divine humanity*. – How far then is that human nature identical with the divine? – How far is human nature in us dependent for its divine strength on the acts of this divine humanity?' (Biswas, *Reconsideration*, p. 475).

p. 78 'Whence are ye, vague desires'. Dated 1849 in Mrs Clough's list of contents for *1862* sent to Norton.

p. 80 Sa Majesté Très Chrétienne (1849–50). The text printed here is a conflation of two manuscripts: a first draft headed 'L[ouis] XV' and a shorter fair copy entitled '*Sa Majesté très Chrétienne*' (previously '*Le plus Chrétienne Roi*'), which is followed as far as possible. (*1974* follows the shorter version exclusively.)

Clough's title refers to the traditional honorific of the Kings of France. 'Le Roi de France porte le titre de Roi *très Chrétien*, prerogative dont on fait remonter l'origine jusqu'à Childebert' (*L'Encyclopédie*, ed. Diderot et D'Alembert, 1751–76, vol. III, p. 379, 'Chrétien'). For Louis XV's use of the phrase, see *Medailles du Regne de Louis XV* by F. le Moine (Paris, 1745), pl. 22: a medal of 1722 bearing the legend 'LUDOVICUS XV, REX CHRISTIANIS-SIMUS', which signifies 'Louis XV Roy très Chrétien'.

Biswas observes 'Obviously Clough started with two separate but related monologues' (*Reconsideration*, p. 335), and Gollin, Houghton and Timko's *Arthur Hugh Clough: A Descriptive Catalogue* (New York, 1968, p. 18) suggests that ll. 93–8 are 'spoken by a bystander, suggesting that in this rough first draft Clough was moving from dramatic monologue toward a possible drama'. The asterisked divisions are editorial.

Of Louis XV of France, John Lough writes, 'even as a child he was both lazy and bored, and always took pleasure in inflicting pain on other people. He always remained timid, afraid of new faces and a bad public speaker. A far from edifying private life did not prevent him from being extremely pious and attending all the religious services required of him' (*An Introduction to Eighteenth Century France*, 1960, p. 159).

'*O templa quam dilecta*' (l. 113) adapts the Vulgate text of Psalm 84:1, 'Quam dilecta tabernacula tua, domine virtutum' ('How amiable are thy tabernacles, O Lord of hosts!')

Origenes Adamantius (*c.* 185–254), the first great scholar among the Greek fathers of the Church, took literally the words of Matthew 19:12 and castrated himself (l. 180).

The King's wish to escape responsibility (ll. 184–6 and *passim*) is similar to Claude's in *Amours de Voyage* (III, 78, 211–13).

p. 86 'I dreamed a dream'. Date unknown. 'The MS of this poem is incomplete; but it has been thought best to give all the separate fragments, since they are evidently conceived on the same plan, and throw light on each other' (footnote, *1869*).

The Shade described in ll. 3–6 is Tiresias in the Underworld (Homer, *Odyssey*, XI).

'Quietly demured' (l. 69) was supplied in *1869* to fill a lacuna in the manuscript.

Like the 'dignitaries of the Church' (l. 80), Edward Hawkins recommended in a letter of 20 November 1848 that Clough read Joseph Butler's *Analogy of Religion Natural and Revealed* (1736) 'for the correspondence between Religion and the constitution of what we call nature' and William Paley's *Natural Theology* (1802) 'for a good proof of the being of a Personal God' (*Corr* I, p. 225). Both books were required reading for candidates for ordination.

p. 89 Easter Day. Naples, 1849. The poem has been printed under this title since *1865*, but of the two manuscripts in Clough's hand one has no title and the other (followed here as in *1974*) is headed only 'Naples, August 1849'. A copy believed to be in the hand of Mrs Clough bears the title used here.

p. 94 Easter Day II (1849?). Although not given on Clough's manuscript, the title has been used since *1865*.

p. 95 'What we, when face to face we see'. Written in 1849 according to Mrs Clough's list of contents for *1862*, but the only datable manuscripts are from 1852/3. The shorter fair copy, MS2, is followed here (whereas *1974* follows *1862*, on the supposition that it may be based on a manuscript now missing).

'Beloved, now are we the sons of God, and it doth not yet appear what we shall be: but we know that, when he shall appear, we shall be like him; for we shall see him as he is' (I John 3:2). 'For now we see through a glass, darkly; but then face to face: now I know in part; but then shall I know even as also I am known' (1 Corinthians 13:12).

In 1847 Clough wrote to his sister Anne, 'I think others are more right, who say boldly, We don't understand it, and therefore we *won't* fall down and worship it. Though there is no occasion for adding – "there *is* nothing in it –" I should say, Until I know, I will wait: and if I am not born with the power to discover, I will do what I can, with what knowledge I have; trust to God's justice; and neither pretend to know, nor without knowing, pretend to embrace: nor yet oppose those who by whatever means are increasing or trying to increase knowledge' (4–23 May, *Corr* I, p. 182).

p. 96 'That there are powers above us I admit'. Date unknown. The sole manuscript is written in pencil but has two ink revisions which are followed here (though not in *1974*, on the grounds that they may not be Clough's): in l. 16 'believe' is substituted for the alternative readings 'suppose' and '[truly?] think'; and between ll. 16 and 17 is deleted the line '(Hypothesis the soul of science is)'.

'And his disciples came to him, and awoke him, saying, Lord, save us: we perish. And he saith unto them, Why are ye fearful, O ye of little faith? Then he arose, and rebuked the winds and the sea; and there was a great calm' (Matthew 8:25–6).

p. 97 AMOURS DE VOYAGE

The text is that published serially, February–May 1858, in the *Atlantic Monthly*, with Clough's corrections from his letters to Norton, where ll. 86–112 of Canto V were added (24 March and 1 April 1859; *Corr* II, p. 565 and *CAKL* 965). The punctuation of the *AM* text, which was done by the printers, is lightened in line with surviving manuscripts, following Patrick Scott's edition (University of Queensland, 1974, p. 19; and p. xiv above). Two corrections from Clough's letters to Norton apparently overlooked by Scott are also incorporated: 'Quitted the sea' for *AM* 'Quitted the ship' (I, 239) and 'our rocks' for *AM* 'the rocks' (II, 42).

Strands of the poem are prefigured in the four epigraphs: (a) *Twelfth Night*,

I, v, 90–91; (b) 'He doubted everything, even love' (the French novel has not
been traced); (c) 'It is refuted by walking' (a common-sense reply to Zeno's
paradox of the impossibility of motion); (d) '[Anacreon] sang full oft his
plaintive strains of love in simple measure' (Horace, *Epodes*, XIV, 11–12;
Clough changes 'amorem' to 'amores' to fit *Amours*).

Three additional epigraphs appear in the first long draft of the poem, two in
Greek and one in Anglo-Saxon: (e) 'The Gods made him a man who was
neither a digger nor a ploughman nor good for anything at all' (Homer,
Margites, II); (f) 'You hanker after an ideal state, but you do not give your
minds to what is straight before you' (Thucydides, *History of the Peloponnesian
War*, III, Ch. 38); (g) 'He who thinks too much about himself is without
courage' (King Alfred's translation of Boethius, *The Consolation of Philosophy*,
VIII). In a letter of 1855 to F. J. Child, Clough suggested an epigraph for the
flyleaf, from Horace, *Epistles*, I, xi, 29: 'Navibus atque / Quadrigis petimus
bene vivere' ('We seek the good life through ships and chariots'; 4 November,
Corr II, p. 511).

Although Pope Pius IX had begun to introduce liberal reforms in the Papal
States, he was forced to flee in November 1848. A Roman republic was
proclaimed on 8 February 1849, and in March, Mazzini, as one of three
Triumvirs, became effective leader of the government. Clough arrived in mid-
April, just before Rome was besieged by the French under General Oudinot.
Despite being defended by Garibaldi's First Italian Legion, the city fell on 30
June. *Amours de Voyage* was drafted during the siege, and its events and
occasionally its phrasing are paralleled in Clough's letters and notebook (see
the full and excellent notes in Scott's edition, pp. 21–37). For example, a letter
of 23 April to F. T. Palgrave explains the references at I, 267, and II, 28:
'[Mazzini] asked me if I had seen anything of the pillaging &c. which the
English papers were acquainted with ... *The Times* he said *must* be dishonest –
for the things it spoke as facts were simply not facts ... *The Times*'s story
about the Belvidere Apollo is simply false. Tell Blackett he may "contradict it
on the highest authority" in *The Globe*. – I fancy it was originally mentioned
as a sort of joke – a similar rumour went about, that the Pantheon was to be
sold to the English for Protestant Service ... Tell Blackett he really must
defend S.P.Q.R. It really is a most *respectable* republic, it really (*ipse* dixit)
thought of getting a monarch, but couldn't find one to suit' (*Prose Remains*,
pp. 141–4).

This is Clough's second long poem written principally in hexameters – the
metre of Greek epic – following *The Bothie* (1848). Classical prosody is based
on quantity, the length of syllables, whereas English verse is based on accent or
stress. There was much debate in the 1840s about whether classical 'longs and
shorts' could be successfully imitated in English. As Clough wrote, 'The accent

of words with us is fixed, with them was in metre arbitrary. So on the other hand, with them, the quantity was fixed and carefully observed; with us it is variable, and greatly neglected' ('Illustrations of Latin Lyrical Metres', *Classical Museum*, vol. IV, 1847; *1974*, p. 553).

Among several attempts to conform to both classical and native criteria – with stresses and quantities coinciding – were a number of contemporary hexameter translations, Longfellow's *Evangeline* (which Clough read in 1848) and exercises by Clough himself such as 'From thy far sources 'mid mountains airily climbing' (p. 213). But despite his experiments Clough believed that in 'Anglo-savage' hexameters, stress and quantity should sometimes clash, as a note in the first edition of *The Bothie* explains: 'The reader is warned to expect every kind of irregularity in these modern hexameters: spondaic lines, so called, are almost the rule; and a word will often require to be transposed by the voice from the end of one line to the beginning of the next.'

The use of mock-heroic hexameters in *Amours de Voyage* invites comparisons between the contemporary siege and legends of Greece and Rome. Among the legendary figures are the sailors who in Book X of Homer's *Odyssey* were transformed into beasts when they drank from the magic cup of Circe, while Ulysses was protected by a herb, moly, given him by Hermes (I, 238–40); and Theseus, who used a thread or 'clue' (I, 245) to trace his way out of the Labyrinth.

Clough also adapts to the modern 'pother' (III, 75–8) the words of classical authors, such as Tertullian's affirmation that 'The blood of the martyrs is the seed of the Church' (*Apologeticum*, 50, 13). Particularly, the all-embracing line of Terence 'I am a man, nothing that is human is foreign to me' (*Heauton Timorumenos*, I, 25) is contracted to the smirking embrace of 'I am a man, I count nothing feminine foreign to me' (III, 158–9).

The siege of Troy is also in Clough's mind. At the end of the poem (V, 218), he invokes the palinode to Chaucer's version of the love story, *Troilus and Criseyde* (V, 1786): 'Go litel boke, go, litel myn tragedye.' And at III, 85–90, he describes the cypress trees that were planted at the grave of Protesilaüs (the first Greek killed in the campaign), which died when they grew high enough to see Troy (Homer, *Iliad*, II, 695–9). These had been described at the end of Wordsworth's 'Laodamia' (1815):

> A knot of spiry trees for ages grew
> From out the tomb of him for whom she died;
> And ever, when such stature they had gained
> That Ilium's walls were subject to their view,
> The trees' tall summits withered at the sight;
> A constant interchange of growth and blight!

Clough read Wordsworth's poem on 18 July 1841 (*Diaries*, p. 170).

Clough had been in Paris during the 1848 uprising. Now, by a twist of fate, the army besieging Rome was that of the sister republic, France (II, 16–23). This betrayal of the ideals of 1789 and 1848 is in Claude's mind when he mentions the September Massacres of 1792 (II, 204), and when, five lines later, he alludes to the dictum 'History is a distillation of rumour' from Carlyle's *History of the French Revolution* (1837; VII, 5). Also quoted are the lines 'If our young heroes fall, the earth will produce new ones ready to battle against you all', from La Marseillaise (II, 59–60). G. M. Trevelyan records that as the French stormed Rome, a band played this anthem 'so that the French might hear it through the cannon roar, and be withered with the irony' (*Garibaldi's Defence of the Roman Republic*, 1920, p. 171, cf. II, 156–9).

In the first canto Claude is little more than a Grand Tourist, expressing, for instance, typical mid-Victorian contempt for Bernini (l. 44). From Murray's *Handbook for Travellers in Central Italy* (1843), he learns that much of Rome's brickwork was once overlaid with marble, and he reverses the boast of Emperor Augustus to express his disappointment (I, 49–50). As a tourist he sees the 'marvellous twain', or Dioscuri, the statues of the Horse Tamers in the Monte Cavallo that are thought to represent Castor and Pollux (I, 190), and the Venus de Medici in the Uffizi, Florence (IV, 18). The statues of Ariadne and the Triton (half man, half fish) in the Vatican Museum make him reflect 'we are still in our Aqueous Ages' (III, 59), a reference to Robert Chalmers's theory in *Vestiges of Creation* (1844) that organic life began in the sea.

Claude also visits the Pantheon – the 'great Dome of Agrippa' (I, 156), and the 'solemn Rotonda' (III, 1) – which was dedicated a Christian church *c.* 609. In the chapter added to the second edition of *Contrasts . . . between the Architecture of the Fifteenth and Nineteenth Centuries* (1841) A. W. N. Pugin had commented that St Peter's showed 'the attempt to adapt classical details to a Christian church, the very idea of which implied a most degenerate spirit' (p. 9n). Such appropriation of the buildings of 'an older, austerer worship' (I, 163, 265–7) puts Claude in mind of classical mythology, and he recites Horace (*Odes*, III, iv, 58–64; but Clough's Latin footnote is slightly inaccurate: 'humero' should read 'humeris', and 'lavat' should read 'lavit'). For a reconciliation of Ancient and Modern, he then turns to the Sistine Chapel, the 'Chapel of Sixtus' (I, 205), because its frescoes show both pagan and Biblical prophets.

Although he feels some of the idealistic spirit of the nascent republic, Claude is not prepared to fight (III, 68–72), and the siege is little more than an annoyance that deprives him of milk for his coffee (II, 100). He dismisses the shooting and uncertainty with the catchphrase of the cynical Mr Jingle in *Pickwick Papers*: 'tiresome, very' (II, 132). Claude is attracted to the Trevellyn party, but whereas his sympathies are with the Republicans and with 'noble

Mazzini' (II, 249), Georgina Trevellyn refers in her letters to 'republican terrors' (II, 318) and 'this dreadful Mazzini' (II, 230), and while he is disappointed with 'St Peter's, perhaps, in especial' (I, 13), she is 'delighted of course with St Peter's' (I, 54).

In the third canto Claude responds to the traditional beauties of Italy, as when, contemplating the hills around Horace's Sabine farm (III, 214–17), he paraphrases his *Odes*: 'Albunea's echoing grotto and the tumbling Anio, Tiburnus' grove and the orchards watered by the coursing rills' (I, vii, 12–14). Here he also admires the Teverone or River Tiber (III, 222). However, some 'uneasy remarks' by George Vernon (III, 240–41, 273) put an end to Claude's relationship with Mary Trevellyn, because, not being Prince Hamlet (III, i, 154), he is not prepared to be 'the observed of such observers' (III, 279). He later consoles himself that there was perhaps 'something factitious' (V, 164) about his feelings for Mary, like those of the players in *Hamlet*.

Claude again alludes to Shakespeare in the fourth canto, when he diminishes Brutus's 'There is a tide in the affairs of men' (*Julius Caesar*, IV, iii, 218) to 'the *love* affairs of mortals' (IV, 33). Here Clough is probably also recalling Byron's *Don Juan*, VI, 2:

> There is a tide in the affairs of women
> 'Which taken at the flood leads' – God knows where

– a sentiment appropriate to Claude's predicament, for he has lost track of Mary Trevellyn's movements.

Unlike Saul, who found a kingdom while searching for his father's asses (I Samuel, 9–10), Claude finds only asses as he searches through several lands (IV, 32). There are several other echoes of the Old Testament. The *AM* text omitted ll. 143–6 of the first canto, because they travesty Isaiah's warning to Sodom and Gomorrah (Isaiah 1:13). In the second canto ll. 57–8 adapt 2 Samuel 1:20, 'Tell it not in Gath, publish it not in the streets of Askelon; lest the daughters of the Philistines rejoice'; and ll. 153–4 travesty the refrain in the early chapters of Leviticus: 'It is a burnt sacrifice, an offering made by fire, of a sweet savour unto the Lord'.

By the end of the poem Claude has shirked the roles of hero and lover, and is once again the tourist, visiting Lake Lucerne ('the Alpine sea'; IV, 76), Florence (V, 1) and Naples (V, 3).

John Goode suggests that the poem is indebted to Goethe's *Roman Elegies* (1795), which also chart a love affair against the background of Rome ('*Amours de Voyage*: The Aqueous Poem' in *The Major Victorian Poets: Reconsiderations*, ed. Isobel Armstrong, 1969).

Eugene R. August suggests that the romantic débâcle in *Amours de Voyage* is based upon Matthew Arnold's fascination with 'Marguerite' and he accepts evidence gathered by Park Honan that 'the real-life counterpart of Marguerite was a young woman named Mary Claude' (*Victorian Newsletter*, Fall 1981). '[Arnold's] love affair took on the aspect of a comedy of errors when he planned to meet his beloved in Switzerland, only to discover (after what confusions?) that he had inadvertently missed her. Already one begins to sense the ironically comic atmosphere of *Amours de Voyage*. But the most obvious clues that Clough had Arnold in view when he composed *Amours* are the names of his would-be lovers – Mary and Claude.'

———

p. 146 'Say not the struggle nought availeth' (1849). Probably written during the siege of Rome.

A detailed description of five of the manuscripts is given by A. L. P. Norrington in *Essays . . . Presented to Sir Humphrey Milford* (1948), but Norrington was unaware of a sixth manuscript in a letter of 29 October 1849 to Thomas Arnold (MS3 in *1974*, reproduced in facsimile in *New Zealand Letters of Thomas Arnold*). Not mentioned by either Norrington or *1974* is a further fair copy with several verbal variants (MS7). Once owned by Charles Eliot Norton, this is now at Wellesley College, and is reproduced in facsimile in *Index of English Literary Manuscripts*, Vol. IV, Part 1 (compiled by Rosenbaum and White, London and New York, 1982).

MS5 (which is reproduced in facsimile in P. J. Croft's *Autograph Poetry in the English Language*, Vol. II, 1973) entitles the poem '*In profundis*' ('In the depths'), adapting Psalm 130 (Vulgate), '*De profundis*': 'Out of the deep have I called unto thee, O Lord'. MS7 entitles it '*Dum Spiro*' ('While I breathe I hope', motto). The poem was published with slight editorial amendments in the *Crayon* (New York, 1 August 1855) under the title 'The Struggle'. It is ironic that this title should have been used, for the earliest draft, MS1 (which is reproduced in facsimile as the frontispiece to *1951*) shows that Clough could not find *le mot juste*: the first line reads 'Say not – the [   ] nought availeth'.

MS6 is followed here, as in *1974* (which adds its own punctuation).

In a revealing article about Clough and Arnold's imagery (*English Studies*, vol. XLVIII, 1967, p. 503) Richard M. Gollin compares ll 6–8 to a letter from C. E. Prichard to Clough on the disarray among Christian soldiers: 'I hope that many fight on the same side, whom the smoke of their own guns hides from one another. But I cannot hope that it may continue so: else they may shoot one another and the enemy be all the better' (3 February 1849; *Corr* I, p. 236).

———

p. 146 'In controversial foul impureness' (1849). *1869* supplied 'great,' (l. 10) to fill a lacuna in the manuscript and omitted 'By' (l. 14) in order to supply 'The coming fate'.

Houghton suggests that this unfinished poem complements 'Say not the struggle nought availeth', using similar metaphors of sea and stream (*Revaluation*, pp. 47–8).

p. 147 The Latest Decalogue (1849). Two very different manuscripts survive. MS1, now in the British Library, is followed here, as in *1974*.

The first twenty lines are a travesty of the Ten Commandments; the final four lines, which have no equivalent in MS2 and were not printed until 1951, travesty the Summary of the Law (Matthew 22: 37–9). Patrick Scott suggests that the poem specifically parodies a rhyme from *Divine Songs Attempted in Easy Language for the Use of Children* by Dr Isaac Watts (*Notes and Queries*, October 1967).

Houghton compares the poem with a letter from Clough to the *Balance* (6 February 1846): 'The very Decalogue itself – the definitive "Thou shalt not do murder," and "Thou shalt not steal," may pass into a very dubious "Thou shalt not do murder, *without great provocation*," and "Thou shalt not steal, *except now and then*"' (*Revaluation*, p. 72n).

p. 149 From DIPSYCHUS AND THE SPIRIT

Drafted during or shortly after Clough's visit to Venice of 1850, at the end of a depressing year as Principal of University Hall, London.

This text is an attempt to recover something like the original inspiration of the early scenes from the mass of manuscript material, none of which was published by Clough. The first continuous draft (MS1) is followed, with occasional insertions from still earlier drafts. (The revisions of MS2, which is followed by *1974*, are less explicit about sexual temptation.)

After Scene IV, Clough wrote 'End of Act I', but he continued to number the scenes sequentially.

The scene-numbering is that of *1974*, although in the manuscript, Scene III begins at II, 64, with subsequent scenes numbered accordingly.

The poem is usually entitled simply *Dipsychus* (pronounced 'die-syke-us'), but the full title, which is used four times by Clough, suggests that the Spirit is no mere facet of the divided Dipsychus but an independent agent (II, 17–21). In the earliest drafts the speakers are named Mephistopheles and Faustulus.

'The Greek word *dipsychus* is one which does not occur in classical Greek, but is used in the New Testament in the Epistle of St James. It occurs twice, at 1:8 in a verse translated in the Authorised Version "A double minded man is unstable in all his ways", and at 4:8: "Cleanse your hands, ye sinners; and purify your hearts, ye double minded." Clough copied these passages in Greek into his early diaries; and when as an undergraduate he wished to describe the evil state of his soul it was often the Greek word *dipsychus* which he used' (Kenny, *God and Two Poets*, p. 139). 'I have felt occasionally so dreadfully double-minded that I do not know how I shall ever get on' (25 March 1838, *Diaries*, p. 29).

When his fiancée reported finding this poem among his papers, Clough wrote from America: 'Dear Blanche, please don't read Dipsychus yet – I wish particularly not. You shall see it sometime – but now, not, please – dear, I beg not, please' (21 December 1852, *Corr* II, p. 350). After his death she was equally reluctant that others should read it (see p. xii). It was first published in the private edition of his poems of *1865* and then in *1869*, but much of Scenes II and III was omitted.

The 'white dome' (II, 7 and V, 287) is that of the church of Santa Maria della Salute. The lines '*Ah comme je regrette . . .*' (II, 40–44) are the refrain from 'La Grand'mère' by Pierre Jean de Béranger (1780–1857).

Sidney Herbert (III, 206), first Baron Herbert of Lea (1810–61), was secretary to the Admiralty, 1841–5, and secretary-at-war, 1845-6 . Balaam's ass (III, 216–27) turned aside from the angel of the Lord and then spoke to Balaam (Numbers 22: 23–34). Christ's parable of the wheat and the tares (IV, 60) is recounted in Matthew 13: 24–30. When the Spirit compares the 'vague romantic girls and boys' with 'Timon's feast to his ancient lovers' (V, 275–83), he is recalling Shakespeare's 'Uncover, dogs, and lap' (*Timon of Athens*, III, vi, 85). The Wordsworth poem he then refers to (V, 295–9) is 'Lines composed . . . above Tintern Abbey', 1798 (ll. 93–7):

> And I have felt
> A presence that disturbs me with the joy
> Of elevated thoughts; a sense sublime
> Of something far more deeply interfused,
> Whose dwelling is the light of setting suns

Per ora (V, 1): For an hour (to the gondolier). *Tre ore* (V, 310): Three hours. *gramolata persici* (V, 313): peach ice-pudding.

Dipsychus's speech 'Yes, it is beautiful ever' (V, 51–7), with its wish that we could 'eliminate only/This . . . demon of craving', echoes *Amours de Voyage*, III, 176–81.

p. 179 'There is no God, the wicked saith' (1849–50). This lyric from *Dipsychus and the Spirit* occurs in Scene VI in *1974*. It was originally printed, standing alone, in *1862*.

p. 180 'From the contamination' (1850). This fragment appears among the drafts of *Dipsychus and the Spirit*. Only ll. 10–19 are printed in *1974*.

p. 180 In stratis viarum I (1850–52). The title, from Virgil, means 'In the paved streets' (*Aeneid*, I, 422). The manuscripts appear among drafts of *Dipsychus and the Spirit*, and one is headed 'By Mephistopheles'. In his letter to Norton of 1 April 1859 Clough asked for this and the following three poems to be grouped together, and provided their title.

'change' (l. 8) is an abbreviation of exchange.

p. 181 In stratis viarum II (1852). The manuscripts appear among the drafts of *Dipsychus and the Spirit*, and this lyric is printed as part of Scene V in *1974*. Bodleian MS Eng. Poet.d.138 is followed here. An apparently earlier manuscript and a letter to Norton of 1859 both give as the first line 'Our luxuries, our gaieties'.

During the Irish Famine of 1847, in his pamphlet *A Consideration of Objections against the Retrenchment Association at Oxford*, Clough wrote: 'At no time whatever, I believe, can our large expenditure upon objects of luxury be justified . . . It were absurd to affect a gloom which does not exist. But it is not absurd to avoid in our enjoyments that which a little reflection can show us to be wrong, hurtful or unfitting' (*Prose Remains*, pp. 277, 289).

p. 181 In stratis viarum III. Date unknown. The manuscript is among the papers Clough sent to Norton in 1859. Introducing it, Clough writes, 'Here is another bit of verse (in Heyne's manner) which should go somewhere near "Each for himself—".'

'Jesus saith unto him, Thomas, because thou hast seen me, thou hast believed: blessed are they that have not seen, and yet have believed' (John 20:29). And cf. Genesis 18:31–2, where God promises Abraham that he will not destroy the city of Sodom if twenty – or even ten – righteous men can be found there.

Cf. 'Easter Day', ll. 126–8.

p. 182 In stratis viarum IV (1850?). The sole manuscript is a single sheet among the Norton manuscripts at Harvard.

p. 183 Peschiera (1850). The fortress town of Peschiera was captured by the Piedmontese in 1848, but the Austrians, whose symbol was the eagle, recaptured it in that year and in 1849 put down a revolt in Brescia.

The opening stanza echos *In Memoriam*, XXVII, 15–16, and Clough imitates Tennyson's stanza form. *In Memoriam* was published anonymously in May 1850, but Clough is reported – in an account 'hovering between fact and fiction' – to have commented 'It must be Tennyson. Who else could it be? And his greatest work!' (A. G. Butler, *The Three Friends: A Story of Rugby in the Forties*, 1900).

p. 184 Alteram partem [The other side] (1850). A sequel to 'Peschiera'. The text followed here is that of MS2 (whereas *1974* follows *1862* on the supposition that it may be based on a manuscript now missing).

p. 185 'These vulgar ways that round me be' (1850).

p. 185 'It fortifies my soul to know' (1850). On 8 March 1842 Clough had written in his diary 'Stat Veritas quantumvis mutemur' ('Truth remains, however much we change'; *Diaries*, p. 196). Cf. *Amours de Voyage*, III, 134: 'Sure that in us if it perish, in Him it abideth and dies not'.

p. 185 July's Farewell (1850).

p. 187 'Go foolish thoughts' (1850/51).

p. 188 ὕμνος ἄυμνος [A hymn, yet not a hymn] (1851). Although MS2 is preferred here (as in *1974*), the reading of MS1 at l. 36 makes easier sense than MS2's 'That scan the fact . . .'

p. 189 '"Old things need not be therefore true"' (1851). 'Where then, since neither in Rationalism nor in Rome is our refuge, where then shall we seek for the Religious Tradition? Everywhere; but above all in our own work . . . I would scarcely have any man dare say that he has found it, till that moment when death removes his power of telling it. Let no young man presume to talk to us vainly and confidently about it' ('On the Religious Tradition'; undated but said by Mrs Clough to be 'from the last period of his life', *Prose Remains*, p. 424).

p. 190 'To spend unsolaced years of pain' (1851). The first stanza was published as part of 'Letters of Parepidemus I' (*Putnam's Magazine*, July 1853; *Prose Remains*, p. 391). The second and third stanzas occur only in the draft manuscript, which is followed here (whereas *1974* follows *Putnam's*).

In a letter of 1850 to J. C. Shairp, Clough wrote: 'The sum of the whole matter is this. Whatsoever your hand findeth to do, do it without fiddle faddling; for there is no experience, nor pleasure, nor pain, nor instruction nor anything else in the grave whither thou goest. When you get to the end of this life, you won't find another ready made in which you can do without effort what you were meant to do with effort here' (19 June, *Corr* I, p. 284).

p. 191 'Dance on, dance on' (1851). In the manuscript Clough changed the refrain of ll. 10, 34 and 46 (though not of l. 22) to read 'but all in vain'.

p. 192 'Because a Lady chose to say' (1851).

p. 193 'If to write, rewrite, and write again' (1851).

p. 194 'But that from slow dissolving pomps of dawn' (1851).

p. 194 'To think that men of former days' (1851). The manuscript is followed here (whereas *1974* adapts *1869*).

After l. 32, the manuscript has, uncancelled, a line reading 'It is, if it be anywhere', and after a draft of l. 37 appears '[It is *deleted*] within the [over-weening *deleted*] mind;'.

p. 196 Seven Sonnets (1851). 'These Sonnets have been brought together from very imperfect MSS. It is not to be supposed that their author would have given them to the public in their present state; but they are in parts so characteristic of his thought and style, that they will not be without interest to the readers of his poems' (footnote, *1869*).

Although *1869* and *1974* each print sonnets IV, V and VI in a different order, the arrangement here is that of the sole manuscript.

In the last line of the first sonnet, 'and' is supplied here for sense; 'perplexity' is deleted in the manuscript. In the second sonnet a manuscript variant in l. 3 reads 'She grants for a possession'. In l. 11 of the fourth sonnet 'sign' was supplied in *1869* to fill a lacuna in the manuscript.

p. 199 Thesis and Antithesis (1851). 'Then be not stern' (l. 11) and 'counsel' (l. 39) were supplied in *1869* to fill lacunae in the manuscript.

p. 200 Sectantem levia nervi deficiunt (1851?). The title, from Horace (*Ars Poetica*, ll. 26–7), means 'My aim is smoothness, but my sinews fail'.

p. 201 'O happy they whose hearts receive' (1851).

p. 202 'Come home, come home!' (1852). An earlier manuscript is composed in six-line stanzas. Clough's second line perhaps echoes Tennyson's 'The Lotos-Eaters' (1832): 'Is there any peace / In ever climbing up the climbing wave?' (ll. 94—5).

p. 203 'Ye flags of Piccadilly' (1852).

p. 204 Mari Magno I (1852). (For title, see note to *Mari Magno or Tales on Board* below.) Sending this and the following poem to Norton in 1859, Clough asked that they be placed last in the collection of his poems.

MS2 is followed here (whereas *1974* follows *1862* on the supposition that it may be based on a manuscript now missing).

Cf. 'As, at a railway junction' (p. 21).

p. 204 Mari Magno II (1852). MS2 is followed here (whereas *1974* follows *1862* on the supposition that it may be based on a manuscript now missing).

A manuscript not recorded in *1974*, but apparently earlier than MS2, is at Wellesley College and entitled simply '*Mari Magno*'. Another manuscript not recorded in *1974*, but of the first stanza only, is printed by Paul McGrane in *Victorian Poetry*, vol. 14, no. 4, 1976, p. 364.

When Clough came to write his long poem *Mari Magno*, he intended to print this poem at the end as '*L'Envoi*'.

Cf. Wordsworth's sonnet 'Where lies the Land to which yon Ship must go?'

p. 205 'Come pleasant thoughts; sweet thoughts, at will' (1852).

p. 206 'Were I with you or you with me' (1852).

p. 207 'How in all wonder Columbus got over' (1852).

p. 208 'That out of sight is out of mind' (1853). After this poem in a letter from America to his fiancée, Clough wrote of his disgruntlement with his uncommunicative friends: 'There, that isn't anything more than a bit of ill humour, against [J. C.] Sharp perhaps, [F. T.] Palgrave and I don't know who else – which I don't the least retain – nor mean to entertain again – I only send it you for the sake of the first and last stanzas' (17 January 1853, *Corr* II, p. 366).

p. 209 O qui me – ! [O who me – !] (1852/3). The two manuscripts are each signed τηλόθεν ('from afar').

Cf. 'Come pleasant thoughts; sweet thoughts, at will' (p. 205).

p. 209 'Upon the water in the boat' (1852/3). Published as part of 'Letters of Parepidemus I', where its theme is introduced: 'Each new age and each new year has its new direction; and we go to the well-informed of the season before ours, to be put by them in the direction which, because right for their time, is therefore not quite right for ours' (*Putnam's Magazine*, July 1853; *Prose Remains*, p. 389). *1974* follows *Putnam's* in omitting the fourth stanza.

p. 210 Veni (1852/3, revised 1861; entitled 'Come, Poet, come' in previous editions). Ll. 28–43 were printed as part of 'Letters of Parepidemus I' (*Prose Remains*, pp. 394–5). A manuscript in ink at Wellesley College but not recorded in *1974* is followed here, although it is probably neither of those referred to in Mrs Clough's note to the poem in *1865*:

During the first three weeks [of his fever] he seemed perpetually occupied with a poem he was writing, the last in his volume of poems; and when he began apparently to recover and was able to sit up for several hours in the day, he insisted on trying to write it out, and when this proved too great an effort he begged to dictate it. But he broke down before it was finished, and returned to bed never to leave it again. A few days before his death he begged for a pencil and contrived to write down two verses, and quite to the end his thoughts kept hold of his poem. Fortunately it had all been completed and written out in pencil in the first stage of his illness, and was found after his death in his notebook.

'Or Rome / The pure perfection of her Dome' (ll. 37–8), cf. 'From far and near' (p. 77 and note).

p. 212 'Nay draw not yet the cork, my friend' (1853). The refrain echoes l. 5 of Matthew Arnold's 'On the Rhine' (published 1852): 'But ah, not yet, not yet!'
    In the light of *Dipsychus and the Spirit* (cf. IV, 51–2), this poem may be read as a meditation upon sexual restraint.

p. 212 'O stream, descending to the sea'. Dated 1858 in Mrs Clough's list of contents for *1862*.

p. 213 'From thy far sources' (1861). The text printed in *1869* is so different from the three surviving manuscripts that it must be from a manuscript now missing, so *1869* is followed here (as in *1974*). This is one of Clough's experiments with classical hexameters (see note to *Amours de Voyage*, pp. 240–41).

p. 215 From *MARI MAGNO or TALES ON BOARD*

The Clergyman's Second Tale (1861). The title is from Lucretius, *De rerum natura* 2 *init.*: 'Suave, mari magno turbantibus aequora ventis, / e terra magnum alterius spectare laborem' ('It is sweet, when the winds are troubling the waters on a swelling sea, to watch from land the tribulation of another').

This sequence of tales about love and marriage resembles Chaucer's *Canterbury Tales*, which Clough read in 1849–50, Crabbe's *Tales of the Hall* (1819), which he read in 1856, and Coventry Patmore's *Faithful for Ever* (1860), which he read in 1861. The sequence was incomplete when he died on 13 November.

Of the tale given here, his widow wrote to Norton on 19 March 1862, 'I believe the Clergyman's second tale was written in one night, while he was staying with the Tennysons in the Pyrenees' (*CAKL* 1122). The tale can usefully be compared to Tennyson's 'Enoch Arden', which was written November 1861–April 1862.

p. 225 Currente calamo [With a flowing pen]. From *Mari Magno*: My Tale.
'Phillip' (l. 47) is the Scottish painter John Phillip (1817–67).

FURTHER READING

The Poems of Arthur Hugh Clough. Second Edition, ed. F. L. Mulhauser (Oxford, 1974).

The Correspondence of Arthur Hugh Clough. Ed. F. L. Mulhauser, 2 vols. (Oxford, 1957).

The Letters of Matthew Arnold to Arthur Hugh Clough. Ed. Howard Foster Lowry (Oxford, 1932, repr. 1968).

The Poems and Prose Remains of Arthur Hugh Clough. 2 vols. (London, 1869). Still the standard source for the prose, and for some letters not included in *Corr.*

The Oxford Diaries of Arthur Hugh Clough. Ed. Anthony Kenny (Oxford, 1990).

Arthur Hugh Clough: The Uncommitted Mind. Katharine Chorley (Oxford, 1962). The best biography to date, though the subject of a detailed critique by Richard M. Gollin in *Essays in Criticism*, vol. XII, no. 4, 1962, pp. 426–35. Miriam Allott is writing a biography for Oxford University Press.

The Poetry of Arthur Hugh Clough: An Essay in Revaluation. Walter E. Houghton (New Haven and London, 1963). The best critical study.

Clough: The Critical Heritage. Ed. Michael Thorpe (Routledge & Kegan Paul, 1972).

INDEX OF TITLES AND FIRST LINES

FOR THE BEST IN PAPERBACKS, LOOK FOR THE 🐧

In every corner of the world, on every subject under the sun, Penguin represents quality and variety – the very best in publishing today.

For complete information about books available from Penguin – including Puffins, Penguin Classics and Arkana – and how to order them, write to us at the appropriate address below. Please note that for copyright reasons the selection of books varies from country to country.

In the United Kingdom: Please write to *Dept E.P., Penguin Books Ltd, Harmondsworth, Middlesex, UB7 0DA.*

If you have any difficulty in obtaining a title, please send your order with the correct money, plus ten per cent for postage and packaging, to *PO Box No 11, West Drayton, Middlesex*

In the United States: Please write to *Dept BA, Penguin, 299 Murray Hill Parkway, East Rutherford, New Jersey 07073*

In Canada: Please write to *Penguin Books Canada Ltd, 2801 John Street, Markham, Ontario L3R 1B4*

In Australia: Please write to the *Marketing Department, Penguin Books Australia Ltd, P.O. Box 257, Ringwood, Victoria 3134*

In New Zealand: Please write to the *Marketing Department, Penguin Books (NZ) Ltd, Private Bag, Takapuna, Auckland 9*

In India: Please write to *Penguin Overseas Ltd, 706 Eros Apartments, 56 Nehru Place, New Delhi, 110019*

In the Netherlands: Please write to *Penguin Books Netherlands B.V., Postbus 195, NL–1380AD Weesp*

In West Germany: Please write to *Penguin Books Ltd, Friedrichstrasse 10–12, D–6000 Frankfurt/Main 1*

In Spain: Please write to *Longman Penguin España, Calle San Nicolas 15, E–28013 Madrid*

In Italy: Please write to *Penguin Italia s.r.l., Via Como 4, I-20096 Pioltello (Milano)*

In France: Please write to *Penguin Books Ltd, 39 Rue de Montmorency, F-75003 Paris*

In Japan: Please write to *Longman Penguin Japan Co Ltd, Yamaguchi Building, 2–12–9 Kanda Jimbocho, Chiyoda-Ku, Tokyo 101*

FOR THE BEST IN PAPERBACKS, LOOK FOR THE 🐧

PENGUIN INTERNATIONAL WRITERS

Titles already published or in preparation

Gamal Al-Ghitany	**Zayni Barakat**
Isabel Allende	**Eva Luna**
Wang Anyi	**Baotown**
Joseph Brodsky	**Marbles: A Play in Three Acts**
Doris Dörrie	**Love, Pain and the Whole Damn Thing**
Shusaku Endo	**Scandal**
	Wonderful Fool
Ida Fink	**A Scrap of Time**
Daniele Del Giudice	**Lines of Light**
Miklos Haraszti	**The Velvet Prison**
Ivan Klíma	**My First Loves**
	A Summer Affair
Jean Levi	**The Chinese Emperor**
Harry Mulisch	**Last Call**
Cees Nooteboom	**The Dutch Mountains**
	A Song of Truth and Semblance
Milorad Pavić	**Dictionary of the Khazars**
Luise Rinser	**Prison Journal**
A. Solzhenitsyn	**Matryona's House and Other Stories**
	One Day in the Life of Ivan Denisovich
Tatyana Tolstoya	**On the Golden Porch and Other Stories**
Elie Wiesel	**Twilight**
Zhang Xianliang	**Half of Man is Woman**

PENGUIN POETRY LIBRARY

Arnold   Selected by Kenneth Allott
Blake   Selected by W. H. Stevenson
Browning   Selected by Daniel Karlin
Burns   Selected by W. Beattie and H. W. Meikle
Byron   Selected by A. S. B. Glover
Coleridge   Selected by Kathleen Raine
Donne   Selected by John Hayward
Dryden   Selected by Douglas Grant
Hardy   Selected by David Wright
Herbert   Selected by W. H. Auden
Keats   Selected by John Barnard
Kipling   Selected by James Cochrane
Lawrence   Selected by Keith Sagar
Milton   Selected by Laurence D. Lerner
Pope   Selected by Douglas Grant
Shelley   Selected by Isabel Quigley
Tennyson   Selected by W. E. Williams
Wordsworth   Selected by W. E. Williams

FOR THE BEST IN PAPERBACKS, LOOK FOR THE 🐧

PENGUIN BOOKS OF POETRY

American Verse
British Poetry Since 1945
Caribbean Verse in English
A Choice of Comic and Curious Verse
Contemporary American Poetry
Contemporary British Poetry
English Christian Verse
English Poetry 1918–60
English Romantic Verse
English Verse
First World War Poetry
Greek Verse
Irish Verse
Light Verse
Love Poetry
The Metaphysical Poets
Modern African Poetry
New Poetry
Poetry of the Thirties
Post-War Russian Poetry
Scottish Verse
Southern African Verse
Spanish Civil War Verse
Spanish Verse
Women Poets